FIRST JUDGMENT

Scott R. Frazer

Copyright © 2023 Scott R. Frazer
All rights reserved
First Edition

Fulton Books
Meadville, PA

Published by Fulton Books 2023

ISBN 979-8-88731-445-7 (paperback)
ISBN 979-8-88731-446-4 (digital)

Printed in the United States of America

CONTENTS

Preface..v
Chapter 1:   First Contact 1
Chapter 2:   A Planet Badly Out of Control.................14
Chapter 3:   Chaperoning Aliens..................................20
Chapter 4:   NASA 26
Chapter 5:   The United Nations 38
Chapter 6:   New York City 48
Chapter 7:   Congressional Hearings............................54
Chapter 8:   Escape 64
Chapter 9:   The Tom Blackstone Show.......................72
Chapter 10: Rescue Operation.....................................81
Chapter 11: Recovery 88
Chapter 12: Lost Worlds..92
Chapter 13: The Lost World of Karul..........................95
Chapter 14: The Lost World of Marshon......................99
Chapter 15: A Visit to the Vatican 106
Chapter 16: Rome 116
Chapter 17: Paris Press Conference 121
Chapter 18: Beijing..135
Chapter 19: Negotiations with China 143
Chapter 20: Do You Think Us Weak?........................154
Chapter 21: The Silent Majority 165
Chapter 22: Gather My Saints Together....................168
Chapter 23: Back to Washington 185
Chapter 24: Departure Day 196
Chapter 25: The Appeal...212
Chapter 26: Liftoff...219
Chapter 27: New Earth..224
Chapter 28: Back to Old Earth 228

PREFACE

Science fiction is a natural format for action books and adventure films. In many cases, science fiction storylines include threats to the very *existence* of mankind. In most adventure movies and books, aliens arrive on our planet with plans of occupation and conquest. Could there be any greater drama than defending our entire planet from an outside threat and saving mankind from destruction?

Ironically, science fiction is also a natural format for considering questions about the existence of God. Astrophysicists may complain about having to answer questions about God, but theology comes with the territory. If you are going to research the universe, people will want to know if you have found God or evidence of His existence there. Many religiously inclined people believe that God has created more worlds than just Earth. According to Genesis, man was made in the image of God, a pattern one would expect Him to follow on other planets. If this is so, then aliens should look *exactly* like us.

By the way, alien visits are not precluded by religion. There appears no evidence in world history that God prevents more advanced civilizations from discovering less advanced peoples. Columbus visited the New World. Cortez conquered the Aztecs, Pizzaro defeated the Incas, and James Cook discovered the Hawaiians. God has separated us from other planets by vast distances, but those distances might only be temporary barriers for a scientifically developed and determined alien species.

In most science fiction stories, the aliens are cast as the bad guys because we can't relate to them. To heighten their repugnancy, aliens in action movies are often reptilian because we *really* can't relate to reptiles. We find reptiles and monster aliens in films like *War of the*

Worlds, Independence Day, V, Alien, Predator, Starship Troopers, and *Edge of Tomorrow*. When you think about it, if aliens looked like cute puppies or Spielberg's ET, viewers would be conflicted at their destruction. But we have no problem watching our movie heroes blowing up lizards and other assorted monsters. So only a few science fiction movies have ever been made with humanoid aliens. In the 1951 black-and-white movie *The Day the Earth Stood Still*, the alien Klaatu appears to be a normal human being who is accidently shot by troops called in to surround his spacecraft. Another movie franchise with a humanoid alien is *Superman*, who looks human...but is really not.

What kind of civilization could we expect of visiting aliens? An extraterrestrial species that could develop the advanced technologies required for long spaceflight must be expected to be socially stable. If not, competing nations would use their technical discoveries to destroy one another in wars on their own planet. Considering the United States initiated a nuclear conflict during World War II and almost began a larger one during the Cold War, we must conclude that planet-wide extinctions are possible. If aliens appear, we can logically expect that they have come from a stable and peaceful society. They have avoided self-destruction and have the means to finance efforts to search the universe. Earth is neither technically nor culturally at that level yet.

I have set the opening scene with a spaceship landing on the lawn of the White House. Veteran science fiction readers may audibly groan as this is a well-worn opening scene used in several science fiction classics. Yet it would be a very logical starting point for a first-contact alien race to visit. It's certainly a more likely beginning than having the aliens land in an Iowa cornfield and telling the farmer to take them to his leader.

Science fiction is a good setting to consider deeper questions about the universe and our place in it. Final judgment is always associated with presenting yourself before God, a topic I would not presume to attempt to describe. However, what if Earth had a truly outside observer—an alien—visit Earth and judge us? This book considers two questions. First, if Earth was visited by extraterrestrial humans, how would we treat them? Second, and a little scarier, would our visitors think that Earth is worth the effort to help save?

Chapter 1

FIRST CONTACT

On Saturday, June 5, 2034, at 8:45 a.m., an extraterrestrial spaceship settled gently onto the lawn of the White House. Air pressure changes caused by the descending vessel scattered trash from the protests and demonstrations of the previous weekend. Signs and placards attached to the wrought iron fence protesting government actions and offering the normal profanities slapped wildly against the iron pickets. The ship's struts sunk deep ruts into the perfectly groomed grass. The ship settled into place and, like a toddler who knew his noise had troubled a group of adults, stayed very quiet.

Indeed, a large number of angry adults soon appeared. Security teams monitoring radar around the White House would later report that the spaceship had appeared out of nowhere. Security guards were the first to surround the ship with drawn handguns. The name of the ship, written in flowing English script on both sides, was *We Come in Peace*. No one appeared to be taking the claim seriously. Sporting full riot gear and drawn guns, Special Forces and Secret Service had soon surrounded the ship as well. Officers shouted at their troops to set up defensive perimeters. Within a few minutes, three Air Force jets thundered overhead. Army jeeps and transport vehicles rumbled up. Rocket launchers were broken out of storage cases. There was a *spaceship* on the lawn of the White House! Security was armed, alarmed, and dangerous.

Though radar was not able to track the final descent of the alien ship, numerous Washington tourists certainly did. Many of them had already had their cell phones out and aimed at the White House, taking panoramic video of the home of the president of the most powerful nation of the world. When a spaceship descended into their frames, tourists were at first perplexed and then delighted. Was that the president's helicopter, Marine One? But where were the rotor blades? A few bystanders started to realize that they had caught video of a history-making event, and many wondered how much their clip might be worth to news agencies. Armed troops had poured onto the lawn and around the craft, adding real action and drama to the videos of over a hundred amateur filmmakers. Within minutes, gawkers around the White House had uploaded the best social media videos they would ever post.

The videos immediately went viral, and social media lit up. Initially, the majority of viewers authoritatively declared that the alien landing video was a hoax. But the starship was easily visible from the front fence along Pennsylvania Avenue, and more cell phone photos were posted with heartfelt testimonies of witnesses to the landing. White House correspondents for all the major networks piled out of their offices to film the craft. Normal daytime television was interrupted by *"Breaking News from the White House"* banners. Soon however, news anchors appeared, all with the opening words, *"We interrupt your regularly scheduled programming..."* Across the country, concerned citizens gathered in front of their televisions. The news quickly spread to the rest of the world as well, of course. Amid the chaos that was occurring around it, the spaceship waited quietly. It gave off no sound, no light, and no venting gasses.

When the ship had landed, the president was immediately moved to the White House panic room or Presidential Emergency Operations Center under the east wing. Less than an hour later, the president, his cabinet, and several White House staff members received an email from the leader of the alien delegation.

To the president of the United States,

Sir, we are a first-contact delegation from our home planet of Parmithia. We are here to determine if diplomatic relations can be established between our two worlds. We come in peace; our ship carries no armaments. We have been immunized against all known earthly diseases and carry no biologic weapons. If allowed, we would like to meet you and your nations leaders in four standard Earth hours. Please respond if these arrangements are acceptable.

Darius

The email was forwarded under strict confidentiality throughout the government and, to no one's surprise, was soon leaked to the Internet. The world was spellbound. This was, after all, the first tangible proof that we were not alone in the universe. Science fiction books and movies had been popular for decades. Most of the world's population had seen the movie versions of aliens that might be exiting the ship at any minute. This would be the news event of the century, and no one wanted to miss it. Within the hour, people were arriving at the White House in droves, crowding the fences to better view the starship.

The size and design of the starship was quite similar to that of the space shuttles that NASA had produced four decades earlier. About one hundred twenty feet long and thirty feet in diameter, the thrusters underneath the craft that allowed it to land safely were apparently used as the main propulsion engine as well. Smaller side thrusters allowed the craft to turn or roll as needed. A smoked glass windshield was visible in the tapered front of the craft, but no one could see into the cockpit. Otherwise, there were no apparent doors or windows. Even more disappointing, there were no protruding pulse cannons or rail guns either. But the party had started, and it seemed that half of Washington had turned out to witness the event of the century. Food trucks, beer trucks, and porta-potties began arriving to handle the crowds. Signs and placards popped up above the crowds, with either the sentiment of "ET Go Home" or "Welcome Starfleet."

The collection of spectators formed three rings around the spaceship. The ring closest to the spaceship was made up of heavily armed Secret Service, Army squadrons, and a few Marines. The country's political leaders had also seen their share of science fiction movies, and they weren't taking any chances now. Granted, the spacecraft had no apparent armaments, but a couple of tanks were brought in just in case. Four-foot cement barricades were placed in a circle around the spacecraft to both provide a defensive wall perimeter and to keep out noncombatants. White House staff and officers loitered behind the troops, chatting in groups. For science fiction buffs, the scene was surreal, right out of the old film reels of the movie *The Day the Earth Stood Still.*

Just outside of the outer fence of the White house compound, a ring of television cameras and reporters formed. Dozens of video cameras poked through the wrought iron fence. News correspondents and cameramen elbowed into the fray to film their exclusive reports from different viewing angles. Foreign correspondents were reporting in their native language, adding to the din. Behind them, the numbers of onlookers and protestors grew alarmingly.

After the initial excitement of the landing, expectations were running high. One hour passed…and then another…yet nothing stirred from within the spaceship. Famous astronomers, military generals, and authors of books about extraterrestrials were questioned remotely as they scurried to airports to fly to the capital. NASA officials were pleased to point out the similarities between this ship and their own space shuttles in their interviews. It seemed this alien race had come up with the same basic design but, obviously being better funded by their governments than NASA, had also developed a propulsion technology that allowed intergalactic travel.

By early afternoon, the crowd started getting restless. TV cameras could only pan the ship exterior for so long, and correspondents at the scene were running out of things to say. One of them made a comment on air that someone needed to go knock on the front door of the ship. What could be taking so long? It was a sunny summer day. The pavements were getting hot, and shade was sparse. Shouts and chants started rising from the bored crowd. Finally, one fleet-footed young man made it over the barricades and sprinted toward the alien ship, waving an American flag. The crowd erupted in screams of encouragement as the trespasser slammed himself into the front landing strut of the ship and started battering it with his flagpole. He was caught and escorted away by two Army rangers in helmets and riot gear.

Finally, at about 12:30 p.m., a door in the middle of the ship cracked open. Commands were shouted. Tank turrets rotated into position, and soldiers snapped their rifles to their shoulders. The crowd quieted and collectively held its breath. Nothing more happened, and after a few minutes, everyone exhaled. Again, the crowd grew restless, but the open door indicated there might yet be some appearance. Finally, the door slowly slid all the way open. Mechanical steps extended from the door threshold and rolled down along the side of the ship to the ground, forming an open staircase. A humanoid figure appeared in the doorway and slowly stepped forward. The world again held its breath. Would the alien be two-headed, reptilian, or a woolly monster?

As it turned out, the world couldn't have been more disappointed. The alien was humanoid, with only two arms, two legs, and one head, all in the expected locations. The visitor looked totally human and could have easily passed for one of the thousands of businessmen walking through the capital. He stood just under six feet tall and wore a dark business suit over a white shirt. The only distinguishing feature about him was his shoulder-length white hair. As the crowd realized that the alien was not alien at all, exasperated exclamations arose. Profanities and accusations that this was a government hoax or the opening scene of a film production were shouted at no one in particular. Across the world, disappointed viewers threw empty soda cans and crumpled napkins at their television sets.

As the alien slowly descended the steps, a delegation of security agents from the Secret Service, Homeland Security, and the State Department cautiously approached and formed a perimeter around the stairs' landing. Stepping to the ground, the alien extended his hand to the officer in charge, who shook it reflexively. It appeared the alien spoke English. He amiably submitted himself to be frisked, to be scanned with a radiation detector, and to have swabs taken of his hands and the inside of his cheek. The samples were bagged and whisked away for analysis.

There had been a short discussion by the military and health officials about putting the aliens into quarantine for two weeks. The surgeon general was still in favor of the delay, but he had been outvoted. If the aliens had wanted to expose Earth to a new virus, there would be easier ways to do it than to send in one of their own. Besides, most voters in the country were sitting on the edge of their seats right now. A quarantine would look weak and paranoid to everyone, including the aliens. A small group of congressmen, Joint Chiefs of Staff, and the president's cabinet now stepped forward.

Once again, the alien shook hands with everyone in the group. Introductions and pleasantries continued. The crowd grew restless again. How could there be small talk with an alien? Were they discussing the weather or how the flight went? This little chat could have been the beginning of any random business meeting and was certainly turning out to be more boring than anyone could have ever imagined.

*****

Standing at the door of the White House, President Gordon Schaeffer looked over the ship, still amazed that the first authentic aliens to visit Earth had chosen to appear during his presidency. He didn't know whether to feel delight or dread, but the latter was winning out. After two hours in the panic room watching the news, he had insisted he be allowed to return to the Oval Office. The aliens' email was obviously written to pacify his administration, like a parent soothing an upset child. To cower in the White House and refuse to meet the aliens would be an admission of fear and trepidation. It would *not* be a good start for negotiations or for future reelection.

The president could feel the restlessness in the crowd. He had forgone his normal Sunday morning jog and the casual khaki slacks and golf shirt he normally wore on his day off. Now he was sported a dark-gray business suit, white shirt, and tie. His graying hair had been carefully combed. Even on his worst days, Schaeffer always made sure he looked presidential. He had a healthy build that his military could respect, yet a kind face that voters appreciated. As the president, Schaeffer understood that crowds of voters must be impressed, governed well…and entertained. Making first contact with an alien race would be the most monumental event in his presidency. History would judge how he handled himself in the next few minutes.

Thousands of people stood outside of the barricades. Millions more watched the broadcasts from their homes…and all of them were getting bored. Schaeffer was certain he did *not* want to be remembered as the man who presided over the greatest disappointment in American history. Something memorable had to be done, and it needed to be done now. The president took a deep breath, straightened his shoulders, and marched out the door toward the spaceship. He was followed by a large retinue of security personnel and staff.

Fortunately, someone had the good sense to have ordered the construction of a speaking platform near the spaceship. Chairs, a podium, and microphones were all waiting. A small number of the White House press corps sat with their television cameras in a roped off area in front of the stage. The president's secretary of state joined the president's parade to report that no weapons, radiation, or biological agents had been found on the alien. The alien had assured the group of inspectors that he was not carrying anything of danger to humans, which appeared to be true.

Schaeffer had met resistance from his advisors in his decision to meet with the alien before full biological and security screens could be run. But he had refused to reconsider. It was important that the country see strong leadership in this first encounter with extraterrestrial life. The president knew that any meeting could be delayed for weeks. It was apparent to Schaeffer that the aliens had landed on his lawn to force this initial meeting. The strategy had worked; the president approached the alien representative at the base of the speaking platform.

The president stepped forward and tentatively shook hands with the alien. He was taken aback at how very *human* the visitor appeared. Could this possibly be an elaborate hoax designed to discredit his administration? But no, that was impossible. The ship had appeared from nowhere and had descended noiselessly, demonstrating technologies well beyond the engineering capabilities of Earth.

"President Schaeffer, my name is Darius, and I am the sworn representative of the planet Parmithia, orbiting the sun you call K127 in your Gemini system of the galaxy. The leaders of my planet send their greetings. It is a pleasure to meet you."

Darius appeared to be a man in his early forties and, with his long white hair, could have easily been the president of some high-tech company out of San Francisco. His English was perfect and precise, with a lilt that sounded like he might have been a native of France, though that was rather unlikely. His eyes were a startling blue. His smile seemed genuine, and he appeared to be very relaxed under the circumstances. He even had a healthy tan to his skin. If this was all a ruse, the president thought, then it was a very good one. In any case, it was time to make an appearance and reassure the voters.

"The pleasure is all mine, Mr....uhm, Darius. Welcome to Earth and the United States of America," President Schaeffer stammered self-consciously. This whole event was surreal. He was speaking before a worldwide audience, with no prepared remarks or idea of what he was doing. Certainly not your typical Sunday... The president shook himself mentally, *Get it together.*

"Darius, before we go into the White House to meet, I was wondering if you could address the citizens of our planet who wish to welcome you here. There is much anticipation to learn about you and the people you represent." Pointing to the small army of reporters, he added, "Those cameras are transmitting video and audio signals to all parts of our planet."

Darius nodded amiably and allowed himself to be directed to his seat on the platform. The president approached the podium, which bore the seal of the president of the United States. Incredibly, the crowd quieted. The show was finally about to begin.

President Schaeffer recognized and welcomed the members of the Joint Chiefs of Staff and congressional leaders who had made the cut to be seated on the speaking platform. He spoke about how Earth had always wondered whether we were alone in the universe and that the events of the past few hours had finally answered that question. He relayed the world's appreciation to Darius for this long-awaited visit. The president paused and realized he had no more information to share. This was obviously not the time for a political speech about the country's problems. In front of the largest television audience ever assembled, this would be the shortest speech of his life.

"So without further ado, let me introduce Darius, a representative of the planet Par…mithia, located in the Gemini system of our galaxy. Ambassador Darius…," the president intoned, rather guessing this would be the appropriate title to bequeath the alien.

Darius arose and shook hands with the president. He stepped up to the microphone, appearing at least to be a veteran politician who had spoken at many such Washington gatherings.

"Citizens of Earth, I greet you and bring you the good tidings from my government of the planet Parmithia, which roughly translates to mean Mother World in your language. I beg your forgiveness for the delay in making my appearance. Given the number of weapons that surrounded our ship, we hoped that delaying our appearance would give you time to calm any concerns or fears you may have had," Darius explained diplomatically.

With a start, President Schaeffer realized that Darius had delayed his appearance for so long because *he simply didn't want to be shot*. In his opening line, Darius had very subtly rebuked the president and the United States for their reception. The president grimaced. What had Americans communicated about themselves when we surrounded our visitors with a ring of armed men, guns, and tanks? We assured them that we were a warlike people and expected others to be warlike as well. Welcome to Earth. Now put your hands on your head and don't make any sudden moves.

Darius continued, "My name is Darius, and I am the leader of this expedition. We are members of the Parmithian Space Exploration Confederation and represent our world in first-contact planetary visits. Since developing the technology to travel the expanses of space, my people have explored the galaxy. We have discovered dozens of planets that support life, some inhabited and others not.

"You may be surprised at my similarity to you. I assure you that I am from another planet. When Parmithian ships first started visiting other developed worlds, we were amazed to find that all advanced civilizations there were human, nearly identical to ourselves. At first, we credited evolution with the ability to produce human species with exactly the same build, bodily features, consciousness, and intelligence on many different planets.

"However, evolutionary forces alone cannot explain the similarities between Parmithians, earthlings, and the inhabitants of hundreds of other planets we have visited. Genetic material, left to its own devices, creates much more diversity than what we witness in humans throughout this galaxy."

Darius paused for a moment, carefully choosing his next words. "Earth has a book of…scriptures which declares that earthlings were created in the image and likeness of that God who created the universe. We Parmithians share that same belief with you."

Pointing to himself and then the crowd, Darius concluded, "The genetics of our two worlds as well as hundreds of others have been directed toward the same end by a Higher Being. It is the only explanation for the overwhelming similarities of the populations of humankind on planets scattered throughout the galaxy."

In his opening statement, Darius had just answered philosophical questions with which humanity had struggled for millennia. For scientists and theologians throughout the world, today had become a landmark event far beyond what they expected. Mankind really was the pinnacle of evolution, but we weren't alone in the universe. In fact, apparently, we weren't even all that special…

Darius hesitated and turned to more practical matters. "Five others from my planet have accompanied me on this voyage. They are still in the ship, but with your permission, I would like to introduce them now."

Five other aliens cautiously emerged one by one from the space shuttle. Based on size and shape, there were three males and two females. Once again, commands were shouted, and soldiers snapped their rifles to their shoulders. From one of the front seats on the speaking platform, General Theo Bart of the Joint Chiefs, bellowed,

FIRST JUDGMENT

"At ease!" obviously irritated by the redundant display of force. Commands were quickly relayed by abashed officers, and rifles were immediately lowered. The team of Parmithians slowly descended the steps and formed a line beside their ship. They, too, exhibited disturbingly humanlike discomfort and nervous energy from the stares of a quieted crowd. One woman was small and blonde; the other was tall and brunette. Both had their long hair braided down their backs. One man was bald. One had a military buzzcut, and another had the unkempt hair of someone who didn't really care about its appearance. All five of them wore dark-green jumpsuits and appeared physically fit.

Darius started the introductions, "I would like to introduce Matthew, my second-in-command and our resident expert on religion and cultures." The bald man smiled uncertainly, stepped forward, and bowed slightly to the crowd. The movement was a little forced, but it was a surprisingly earthlike greeting. Matthew had the slight build one might expect of a cleric and the calm, impervious expression one would expect of a monk.

"Newton is our ship's engineer." A large man with darker skin, an impressive build, and a precise military haircut stepped forward and raised his hand in greeting, quickly stepping back and assuming a parade rest stance.

"Amelia is our navigator and pilot." The brunette woman stepped forward, smiled, and waved. Amelia's flight suit accentuated a rather attractive figure, and her smile was dazzling. Wolf whistles erupted from the crowd, with shouted invitations to come on over and join the party. Amelia laughed as if enjoying the attention and reluctantly stepped back into line.

"Friedrich is our social statistician and cook." The tall, lean man with the unkempt blond hair stepped forward and raised a hand. He seemed to be studying the crowd even more intensely than they were looking at him.

"Our newest team member, Teresa, is our team apprentice and intern." The small, blonde woman, who was quite pretty but looked barely old enough to attend college, stepped forward and waved timidly. Again, there were wolf whistles, whoops, and shouts. Teresa blushed deeply, quickly stepped back in line, and looked at her feet. She didn't appear to be much of a party girl, and the crowd soon quieted.

Darius continued, "We have each chosen a name from Earth's history that best represents our individual roles and missions. It has taken us five Earth years to arrive here on your planet. During that time, we have studied Earth's transmissions. With some computer assistance, we have all learned your English language. We have studied your culture, religions, literature, and history to better understand you. Each of us has learned a second language as well."

Darius smiled as if sharing a private joke about Earth that he and everyone would find amusing. "Actually," he continued, "it was your transmissions that led us here in the first place. You see, Earth is a very noisy planet. Electromagnetic broadcasts on numerous frequencies fill your entire quadrant of space. Our learnings about Earth were made possible by listening to those broadcasts. As we drew closer to Earth, we were even able to download information from your computer networks."

The crowd stirred. Were these aliens spying on Earth? What right did they have to listen in on our public broadcasts? Did they listen to personal cell phone communications? The recurring plot of numerous sci-fi movies was hard to dismiss. Was this an advance team of aliens arriving to scope out how to conquer our planet?

"President Schaeffer," Darius said as he turned slightly toward the president, "please know that we come in peace. We are here to learn more about your planet, cultures, and lifestyles. Thank you for this kind reception."

Darius then sat down, much to the surprise of the president and everyone else on the platform. It was expected that the alien would speak for at least an hour. More bothersome, where were the assurances of establishing close diplomatic relations and trade agreements with Earth? Wasn't that the goal of such extraterrestrial visits?

The president struggled to gain both his feet and his composure. Patting his hair to make sure it was perfect, Schaeffer walked calmly to the podium. He touched the presidential lapel pin he wore, reminding himself who he was. He knew his next words would go down in history as the most important speech of his career.

"Ambassador Darius, we wish to thank and congratulate you and your team for completing your five-year voyage to our planet. We appreciate the effort and the interest that you have in establishing relations with Earth. We hope it will be a rewarding and mutually beneficial, uhm…partnership. We welcome your interest in learning about our planet and people and will extend every resource to help you in that effort…"

Shouts and crashes of metal on metal resounded from behind the northwest section of the security fence. Schaeffer glanced quickly over his shoulder. He was annoyed by the disturbance but confident that his security and staff would quell this noisy interruption. He was grievously mistaken.

Chapter 2

A PLANET BADLY OUT OF CONTROL

Major Phillip Casaverde, a member of the Army diplomat relations team, stood at parade rest with other lower-ranking military officers who also did not qualify for a place near the speaker's platform. Phil was twenty-eight years old, which was young for his rank and position. After graduation from West Point, an extraordinary gift for languages had directed his career into diplomatic relations, mostly coordinating security for visiting diplomats. When multinational delegations came together, it was impressive that the US Army could assign an attaché who could speak to them in their native tongues. Phil's commanders had promoted him to keep him in government service and out of the hands of higher-paying foreign contractors.

Casaverde enjoyed being in the Army, though he had still not decided if it would be a life-long pursuit. His dark hair was military length but just barely. His boyish face had the square jaw of many military men, yet was more comfortable in a wide grin than in the serious frown expected when standing at attention. Phil was subtly stretching his back from side to side, trying to work out the developing soreness from his workout early that morning. While being a language nerd came naturally, staying in physical condition to meet the requirements of military service did not. Deep inside, Phil believed that only a strict regime of diet and exercise stood between him and pudgy.

In his job in diplomatic security, Casaverde's main responsibilities were to escort and protect foreign government leaders during their visits to Washington. The job was often routine, but lately he had been forced to hustle dignitaries around rallies protesting the politics and actions of his charges. Having foreign presidents and ambassadors see violence, looting, and burning cars in the streets of the capital tended to lower their respect for the United States. Demonstrations were rarely peaceful anymore, and preventing serious harm to ambassadors was getting more and more difficult.

Normally, welcome receptions like today's were beyond tedious, which had to be expected when working for the diplomatic corps. But today was infinitely more interesting. After the spaceship landing, Phil had spent the day calling in favors and appealing to his commanders to gain admission to this event. Phil had been a big fan of science fiction all his life. Though the special effects of *Star Trek*, *Star Wars*, and *Battlestar Galactica* were old and outdated, he had watched them all. He had read virtually all the works of sci-fi greats like Isaac Asimov, Robert Heinlein, and Arthur C. Clark. Now he was standing less than twenty yards from a functioning spaceship from another solar system! It was surreal, like being unexpectedly transported into the future. Standing in the hot sun in his dress uniform was a small price to pay for such an experience.

A few acquaintances approached and tried to talk with him, but Phil was too distracted to carry on even a simple conversation. Finally, the major excused himself and discreetly slipped to the very edge of his group, getting as close as possible to the spacecraft and the team of alien visitors. He was trying not to stare like a kid in a candy store. President Schaeffer was speaking again, and it looked like he would go on for a long time. Casaverde could hardly blame him though. His commander in chief had the attention of the entire world, and this was a unique event that would almost certainly improve both his ratings and the standing of the nation on the world stage. The president's voice carried across the White House lawn.

"And when the time is convenient, we will schedule meetings for you with our other world leaders to discuss potential trade agreements. You will certainly want to meet with our United Nations and…"

Rattling fences and shouting had continued to interrupt the president from the far northwest corner of the White House lawn. Suddenly, in a concerted action, the ends of about two dozen aluminum ladders swung into position above the top of the security fences. Green military-surplus canvas bags came lobbing over the fence. Men dressed in an assortment of military camouflage, bulletproof vests, Harley-Davidson jackets, and black ski masks poured over the ladders and dropped to the ground. The invaders ran to the bags and removed assault rifles, handguns, clubs, and even a few swords. Several of the intruders carried American flags; others carried placards communicating their demands.

"Take Back America!"

"Repel the Aliens!"

"We Will Not Be Assimilated!"

A couple of gunshots rang out in quick succession as one protester sought to clear the immediate area of bystanders. When enough attackers had clambered over the fence to sufficiently bolster their ranks, the insurgent group started its attack. In what was obviously a preplanned strategy, the invaders split into two groups. The smaller group headed toward the speaking platform and the gathered national leadership. The larger group headed toward the spaceship and its crew. Screams, shouted orders, and more gunshots filled the air. Rookie cameramen panicked and scattered, while veteran reporters repositioned their cameras for better viewing angles. Many people instinctively ran toward the expected protection of the White House.

Into the bedlam, Major Casaverde reacted without thinking. His job had taught him that his first priority was to protect the dignitaries. The president and other national leaders had plenty of protection around them. Phil leapt over the cement barricade and broke into a hard sprint toward the team of Parmithians standing by their ship. This was madness! Protestors were *never* to be allowed to get this close to foreign diplomats.

FIRST JUDGMENT

The president was immediately covered by his Secret Service agents and was rushed off the stage. The president resisted at first, still in denial that the greatest embarrassment of his presidency was unfolding. This was *not* how the first contact with an intelligent alien species was supposed to go. History would blame him and his administration for this catastrophe. These alien visitors could possibly provide solutions to many of the world's problems, and yet Americans were attacking them with guns!

Darius broke off from the fleeing group, rushed to the microphone, and shouted to his crew members, "*Macchew, shacersamonte asta' ferett!*" The bald Parmithian met his captain's eyes, nodded, and started to herd his colleagues onto the staircase and toward the safety of their ship. They were taking the steps two at a time and making good progress. They had almost reached the top when several more shots rang out, mostly pinging ricochets off the side of the ship. One bullet did not.

Casaverde had been watching the group, inwardly cheering their escape. Then he saw the brunette woman—Amelia?—take a bullet to her leg and stumble badly. Her team lunged to assist her, but her injured leg buckled, and she cartwheeled over the chain banister toward the ground two floors beneath her.

Major Casaverde was still in a full-out sprint when he saw the Parmithian woman start her fall. Though his plan had been to go up the stairs, he ran past the landing. The logical part of Phil's brain pointed out how ridiculous it was to think he could actually help this woman. She was falling fast, and he had no time to stop to position himself for a catch. Phil was gasping for breath by now. What was he thinking? More shots rang out, several of them hitting the spaceship behind him. He was under enemy fire…

Unexpected but welcome, Phil felt a surge of adrenaline hit his brain. Suddenly…the outside world dropped into slow motion. Gunshot blasts and shouts were muted. Phil's breathing became easier. Phil felt like his body was moving through a slow-motion scene from one of his favorite action movies.

The falling woman had about twenty feet to fall, and Casaverde had about that far to go to get to her. His mind was racing, and he realized he wasn't going to quite make it in time unless... Casaverde took three more bounds and launched into a leap as if he were expecting to fly. Phil's mind took a moment to appreciate how wonderful adrenaline was in emergencies like this. Watching her intently, Phil calculated Amelia's cartwheeling motions and adjusted his arms to grasp her most securely upon their impact. Still imitating Superman, Casaverde gathered the woman, who was still falling in slow motion, into his arms. In a single motion, Phil pulled her into a close embrace and twisted his head and shoulders hard to the right. He had just enough time during the short descent to perform the midair half twist he had initiated.

Phil's short flight then came to its predictably swift and painful end. The major landed flat on his back, cushioning the impact for the brunette woman in his arms. The impact extinguished Phil's world of slow motion and returned him to normal space, time, and sound. He skidded along the grass, spreading his legs to prevent rolling on top of the injured woman. Held tight against his chest, the woman made no sound upon their impact. Major Casaverde, on the other hand, gasped loudly as his breath was knocked out of him. He labored to draw air back into his lungs even as he struggled to his feet.

The major gathered up the woman, threw her over his shoulder in a fireman's carry, and charged up the narrow steps. Phil's vision narrowed and darkened from the lack of oxygen. The bald Parmithian helped pull them through the door and closed it quickly behind them.

A contingent of troopers in bulletproof vests had headed off and surrounded the intruders. Many of the attackers had already dropped their weapons and were kneeling and holding their hands above their heads. Only a few shots still rang against the fuselage of the spaceship.

Still watching intently from the speaking platform, Darius realized that his team was now safe. A ship that could deflect asteroids during space travel could certainly repel bullets from the guns of this scroungy group of misfits. General Bart, in full military dress, was an imposing sight as he approached Darius with a fully armed squad of Army Rangers behind him. Politely and calmly, he asked,

FIRST JUDGMENT

"Ambassador Darius, will you please follow me?" The general turned and walked quickly toward the White House. Darius joined him quietly, but inside he was fuming at this reception. He and his team had learned in the last five years that the Earth was a planet teetering on the edge of self-destruction. But the situation now appeared far worse than they had expected. In his entire career of first contacts, he had never seen this level of undisciplined aggression. The United States of America was reported as one of the largest and most stable governments in the world. How could it, and possibly the whole planet, be so out of control?

Chapter 3

CHAPERONING ALIENS

Two days later, Major Casaverde received orders to report to the office of General Theodore Bart at the Pentagon. Washington was in chaos. The Parmithians had stayed cloistered in their ship, though Phil could hardly blame them. They had refused all offers of food, supplies, or medical assistance, reassuring the president that Amelia's wound had been treated. Casaverde had gotten to stay on the ship for only a few minutes. When the shooting stopped, Matthew had politely escorted Phil to the door. In his dazed condition, Phil did not really appreciate he had been the first earthling to ever see the inside of an alien spaceship, and he could recount very little of his visit in follow-up interrogations.

A right-wing splinter group called The Militia had taken responsibility for the attack. The Militia was an assortment of pro-gun, promilitary, yet antigovernment extremists known for their deep-seated paranoias. The attackers saw threats around every corner and kept their guns ready to fight them. Aliens, even peaceful ones, easily met their standard for a threat to their country and their freedom to bear arms. Simple xenophobia provided the justification for their attack. The group firmly denied they were attacking the president. According to their statement, they had sought to "remove the threat of an alien invasion by eliminating their scouting force and sending the message that patriotic Americans will not be moved from their homes." Three Secret Service agents had died in the battle, and several soldiers were wounded. Twenty of the marauders were killed, and twice as many were seriously injured.

Social media was enjoying record-breaking numbers of postings. Everyone had seen videos of the attack, and everyone had their own opinion about it. A large contingent still believed the whole event had been staged and there were no aliens. Right-wing groups generally supported the actions of The Militia, calling for the president to nuke the spaceship sitting in his front yard. Left-wing groups condemned the attack and called for US military to stay out of future negotiations with the Parmithians. Scientists around the world pled for world leaders to appreciate the technology that might be provided by a space-voyaging civilization such as the visiting aliens. Demonstrations occurred throughout the world either radically for, or radically against, the Parmithians. Numerous foreign countries, hoping to get their hands on alien technology, demanded the Parmithian delegation be sent to them for their own safety.

Major Casaverde arrived at General Bart's office and was escorted to a small conference room. Awaiting him was the general and a woman who Casaverde first thought to be a stenographer there to take notes. She wore dark-rimmed glasses, and her auburn hair was pulled into a tight bun. She sat ramrod straight with a laptop on the table in front of her, apparently ready to do her job. Casaverde noted the woman wore a major's uniform, which was odd. The general made quick introductions.

"Major Casaverde, I would like you to meet Major Allison Heroux. Like you, she works here at the Pentagon, reporting to me and coordinating our participation in diplomatic relations with the State Department. Major Heroux, this is Major Phil Casaverde."

Casaverde shook hands with the young woman who still looked more like a stenographer than an army major. She was certainly attractive enough, but slight of build. Her glasses gave her the look of an intellectual. Could she convince soldiers to follow her into battle? Could she yell or be yelled at? When Major Heroux looked helplessly back to the general, Casaverde realized he had been inadvertently staring at her and holding the handshake for an uncomfortably long time. Phil felt himself blush deeply as he released his grip and stepped back.

Everyone seated themselves. By authority of rank, General Bart took control of the meeting. The general was pure military. His face bore the wrinkles of a lifetime of outdoor service in lands where the sun was especially harsh. A large man, his muscles were slowly turning to fat with age. His integrity and patriotism had never been questioned. No one would dare. Bart ran his hand through his thinning gray hair and then cleared his throat in a way that called for both silence and attention.

"Due to severe failures of our own White House security, our reception of the Parmithian delegation has been generously compared to a dumpster fire. We have attempted damage control, but the Parmithians have been unresponsive. Finally, this morning, the president and I received the following correspondence from Ambassador Darius. I would like to read it to you."

President Schaeffer and General Bart,

> *Despite the poor start of our initial meeting, my team and I would like to continue our mission on your planet. We would like to visit certain organizations and governments of this world and request your assistance in making the arrangements for our travel and meetings. For security reasons, my team and I have decided to travel in our own ship and sleep in it at night. If you could find places for us to land and keep our vessel safe, we would appreciate it.*
>
> *We would like to convene meetings with the political leadership of each city we visit but reserve the right to meet with select citizens of those countries as well. A small personal security detail would be appreciated, not to exceed one guard per member of my team. Too much military presence stifles the purpose of our meetings.*

FIRST JUDGMENT

> *We thank you for your efforts in helping us to evaluate your planet. We wish to thank you for your hospitality and especially want to recognize the courage and response of Major Phillip Casaverde. He saved our dear Amelia from more serious injury or death.*
>
> Sincerely,
Darius

Holding up a second paper, General Bart added, "Darius included a list of organizations, governments, and individuals across the world that he would like to visit. It is quite a list, and the visits will take several weeks. This is to be considered highly classified information." The general sat back in his chair.

"First, Major Casaverde, you are to be commended for your heroic rescue of Ms. Amelia. You prevented this disastrous first contact from becoming an irrecoverable tragedy. Darius chose to recognize you personally in his email. We believe he would appreciate having you lead his security team…as would I. For the next several weeks, you will escort the Parmithians wherever they wish to go and run security for them. You will report to me personally and prevent any further attacks on our guests."

Phil flushed at the praise and rejoiced at the assignment. Inwardly, he knew the rescue had been extremely lucky; he didn't remember doing any actual thinking at all. Yet now he was going to be allowed to accompany extraterrestrial visitors in their first contact with Earth. Some dreams did come true.

The general turned to Major Heroux and continued, "Major Heroux, your assignment is to assist the Parmithians in any and all arrangements they wish to make. You will set up meetings, schedule meals, arrange transportation, and organize anything else needed to make this world tour successful, coordinating with Major Casaverde for security."

Allie nodded, a little wide-eyed at the assignment.

"You will both keep your ears and eyes open. Darius mentioned that they are evaluating our planet, but we have no idea what that means. Evaluating us for what? Why are they here? Any bit of intelligence on the Parmithians' mission, their priorities, or expectations is to be reported to me immediately. I will pass those reports directly to the president."

As his excitement about the assignment diminished, Major Casaverde realized what he would be up against. The Militia splinter group would *not* be the only dissident organization gunning for the Parmithians. What was the general thinking?

Phil blurted, "General, I would like to request the Stryker Brigade Combat Team accompany us on these visits."

General Bart looked at Phil as if he was reconsidering the assignment he had just made.

"Major, I think that 3,600 highly specialized troops are not what Darius wanted when he stated that the security team is to be restricted to *six* people. I suspect that Darius wants to set a particular tone to his meetings, and the presence of a brigade of heavily armed troops is not conducive to his expectations!" General Bart fixed Phil with a stare that he dared not return. "Major, do you know the three main reasons you and Major Heroux have been chosen for this assignment?"

Half of Phil's brain clamored for him to *stop talking*, but the stubborn half continued, "Well, sir, I imagine that as majors we are high enough in the command chain to know how to get things done, but low enough not to complain about an impossible task."

"No, Major, that's only the fourth reason! The first was that your heroic actions endeared yourself to Darius and his team. Second, you're an experienced security man who happens to speak several languages, which could be essential during your visits. Third, Major Heroux here is the most organized, clear-thinking officer that I know, who I trust will attend to every detail of these meetings. Our president has forcefully expressed his desire for a successful mission by the Parmithians, and if you have to move heaven and earth, *he will have it!*" General Bart paused. Casaverde remained silent. The general calmed himself and looked down at his hands. He knew the risks inherent in his orders. His voice quieted a bit.

"Majors, these aliens obviously have technology above and beyond our own. Think of what it could mean to our defense, energy production, and even space travel. Every country on Earth wants the technology represented by that spacecraft. The Parmithians chose to visit the United States first, an initial advantage that we bungled badly. I am asking you two to help America recover from that setback. Major Casaverde, security will have precedence in all decisions. If you even smell a hint of danger, get the Parmithians to safety no matter who is inconvenienced."

"Yes, sir," Phil said immediately, trying to reverse the negative attitude he had portrayed earlier.

The general continued, "You have my private number, so call me if any need arises. One more detail. Major Casaverde, you are a good-looking fellow, and I am sure you are an accomplished ladies' man. However, that skill won't be needed on this assignment. Do I make myself clear?"

"Yes, sir. No hitting on the alien women."

"Very good. Well…if there is nothing else." The general rose from his seat to signal the end of the meeting but then paused. For a moment he looked older…and sadder. "Majors, I was very embarrassed at the reception we provided for the Parmithians two days ago. Our world is going to hell, and we clearly demonstrated that fact to our guests. I will be very displeased if anything similar happens to our visitors again. Do I make myself clear?"

"Yes, sir," both majors responded in unison.

The general looked down at the paperwork in his hand and smiled for the first time in the meeting. "At least you aren't going too far on the first leg of your journey. According to the list, Darius wants to give NASA a tour of his spaceship. Enjoy your travel."

As they filed out of the conference room, Major Heroux looked up at Casaverde and gave him a wistful smile. He smiled back, certain they were thinking the same thing. This assignment was a career maker or career breaker, with a couple of inches of upside opportunity and miles of downside opportunity. Granted, the alien reception had been a catastrophe, so things must surely get better. Really, what else could go wrong?

Chapter 4

NASA

NASA's Goddard Space Flight Center is located in Greenbelt, Maryland. The GSFC included unique research laboratories for designing spacecraft and developing other technologies for traveling and operating in space. An elite engineering group was onsite to build out those designs. For some reason, Darius and his crew had wanted to start out their Earth tour here, so arrangements were made for a visit on Thursday, three days later.

Every employee at the Goddard Center was more than thrilled at the prospect of a visit by aliens and their starship. NASA had suffered severe budget cutbacks in the past few years as federal funds had been required to fund swelling welfare programs. Layoffs had become regular occurrences, and the mood at Goddard was not hopeful. Most of the highly intelligent men and women at Goddard had come to question their decisions to become rocket scientists. Having the world turn its attention back to space travel because of an alien visit was more than a little heartening. The fact that the alien's first visit was to *their* facility was absolutely thrilling. The alien visit would provide great publicity, a unique opportunity for learning… and a needed distraction. Scientists, engineers, and technicians cancelled all vacation plans and dental appointments during the week. Arrangements and approvals for the visit were made in record time.

FIRST JUDGMENT

Though the meeting was three days off, the Parmithians moved their ship to Goddard the very next day. Security around the White House and spacecraft had been doubled and then doubled again. Secret Service agents and Army troopers were bumping into one another. The spaceship had become a distraction for the entire executive branch of the government. Everyone in the White House agreed it was time to move the starship to a less public location. Early Wednesday morning, the *We Come in Peace* lifted quietly off the White House lawn and flew northeast.

As directed, the Parmithian ship landed in the main parking lot of the Goddard Center and had sat there for the rest of the day. There had been no further communications. Once again, concrete median barriers were placed around the ship. Troops from Andrews Air Force Base manned security positions at the front gate, parking lot entrance, and all around the ship.

Darius had agreed to give three tours with twenty people in each tour and then to give a seminar in Goddard's main auditorium. As the sun appeared above the horizon, Major Heroux stood at the back exit of the large command tent, which had been set up with tables, chairs, and two full-size metal detectors.

Allie had needed to make only a few arrangements for this visit. Major Casaverde had made all the security assignments. NASA had made the other arrangements, including which of their principal scientists and engineers would be included on the tours. Allie was accustomed to being the main organizer for such events. She kept thinking there was something she should be doing.

Allison watched as NASA technicians, scientists, and engineers walked around the security perimeter, gawking at the *We Come in Peace* starship. Only a few would be allowed to enter the ship, but everyone was permitted to take photos of its exterior. Selfies were being taken from every angle available. Allie saw Phil Casaverde slowly work his way through the crowd and flash his identification to the Army troopers. He spotted her, changed direction, and quietly joined her in the command tent. For several seconds, Phil gazed at the myriad of sightseers but said nothing. He rocked back and forth on his feet, and Allie could feel the agitation radiate from her counterpart. Allie folded her arms, glanced at him, and waited patiently.

Gesturing toward the crowd meandering around the ship, Phil groused, "You know, Major Heroux, I was against this unrestricted access to the ship. This is just a political goodwill visit. Darius sent me a personal email and…how *did* he get my email address by the way…and explained that he wants to show NASA and the US military that the Parmithians have nothing to hide. Darius figures if he can sooth NASA into reporting their ship has no hidden weapons, it will make their visit safer and easier. He instructed me to allow anyone on base to see and even touch the ship! We have several hundred people here, any of whom could be an enemy infiltrator. Did you know video cameras are being allowed on the tours inside the ship? The Parmithians have no appreciation for security precautions. How they made it safely to Earth is beyond me!" Phil stopped and took a deep, cleansing breath, aware he had been ranting. He closed his eyes, dropped his chin to his chest, and smiled apologetically. "Okay…sorry about that. I'm pretty sure this wasn't your fault…"

Allie giggled and sighed heavily. "Well, Major Casaverde, I can appreciate your frustration. I'm the event coordinator with nothing to coordinate. NASA has been doing my job for me." Allison threw up her hands in mock frustration. "I mean, really, it's maddening."

"Major Heroux, sarcasm does not become you," Phil said gruffly, and then he paused. His next words were barely a whisper, "I get to go into an alien spaceship today, which has been a dream of mine since I was a little kid. I just don't want anything to ruin this…" Phil cleared his throat and squared his shoulders, remembering who he was and why he was here. He looked at Allison and asked, "Do you really want to help?"

Allie did not even pause. "Yes! I'll do anything… Well, almost anything," she finished, realizing who she was talking to.

"The first tour will be arriving at oh-eight hundred. If you could escort our guests through security and establish a queue to the door of the spacecraft, I would appreciate it. And…please keep an eye out for security threats."

FIRST JUDGMENT

By 8:00 a.m., the first tour was standing in line, eagerly waiting for the doors to open. Security checks had gone well; everyone had been cooperative. This could have been a new ride at Disneyland; there was so much excitement in the air.

Casaverde followed each group as it made its way through the ship. All three tours were uneventful. Newton, the ship engineer, played tour guide and kept a running dialogue of each room and its purpose. The ship had several floors since the backend of the ship always had to be the floor. The bottom floors contained engineering, storage, water treatment, atmosphere control, heating, and propulsion. The very top of the ship was the bridge. Two floors below contained the kitchen, crew quarters, and a large common area for meals and meetings. Major Casaverde noticed the walls were painted in calming natural colors and pastels—browns, whites, and blues. It appeared that human response to color was built into our genes.

The tour had started on the top floor and made its way down. Guests were allowed to touch pipes, examine control panels, and ask questions. Several times Casaverde had felt that he was on a tour of a naval cruiser. Doors, hatches, and even light switches were placed in all the logical places. The final stop on the tour was the engine room at the bottom of the ship.

Ship engineer Newton waited until everyone had entered the room and then pointed to a large sphere that dominated the room. With a diameter of at least twenty feet, the face of the sphere was covered with a thick but clear crystalline polymer. The back of the sphere appeared to be made of thick stainless steel. There were two huge mountings attached to each side, capable of rotating the orb in any direction. Large cables, metal boxes, and a couple of possible transformers were attached to the steel half of the sphere.

Newton waited for the excited discussions to quiet down. "This is our dark-energy drive. As you can see, the drive is pointed straight down now as we used it to control our descent during landing. The mountings allow very precise movement of the drive, which is required for successful navigation. For the short times when directional changes are required, we strap into flight chairs. We will explain…a little more about this propulsion system in the seminar that follows the tours. I'm sorry, but I cannot answer any questions about the drive right now."

Newton had been very forthcoming about every other aspect of the ship. His refusal to talk about the engine that allowed faster-than-light space travel was an immense disappointment. Questions were shouted out anyway, but Newton refused to acknowledge them. It was painfully obvious that Newton felt bad about disappointing these engineering comrades who were so enthusiastic about his ship.

The last tour was exceptionally loud. Holding up his hands and shrugging, Newton told the last tour, "I'm sorry. I really am. We will explain everything in the seminar."

*****

The auditorium was less than half full after everyone had arrived for the seminar. This building had been constructed several decades before. In those days, the United States had been serious about space exploration and the Goddard Space Center had boasted four times the number of employees it had today. But the audience was well educated and appreciative that their alien visitors had chosen to visit their location. Major Casaverde expected no security problems. He and Major Heroux sat together in one of the back rows. The audience immediately quieted as Newton stepped to the microphone.

"Hello, everyone. For those of you I have not met, my name is Newton. I am the ship engineer of our first-contact team from the planet Parmithia. The star craft outside that some of you have toured is named the *We Come in Peace* because we want to make it clear from the beginning that we do come in peace. We are here to learn of your planet and, if we can, help you with some of the issues you face today. Parmithians have visited dozens of humanoid worlds, and we have some knowledge of how societies evolve."

Newton clasped his hands together, apparently quite at ease in front of an audience. He smiled and continued, "I would like to introduce you to our team and ask that each stand."

Phil and Allison looked at each other, realizing that they would benefit from these introductions as much as the rest of the audience.

Their alien charges were still quite unknown to them. Gesturing to each of the team in turn, Newton began the introductions. "Darius is our mission leader. He specializes in first-contact protocol and strategizing how we might benefit the populated worlds we encounter."

Darius rose confidently, lifted a hand in greeting, and took his seat again. An appreciative applause broke out for the man who had led the mission to planet Earth.

"Matthew is our expert in religion and culture. He assesses the influence of theological and cultural beliefs on societies and their governments."

Matthew stood. Holding his hands behind his back, he nodded his bald head in greeting to each side of the auditorium. Casaverde noted that Matthew wore a light-colored robe today, the first time any of the crew had departed from Earth styles of dress. He certainly looked the part of the theological scholar.

"Amelia is our ship's pilot. She also handles navigation and helps me maintain control systems. She chooses the flight plan to our destination and flies us there."

Amelia stood gracefully despite the cast that was clamped to her left thigh. She flipped her dark hair out of her eyes and gave the crowd a big smile and a wave. Today, Amelia wore a curve-fitting, spandex-like flight suit. The men in the audience stared and applauded appreciatively. This was the first good look Casaverde had gotten of Amelia since he had rescued her in Washington.

"Wow, she's gorgeous...," Phil mumbled.

The scientist sitting next to Allie grinned and leaned over her to respond to Phil's comment. He whispered, "She could only be more attractive if she was green."

Phil smiled and whispered back, "No, no, she's not from Orion. She's from Parmithia!" and laughed at his own joke. The fellow science-fiction enthusiast slapped his leg and chuckled softly at the shared cultural reference.

Phil caught Allie's frown and shrugged. "*Star Trek*!" he whispered as if it should have been obvious.

Allie glanced at both men, looked forward, and whispered back, "Nerds."

"Friedrich is our social statistician. He develops working models of how countries interact with one another. His models help us predict how your planet might benefit from Parmithian influence and technology. He assists in engineering. He is also the ship cook who makes us dinners that we anticipate and appreciate each evening."

Friedrich stood up and waved both arms over his head. Light laughter filled the auditorium. Friedrich was tall and gangly. His hair was in disarray, and everyone in the auditorium liked him immediately. He wore blue jeans and a T-shirt and could have easily passed for one of the NASA scientists. Casaverde wondered at the description of a social statistician, feeling Friedrich's role was somehow more important than it sounded.

"Finally, please let me introduce Teresa, our mission intern. This is Teresa's first voyage, and she is tasked with learning how to do Matthew's job as a specialist in religion and culture."

Teresa stood shyly, pushed her dark-blonde hair behind her back, and waved her fingers. She looked like a college student, so it wasn't hard to think of her as an intern. With introductions complete, Newton was ready to begin his lecture.

"We have spent the past five years flying here to Earth. We spent that time studying your world history and cultures. We learned English. As Darius mentioned in Washington, we tapped into your Internet and read all we could about you. I have been asked to summarize for you some of our technology, so here we go."

On a large screen behind him, Newton displayed an overview of the ship's systems and proceeded to describe each section—navigation, water and air recycling, food storage, and meal preparation. It was apparent that Newton was enjoying himself. He rattled through several more slides, detailing how different systems worked. Most of the audience took notes, though the presentation was being recorded for later viewing. Casaverde enjoyed the explanation of the navigation system but struggled to understand the technical details of communications.

The seminar had been scheduled for ninety minutes, and the time flew by. Many of the scientists had been glancing at the clock nervously. One brave soul suddenly stood up and interrupted,

"Newton, I apologize, but...my name is Dr. Tom Guggenheim. We are happy to report that many of the systems you have described are similar to the technology that we developed for our own space shuttles. You have described your advances in those areas quite well, and we look forward to more discussion. Forgive the pun, but it is your propulsion system that is light-years ahead of where we are. Can you please tell us about the dark-energy drive?"

Newton smiled self-consciously and glanced up at Darius, as if for permission to continue. Finally, he replied, "Like here on Earth, but a couple hundred years ago, Parmithian scientists discovered a previously unknown force that is pushing galaxies away from each other. The big bang, as you call it, created our universe about 14 billion years ago and initiated its expansion. However, the universe is expanding at a rate much faster than it should, even considering the force of that big bang. Earth scientists have called this repulsive force dark energy because like dark matter, it is very hard to detect, measure, and characterize. Yet we realized the force behind dark energy must be strong as it moves entire galaxies away from one another. While gravity pulls objects together, dark energy pushes things apart. Unlike gravity, whose force drops off greatly with distance from the mass of a planet or sun, dark energy is barely affected by distance."

Newton's voice betrayed his awe of his topic. "Dark energy can best be compared to magnetic force. Magnets attract or repel one another, depending on their poles. Both forces are very similar, yet opposite, just like gravity and dark energy. Like gravitational waves, dark energy is generated by the mass of solar systems and galaxies. It is all around us. However, dark energy exists outside of our normal space-time, so it cannot be detected by technology we developed for normal space-time."

Newton was obviously excited about his topic. His hands demonstrated how forces worked to attract or repel.

"In fact, dark energy forces are so similar to magnetic forces that magnets can be used to focus and amplify dark-energy forces. Our dark-energy drive is essentially an electromagnet with shifting poles and amplitudes that constructively interfere with dark-energy forces and strengthen them exponentially. The modified dark-energy pushes against objects of our choosing. Since dark energy never stops and large distances don't weaken it, when the drive is engaged, the ship moves faster and faster away from the sun it is pushing against."

Newton might have been a physics teacher lecturing a college class. Now using his hands to portray the sun and a departing ship, he continued his lesson. "To come here, we pointed our dark-energy drive at our own sun and engaged the drive. The sun, being so massive, moves imperceptibly—less than millimeter. But our ship, with millions of times less mass, is pushed with ever-increasing force. Our ship continuously picked up speed as the dark-energy force accelerated us away from our sun. The buildup of dark energy around the drive gradually generates a forcefield that engulfs the ship. That field creates its own space-time, so the *We Come in Peace* spaceship is not limited by your physicist..." Newton checked his notes. "Albert Einstein's equations that restrict a ship's speed to that of light. Dark energy allowed us to go faster than light speed and arrive here in five years instead of five lifetimes."

Still using his hands to represent his ship and our sun, he continued briskly, "About a year ago, as we approached your solar system, we turned the ship around so that the dark-energy drive was pointed at your sun. Then we started the braking process. When we got close enough to your planet, we pointed our drive at Earth and controlled our descent onto a spot outside of your..." Newton checked his notes again. "White House."

Newton paused his lecture to catch his breath and allow for questions. For a moment, the room was silent except for dozens of pens furiously scratching out notes. Noting their opportunity, hands started to shoot up. Newton again recognized Tom Guggenheim, who asked the follow-up question that Newton was dreading.

"Newton, this is absolutely fantastic," Tom gushed. "So what magnetic amplitude programming do you use? How does the drive do what you just explained?"

Newton looked down at his notes as if he might find an unexpected answer there. He was clearly embarrassed but finally looked up to look at his questioner. "Dr. Guggenheim... I do not know."

FIRST JUDGMENT

After a stunned moment of silence, laughter and guffaws erupted from the audience. This had to be a joke, of course. It was apparent that no one believed Newton. Dr. Guggenheim smiled and again took the lead. "Newton, you're the ship's engineer! You must know how your engine works!"

Darius rose from his seat, bringing the authority of the mission commander with him as he stepped to the podium. Newton stepped back to allow his commander to speak.

"Dr. Guggenheim, besides the general theory he has just explained to you, Newton really does not know how the dark-energy drive works. None of us do. We were purposefully not taught anything about the drive. What's more, the drive cannot be opened. If someone manages to open the drive to examine its contents, it will explode. The effect of the energy released would destroy thousands of square miles from the point of the explosion and possibly alter the orbit of your planet."

Guggenheim paused, disbelief and disappointment etched on his face. "But *why* would your people do that?"

It was Darius's turn to pause. These men and women, so much like the scientists at Parmithia's own Space Center, deserved to know and to understand. This announcement, painful though it be, was the real reason for the visit to Greenbelt NASA. The world had to understand the reasons for their visit.

"The maturity and social stability of any people must keep up with their technology. If not, that technology will eventually be used to destroy that people's enemies. Entire worlds have been lost due to this imbalance of technical knowledge and moral determination. Your own Earth faced such a possibility in 1962 when the United States and Union of Soviet Socialist Republics almost started a nuclear war that could have destroyed your planet. Technology had outpaced the maturity and wisdom of your people and its military leaders. Only last-minute actions by Presidents John F. Kennedy and Nikita Khrushchev diverted a disaster that would have killed billions of Earth's people.

"Dr. Guggenheim, your planet is a world of incredible turmoil. Within your own country, you have armed protests, riots in the streets, and violent skirmishes every day in hundreds of locations. Parmithia will not be responsible for potentially destroying millions of human lives. Thus, our team cannot reveal the workings of our dark-energy drive even under torture. The drive cannot be opened for examination, for it will self-destruct."

The audience demonstrated a wide range of emotions. Some shook their heads in disbelief. Others nodded, recognizing the wisdom of the Parmithian cautions.

Darius then delivered the message he had come to NASA to deliver. He continued, finding it hard to look at his audience. "While we can share other technologies with Earth, our present judgment is that we will not provide you with our dark-energy drive technology. As a planet, you don't have the social maturity, wisdom, or self-restraint to be trusted with such power. With it, you could destroy yourselves or, even worse, take it to other inhabited worlds to destroy lives there. We have learned by sad experience that worlds with high technical competence, but low moral maturity will try to steal our dark-energy drives or force our people to reveal its secrets. To prevent such seizures, Parmithian leaders have made it impossible for us to divulge how to build a dark energy drive."

Dr. Guggenheim looked around at his colleagues in the auditorium. Most appeared dumbfounded; several were wiping tears from their eyes. Conflicting emotions were evident in Guggenheim's face and voice. He hesitated as he struggled to regain his composure. Everyone in the auditorium knew their director of science operations could make iron-clad scientific arguments. The man was a genius. However, this was a moral and social conclusion that he could not refute.

Guggenheim sighed and looked up from staring at his hands. "I would very much like to be able to argue with you about our country's readiness to utilize dark-energy propulsion. But I cannot. As a country, we have lost our nerve for space travel. Our government has been distracted by problems nearer to home, but those problems never cease. NASA doesn't have the resources to make significant advancements in science."

Dr. Guggenheim sat down, realizing he had probably been more truthful than he should have been. The audience sat in uncomfortable silence. Nothing more could be said, so Newton thanked everyone for their attendance and closed the meeting.

Phil saw that Darius had accomplished his goal of proving to NASA that their starship was not a danger to Earth. But with the revelation that they would not share dark-energy technology, Darius had also informed the leaders of Earth that Parmithians had a low opinion of their planet. The Earth they had found so far was simply not morally mature enough to be trusted with advanced technology. While probably true, Phil realized, certain citizens of Earth were going to be very unhappy about that conclusion.

Their next visit would be to the United Nations headquarters in New York City. Some of those unhappy people would certainly be there.

Chapter 5

THE UNITED NATIONS

For providing security for outside visitors, New York City had to be one of the worst places in the world. Traffic could wreck exit strategies in mere seconds. People were everywhere, so entrance and exits were always observed by someone and immediately posted on social media. Even worse, New York City had become a center for ongoing protests, violent demonstrations, and open conflict between opposing groups. Ground zero for all international protest activity was, of course, the United Nations building, which the Parmithians had chosen for their next visit.

Over the weekend, Majors Casaverde and Heroux had made their plans. The starship and its crew had moved to West Point Military Academy early Sunday morning when traffic was lightest. The next morning, Casaverde and Heroux pulled up to the ship with an entourage of five black security SUVs. Agents exited the vehicles and established a perimeter around the base of the star craft's stairway. The six Parmithians exited the ship and descended. Major Casaverde looked at the group, blinked, and then looked again. Gone were the work uniforms the crew had been wearing at the disastrous White House reception and the more casual dress for the NASA visit. The four alien men sported dark pin-striped suits. Amelia and Teresa both wore designer dresses, which seemed to fit them *really* well in Casaverde's opinion. Both wore their hair up. Though the entire world had seen the Parmithians the week before, it was unlikely anyone would recognize them today.

"Phil, please quit staring and close your mouth," Allie instructed as she walked up to him. After several days of working together, they had agreed to be on a first-name basis in casual settings. Allie continued, "I thought it best that our alien friends look a little less alien, so I took some clothes over for their selection last night. Amelia, Teresa, and I had a wonderful time trying on dresses and making adjustments. I decided that new clothes would draw less attention to ourselves. Nod blankly if you agree." Casaverde tried to shoot her a look of exasperation, but he was too impressed by her forethought to make it work.

"Good thinking," he answered, shaking his head to clear his mind.

Darius approached them. He was wearing a charcoal-gray suit and matching fedora to cover up his signature long white hair. "Shall we go?" he asked. "I would like to chat with members of the Security Council before our meeting with the General Assembly." Assignments were made, and everyone piled into their assigned SUV.

As leader of the security team, Casaverde rode shotgun. Darius was going over papers with Matthew in the back seat. When he glanced into the rearview mirror, he noticed Amelia staring at his reflection. He caught his breath, but his brain froze. General Bart had been wrong; Phil Casaverde was no ladies' man. He considered himself terrible at small talk and knew from experience that a pretty face stopped his brain functions. Amelia smiled, but she did not break her reflected eye contact.

"Major Casaverde, I have not had the opportunity to express my gratitude. According to videos of my fall, had you not caught me, I would have landed on my head. You probably saved my life, so... thank you for your bravery."

Phil smiled weakly and managed to respond, "You're welcome, ma'am. I was lucky to have been close."

Amelia smiled back. "Well, it was not all luck. I noticed you moving closer to the ship even before the attack."

Phil blushed. "Ma'am, I have been a fan of science fiction and space travel all my life. I thought that being close to a real spaceship was a once-in-a-lifetime opportunity, so… I tried to make the most of it."

"Major, please stop calling me ma'am. You saved my life, so please call me Amelia. I must ask a question… From the videos of my fall, your ability to catch me in midair and then take the blow of our landing was an extraordinary feat. Are you a gymnast, or do you practice catching people as part of your military training?"

Phil smiled more broadly now. "Fortunately, I had an adrenaline burst as you were falling. Everything appeared as if in slow motion, so I was able to wrap my arms around you and roll you on top of me in the air."

Amelia pursed her lips. "Well," she sighed, still not breaking her gaze, "I wish I had been conscious enough to have more fully enjoyed the moment. It could have been so delightful for both of us."

Phil blushed furiously and suddenly found mundane activities going on in the street that demanded his full attention. As they approached the UN building, Phil saw the fringes of a protest march. Many of the placards read "Feed Africa," referring to the famines sweeping across the continent again. To flee from the heat of global warming, agriculture had been moving northward for several decades, and Africa had run out of room. Relief food supplies had been scarce and slow to arrive.

Parking in the underground garage and walking to the United Nations conference room was peaceful. In their New York disguises, the alien party blended in perfectly with dignitaries and ambassadors from around the world. With thirty minutes to spare, the group entered the main meeting chamber, where Major Casaverde was reminded of how fast he could lose control of a security situation. The Parmithians immediately split up, recognizing, and then approaching ambassadors from various countries.

Phil hated surprises, which always threatened his control of a situation. Fortunately, he was ready for this one. Each member of his security team—four men and two women—had been assigned to escort a single Parmithian when needed. He spoke into the microphone on his collar, "One-on-one defense. Move *now*!" He himself quickly followed Darius, who was already introducing himself to the secretary general.

Networking continued for the half hour, and then it was time to begin the meeting. Everyone took their assigned seats, and Secretary General Guillermo Himes called the gathering to order. In his heavily accented English, he welcomed everyone to the meeting and gave special recognition to the first delegation from an alien planet to the United Nations. The agenda had been cleared for this meeting, and the secretary soon invited Darius to take the podium. Darius essentially reiterated the speech he had given in Washington and ended his briefing. "So in the end, we are here to evaluate the state of your planet and how we might be able to best assist your population. Thank you."

Darius knew that there was to be questions; in fact, he had counted on it. A chorus of voices demanded to ask a question. Secretary Himes leaned forward to his microphone. "Time has been set aside for questions. The chair recognizes Ambassador Winston Hall of Great Britain," he intoned gravely.

Mr. Hall stood slowly. He wore a three-piece suit and stuck his thumbs in the vest pockets. His glasses were perched on the end of his nose, causing him to look down that nose at the Parmithian commander.

"Ambassador Darius, Great Britain welcomes you and your team to our planet and the United Nations. We hope that your visit benefits all countries represented here today. I listened to your address in Washington several times and now your words today. But we are missing an essential piece of your narrative. So I must ask you now. What are your intentions with this world? Do you plan to conquer Earth as so many of my people fear? Do you plan to arrange trade agreements with us? Will you allow earthlings to visit or emigrate to Parmithia?"

Darius hesitated only briefly, "Ambassador Hall, we are certainly not here to conquer Earth. It is not our way. Parmithians do not believe in war and only resort to violence when it is forced upon us. Depending on how much of our technology we are willing to share, we may negotiate limited trade with you. We may also help you to preserve parts of your culture. But we will not allow anyone from Earth to visit Parmithia."

Ambassador Hall was miffed as only a British aristocrat can be miffed. He straightened his back and stared at Darius incredulously. Tilting his head back and looking down his nose even further, he asked, "Am I to understand that you do not want any type of cultural exchange with Earth? How dare—"

Darius continued, interrupting the Brit in midsentence, "Ambassador Hall, according to my studies, Great Britain has a rich history of taking civilization to many parts of this world. Your people colonized Africa, China, Canada, the United States, and other lands. You brought order and laws to those lands. But your people know the dangers and difficulties of trying to merge cultures. Your history is full of wars and violence that threatened the very existence of large populations."

Ambassador Hall remained speechless, unprepared for a review of his nation's history.

"We, too, have learned to be very careful about first contacts with alien cultures even if they are humanoid and as similar to ourselves as you. Because while our DNA is undoubtedly very similar, Earth and Parmithia share no history or cultural heritage. This distinguished group of leaders of the United Nations represents many countries. But as a world modernizes and exchanges immigrants, its cultures become more and more similar. Every large city of your planet now has high-rise buildings, billboards, and too much traffic. We do not wish to have a cultural exchange with you. Our culture is unique to our planet, and we wish to keep it that way."

The General Assembly sat in silence. Darius had just made it clear that Parmithia did not want their culture to be tainted with any aspect of Earth's practices and beliefs. Some of the ambassadors were obviously bemused and even sympathetic to the news. Other leaders, especially the older members of the council, were furious. A burst of exclamations and requests to speak were directed at the secretary general. Ambassador Hall took his seat, too angry to continue his questioning. Calmly, the secretary general made his choice.

"Ambassador Joao Ferreira from Brazil, you have the floor," he calmly announced his decision, hoping Ferreira would quell the outburst. However, Ambassador Ferreira was not in the mood to quell anything.

"Ambassador Darius, *what*, may I ask, is it about our culture that you find so distasteful about our society? How are we so different?" he challenged.

Sitting to the side of the podium, Phil and Allie looked at each other. This discussion was already not going well. Phil started checking out exit points should the need arrive. Allie touched his arm to get his attention and calm him. She leaned into him and whispered, "I believe Darius is leading the discussion in the direction he wants it to go. This is purposeful. There is a reason Darius wanted to come here, and it wasn't just so he could shake a few hands and chat."

Darius conferred briefly with Matthew, who was sitting on his right hand, and then Amelia, who was sitting on his left. Both shook their heads slightly, but Darius met their eyes and whispered resolutely in response. Matthew shrugged. Amelia covered her mouth with her hand and gave the assembly a worried glance.

Darius cleared his throat and took a deep breath. "Ladies and gentlemen of the United Nations, please do not take offense to our laws and the need we feel to protect our culture. We have made many sacrifices to develop a society that seeks after the highest principles attainable in this plane of existence."

The Brazilian would not be dissuaded. "How do you think your society is superior to ours?" he asked bluntly.

Darius was unflappable. He paused, drew a deep breath, fixed eyes with Ambassador Ferreira, and responded, "Sir, the differences between our societies run deep. May I give you an example of a practice on Earth that we find especially…reprehensible? One of the requirements of a Parmithian technology transfer is that Earth must right this wrong."

The Brazilian ambassador flushed in anger. Didn't this alien have any respect for this body of world leaders?

"And what would that practice be?" he spat.

Darius's voice turned cold. "Sir, what laws do you have in place to assure your children are raised in happy homes with loving parents?"

Ambassador Ferreira paused for several seconds, obviously befuddled by this unexpected turn in the debate.

Darius continued, "What punishments do you inflict on a father who does not support or help raise his children? During our study of Earth societies, we found a disturbing number of single-parent families. How can you allow this?"

Ambassador Ferreira looked for support from his comrades sitting around him. Most of them were shaking their heads and shrugging their shoulders. He answered defiantly, "If a man divorces his wife, he is legally required to provide financial support for her and his children."

Darius continued, allowing more emotion to creep into his voice in his response. The fact that he was addressing a council of powerful leaders of the planet did not seem to intimidate him at all. "So you recognize a five-minute wedding ceremony to be legally binding, but the birth of a child does not legally bind the baby to its parents? You have no laws that require a child's father to provide paternal support for his child?"

"We have no criminal laws requiring an unmarried father to support his child," Ferreira admitted.

"Ambassador Ferreira, when a baby is born in Parmithia, the father and mother must sign documents that pledge that they will provide for the child's physical *and* emotional needs. If the parents decide to divorce, their separation does not affect their contract to provide continual parental support to their children. If either parent decides to abandon the family and not provide support, they are arrested. If, say, a detained father does not wish to return to his family and continue his paternal role, then his assets are seized by our government. If those assets are enough to provide for familial support of the child until adulthood, the father is released to make his own way in the world."

"And if the monies are *not* sufficient?" Secretary General Hall interrupted, too caught up in the story to contain himself.

Darius continued unapologetically, "Then the parent's salary is garnished until the child's needs are met. If the parent has no job, he or she is provided one at a farm, a manufacturing plant, or a government facility. Food and shelter are made available at the workplace for a small charge. The rest of the parent's pay is diverted to pay foster families who provide for the physical and educational needs of the child until adulthood. If the father has abandoned his family, then a foster father is provided to give the needed paternal support. Once the parent has provided the monies required by law for raising a child, he or she is released."

"That is *barbaric*!" cried the Brazilian ambassador. "On Earth, men are jailed for crimes that they commit, not simply for avoiding responsibilities."

Unfazed by the disdain of Ferriera and most of the audience, Darius continued his chastisement, "I beg to differ with you. Most of the countries represented here do incarcerate citizens for *not paying their taxes*, which is also a simple avoidance of responsibility. Apparently, the nations on this planet think that their taxes are more important than their future generations."

For the first time since meeting him, Phil heard real emotion in Darius's voice. Darius seemed incredulous that he needed to explain such a simple concept to learned men. Yet there was anger in his voice as well—anger at the short-sightedness of an entire planet. A few of the ambassadors looked thoughtful as they contemplated the charges, but most of the audience was beyond angry.

Darius took a cleansing breath and turned to more logical argument. Taking the tone of a college professor, he adjusted his argument. "Our evolutionary paths have been directed to be nearly identical. To create more complex creatures than fungus and bacteria, that path had to turn to sexual reproduction. With a mother and a father, sexual reproduction doubles the number of genes from which offspring can be created, exponentially increasing the diversity of that offspring. As a species, mankind has triumphed because evolution gave us better brains. But larger brains come at a price. First, our childhoods are longer than any other species. Most mammals reach adulthood within a year or two of birth. Human brain development takes far longer, requiring seventeen Earth years to achieve maturity.

"Secondly, much of our larger brains are dedicated to developing and dealing with *emotions*. Having *two* parents not only improves a child's odds of genetic diversity, it *should* also double the amount of attention and love a child receives in childhood. Sons learn to respect women from their relationship with their mothers and how to be good men from their fathers. Daughters need mothers to learn to become women and fathers to teach them what to look for in a companion. Biology and evolution gave us two parents for many reasons. Do you think yourselves wiser than the established patterns of life?"

Darius paused to take a breath, but only a very short breath. He resumed his attack on the Brazilian representative, "Ambassador Ferriera, in your opinion, which is the most important generation?"

Ferriera paused, again confused by the unexpected direction of the question. "That generation would be mine—the generation that leads our nations."

Darius paused, looking disappointed. He responded a bit more quietly, seeming to wonder if he should resign himself to the futility of this lecture.

"On Parmithia, we consider the most important generation to be the *next* generation. As older generations age, they become less relevant and far less important to the future of a planet. Members of the older generations *die*. They leave behind only the teachings and influences they have had on their children and their children's children."

Darius sighed and placed his hands flat on the lectern in front of him.

"Parmithians believe each generation has a responsibility to provide a clean planet and a loving, educational childhood for the *next* generation! This priority affects *all* decisions we make, be they about our environment, economy, or use of natural resources. If a man fathers a child for which he takes no responsibility, he is undermining the ability of the next generation to solve future problems and issues. It is a crime akin to treason. Strong two-parent families are important to Parmithians and certainly more important than the collection of taxes."

Darius paused and dipped his head, as if regretting his last remark. The entire gallery of representatives from the United Nations was silent. Then the secretary general witnessed one of the strangest sights he had ever seen in his years of service at the United Nations. About twenty delegates stood up and applauded Darius's speech, making clear their agreement with his words. About one hundred representatives, including Joao Ferreira of Brazil and Winston Hall of Great Britain, gathered their belongings and stormed out of the conference hall, making clear their indignation. Who had given this alien the right to judge Earth?

Chapter 6

NEW YORK CITY

For the next several days, each member of the Parmithian team held one-on-one meetings in small conference rooms in the Four Seasons Hotel. At Darius's request, Allie had reserved the rooms but had not scheduled any meetings in them. Darius made it clear that Phil and his security team were not invited to the meetings and were to remain posted outside of the conference room door of their assigned charge. Each visitor was checked for weapons and cell phones as Darius had strictly forbidden any recording devices in the meetings. At his own discretion, Casaverde took photos of each visitor. General Bart would want to know with whom the Parmithians were meeting, and the major dared not be unprepared for the question.

Phil recognized several visitors from the meeting at the United Nations, all of whom had applauded Darius's speech. There were several foreign political leaders of countries friendly with the United States. He also recognized several business tycoons and a couple of directors of philanthropic agencies. But most guests looked like common laborers who had just come in from their farms for their interview. The guest list really didn't make any sense to Casaverde. If Darius was planning a conquest of Earth, then he was meeting with all the wrong people.

Darius's remarks at NASA and in the United Nations had both become public record. Pirated videos of his speeches were posted on social media and immediately went viral. It soon became apparent that earthlings did not like to be criticized. Headlines had turned nasty.

"Parmithians Say Earth Will Not Be Trusted with Dark-Energy Technology!"

"Parmithians Chastise United Nations for Deadbeat Parents!"

"Don't Make Plans to Visit Parmithia. You are NOT Welcome!"

News broadcasts invited authoritative guests to speculate on why the aliens were not even trying to spread goodwill and establish peaceful trade with their home planet. Whether one believed that the aliens were on Earth to establish trade relations or to scout for an invasion, harshly criticizing the whole population didn't seem to be a smart move. True, child psychologists had been decrying the problems of children in single-parent homes for decades. Social workers reported that the problem was growing worse every year. As the first outside observer the Earth had ever had, Darius had called out an entire planet for the way it treated its children.

Predictably, the popularity of the Parmithians plummeted. Political leaders in the United States and several foreign countries felt safe in expressing their disgust at Darius's judgments. A few politicians and church leaders had the courage to suggest that laws might be strengthened to make fathers more responsible for the support of their children. In the end, their comments were drowned out by a general outrage that preoccupied news and social media outlets.

While Phil, Allie, and the rest of the security team had stayed at the hotel each evening, the Parmithians had been shuttled to their ship at the end of each day. There had been little time to socialize. On Friday, their last day in New York, Darius invited Majors Casaverde and Heroux to an early dinner with the entire Parmithian team. Phil and Allie agreed but, to maintain security, stipulated that the dinner be catered in one of the private conference rooms in the hotel. With their new notoriety, the Parmithians would certainly be recognized in a public restaurant. With their falling popularity, confrontations could be expected.

In the last few days, Phil and Allie had formed a working relationship with the Parmithians. Neither side felt like the other was so alien anymore. Yet there was also an appreciable amount of tension in the room. Phil knew that many people in Washington were unhappy with the events of the past week. He and Allie were being held responsible by many of them.

Finally, Allie decided that the strained silence had gone on long enough. Addressing the whole group, she decided it was time to break the ice.

"In his speech in Washington, Darius said that you have taken earthly names during your stay that have a special meaning to you. I think I can guess those historical figures whose names you have taken. Teresa, let's start with you. Given your study of our religion, I would say you have taken the name of Teresa in recognition of Mother Teresa, a famous Roman Catholic nun."

Teresa smiled at Allie, pleased with the happier turn in the conversation. "Yes," she agreed, "Saint Teresa of Calcutta founded her own charitable organization but insisted on personally working with the poor for her whole life. She is an inspiration to all those who seek to do God's will. She represented a life and mission that I wish to follow."

Allie glanced over at Matthew, who was sipping his wine and obviously enjoying the shift in the discussion as well. "Matthew, I am guessing that you must have taken your name from the first Gospel writer of the Christian New Testament. He didn't have a last name either, just Matthew."

Matthew smiled and nodded. "Christianity and its message of kindness, charity, and spiritual truth is actually quite similar to our religious beliefs in Parmithia. Taking the name of Jesus would have been…highly presumptuous. Matthew was a man with flaws, but in the end, he was a loyal disciple of the man he believed to be the Savior of the world."

Allie folded her hands in front of her and nodded at Matthew. "It's a very appropriate name for you."

Allie looked toward her newfound friend Amelia. "Amelia, our pilot, must have taken her name from another inspirational pilot named Amelia Earhart."

Amelia smiled, cocked her head, and looked at Allie. "Correct yet again! Yes, Amelia Mary Earhart was the first female pilot to fly solo across the Atlantic Ocean. She set numerous other aviation records and wrote best-selling books about her experiences. In an attempt to become the first female to circumvent the globe, she disappeared over the Pacific Ocean in 1937. She is quoted as saying that 'the lure of flying is the lure of beauty,' and I couldn't agree more."

Allie's tactic to reduce the stress level in the room seemed to be working. Each member of the Parmithian team had obviously spent considerable time contemplating their earthly names. Having Allie recognize the appropriateness of those names pleased them. The tension in the room began to dissipate.

Amelia caught Phil's gaze and held it. "Coincidentally, the name Amelia is also very close to my Parmithian name, which is pronounced Amelshia."

Phil smiled, nodded thoughtfully, but said nothing. He felt that Amelia had just purposefully shared her name with him personally. His heart was beating so fast he forced himself to drop his gaze and take a deep breath to calm himself. This woman was more distracting than he thought possible.

Allie continued to share her conclusions, "Friedrich, your name is a little more shrouded in history. I admit to running an Internet search on it. I would say the name you have taken is in honor of Johann Carl Friedrich Gauss, a German mathematician. According to Google, and I quote, he influenced number theory, mathematic construction, and modular arithmetic. I don't know what any of that means, but it seems to fit with your personality."

Friedrich looked up from his meal, suddenly blushing furiously from Allie's smile and focused attention.

"Ye...yes," he answered haltingly. "You are correct. Carl Friedrich Gauss was a great mathematician who helped establish the foundation of statistics. As a fellow statistician, I feel his work remains somewhat unappreciated."

Allie had noticed the interchange that had just occurred between Phil and Amelia. She could not contain her own curiosity and asked, "So if I may ask, Friedrich...what is your Parmithian name?"

Friedrich gazed at Allie for a moment and seemed to come to a decision. "My real name is… Tobiagentrium Lodentious," he replied, "which may help explain why we took Earth names for our visit."

Allie nodded and smiled. Friedrich was a genuinely nice man, obviously very intelligent. She had always been attracted to intelligent men… Allie snapped out of her reverie and sat up straight in her chair. She flushed at the direction her thoughts had taken her. She looked around the room, anxious to move on. Allie's eyes finally rested on Newton, who was sitting right next to her.

"And, Newton, our engineer. Your choice of name could only have come from Sir Isaac Newton, the famous English astronomer who formulated our laws of motion and gravity."

The big man returned Allie's smile and nodded as he swallowed a bite of his second helping of food. "Isaac Newton was a great man to emulate. His accomplishments were amazing for his time. He was a philosopher as well. My favorite quote of his was '*I can calculate the motion of heavenly bodies but not the madness of people.*'"

"Which is a very good segue into another topic we must discuss," Phil interrupted, bunching up his napkin and throwing it on his plate.

It had been obvious that Phil had been fuming through the whole meal. He caught and held Darius's eyes.

"Darius, I have to ask you, are you visiting Earth to calculate the madness of our people?"

The lighter mood of the discussion immediately evaporated, and Allie couldn't help scowling at Phil. Phil didn't notice; he was looking at Darius for answers. The Parmithian commander returned Phil's stare but did not offer a reply.

Phil continued his attack, "Sir, Major Heroux and I talked to President Schaeffer and General Bart this afternoon. They would like to know, in their own words, 'what the hell is going on.' Since they last saw you, you have withdrawn the offer of your greatest technical advancement to NASA. You have offended the United Nations General Council, most of whom stormed out of the assembly hall. The White House is receiving calls from our closest *allies* calling for the termination of your tour and warning us of dangers to your safety should you try to visit their nation."

Everyone looked to Darius, who was chewing his last bite of dinner. He hesitated, contemplating his answer as he swallowed his food. He wiped his mouth and hands with his white linen napkin and finally looked up. In a terse and unapologetic tone, he replied, "Major Casaverde, you should let President Schaeffer know that a standard first-contact visit is scheduled to last from four to six Earth weeks. During that time, it is the mission commander's responsibility to decide if the planet being visited has the social organization, maturity, and morality to be trusted with Parmithian technology and assistance. The Earth is not to that point yet. With some work, I think it could possibly become so. I believe Earth is neither socially mature nor morally responsible because your citizens have *never been required to discipline themselves.* The challenge given to the United Nations was just one of the requirements that will be made of Earth. You will either meet those requirements or you won't."

Darius turned to face Allie. "Major Heroux, in answer to your question regarding our chosen names, I took the name Darius from an ancient king of Persia. He reorganized his empire and its leadership. He created a new monetary system, built roads, and oversaw the construction of new buildings and government. Because of him, the Persian Empire was unified and elevated to a previously unattained level of civilization. That is what I am trying to do—elevate Earth to a new level of civilization."

Darius stood, making it clear this conversation was over. "Major Casaverde, make no mistake about it. Your planet *is* being judged. If Earth cannot redirect itself to become more socially stable and morally responsible, then Parmithia cannot share any of its technology. We will not help you fix your significant technical problems because your cultural irresponsibility will lead to your self-destruction anyway. So what's the point? You and your leadership might expect more of the same discomforts you felt at the United Nations meeting. We will appreciate transportation to our ship in the morning, and we will see you in Rome tomorrow night."

With that announcement, Darius walked out of the room.

Chapter 7

CONGRESSIONAL HEARINGS

The next morning, Phil and his security team escorted the Parmithian team from their rooms to the hotel lobby. Phil had some unexpected news, and he had decided that a public place would reduce the likelihood that Darius would explode at him in anger. He stopped in the middle of the lobby. The Parmithians and the security team gathered around him, perplexed at the delay. Phil closed his eyes for a moment, gathered himself, and made his announcement. "We are not going to Rome…at least not right now."

Darius opened his mouth to protest, but Phil rushed ahead with his explanation, holding his hands in front of him to deflect any argument.

"General Bart called me late last night. The Congressional Committee of Extraterrestrial Affairs, which formed the day after you arrived, has issued subpoenas for each of you…and for Major Heroux and myself. Your comments to NASA and the United Nations have raised concerns that your visit will not provide Earth with opportunities to…share technology and commerce. We are to appear before the committee at 9:00 a.m. on Monday morning. Your ship and a government jet are standing by at Andrews Air Force Base to take us all to Washington. Congress has subpoena authority, and President Schaeffer and General Bart formally request that you comply."

The Parmithians all looked to their leader. Darius nodded thoughtfully and sighed. Resigned to the new reality, he answered, "Then let's go," and continued his walk to the exit of the hotel.

*****

After the arrival of the Parmithians, Congress had selected members of the new Committee of Extraterrestrial Affairs and several subcommittees to write laws to govern America's trade and interaction with the new planet. There was much to consider. Would Parmithians be allowed to patent their technologies, or would their discoveries need to be transferred to a US corporation? How would taxes be collected on Parmithian trade? It was almost certain that a new cabinet secretary post would be needed. Many congressmen saw Parmithia as the very break they needed to further their political careers.

The first shock came when the Parmithians admitted to NASA that they couldn't—or wouldn't—share their dark-energy technology. To add insult to injury, they announced at the United Nations that they weren't planning on establishing diplomatic or commercial ties either. Apparently, there was to be no trade, no embassy, no tariffs, and no taxable profits! The Parmithians obviously needed to recognize the vast opportunities that lay before them. A hearing was scheduled, and subpoenas were issued. Members of the Senate Judiciary Committee and the Committee on Commerce, Science, and Transportation were invited to attend. The meeting would be broadcast through normal C-SPAN and news channels.

The meeting was to be held in the Central Hearing Facility of the Hart Senate Office Building on Capitol Hill. At 8:30 a.m., Phil, Allie, and the Parmithian team were looking for their assigned seats. The men all wore suits for the occasion in colors ranging from navy blue to light gray. Amelia was dressed in a bright-green dress with a flowered scarf; Teresa was dressed in a blue skirt and white blouse. Phil had rather expected the group to all be in uniform. It was almost as if someone was trying to emphasize that the Parmithians were all different individuals, certainly not a military strike force to be opposed. Phil turned and looked at Allie, immediately realizing she had worked her wardrobe magic again. That woman attended to so many levels of detail it was embarrassing.

Phil and Darius had been seated next to each other at the witness table, each with their own microphone. The rest of the team sat behind them. Allie positioned herself directly behind Phil. Matthew sat directly behind Darius, both close enough to whisper advice. Phil turned to Allie. Only half-jokingly, he asked a favor. "Would you consider changing places with me?"

Understanding the pressure Phil was under, Allie smiled kindly, "You are the ranking major, so no…but I'll be right here should you need me."

Senator Douglas Croft, from the great state of Virginia, was the head of the Congressional Committee of Extraterrestrial Affairs. Croft was one of the oldest members of the Senate. Yet he had aged gracefully, sporting a full head of white hair. He had the puffy physique and bronzed tan of someone whose workouts took place on the golf course. His glasses sat atop his head, ready for use. It was time to begin, and the camera teams had all indicated they were ready to go. Croft cleared his throat to gain everyone's attention and spoke into his microphone, "Ladies and gentlemen, it is time to begin. Could everyone please take your seats? Remember to silence your cell phones. If this meeting is interrupted, someone will be asked to leave."

After a cacophony of the sounds of sliding chairs and settling bodies, Senator Croft brought the meeting to order. He introduced himself, other members of the committee, and recognized other notable guests.

With the preliminaries out of the way, the senator began the interrogation. "This meeting was called to conduct an investigation into the statements and intentions of the foreign delegation from the planet of Parmithia. We would like to keep these proceedings informal, but the committee does have some specific questions they would like answered. We are going to dispense with an introductory statement by the witnesses and go directly to our questions. Ambassador Darius will be the spokesman for his group. Major Phillip Casaverde has led security and travel for the delegation and is also available to answer questions. Each committee member will have twenty minutes to ask their questions. As the chairman of this committee, I would like to ask the first question."

Senator Croft moved his glasses to the bridge of his nose, looked down at his notes, and carefully read his question word for word, "Ambassador Darius, you have made comments the last few weeks that indicate that Parmithia may *not* be willing to enter into diplomatic relations and trade agreements with the planet Earth. These are very disturbing implications for our nation as we see potentially great opportunities of mutual benefit for our two peoples. My question, sir, is can you explain what you meant by your statements? What are your intentions in visiting our planet and, more specifically, our country?" Senator Croft looked up from his notes and nodded to the Parmithian leader.

Darius, who had no notes, looked at the committee and then carefully and diplomatically crafted his response to its chairman. He leaned forward to speak into his microphone. "Senator, I appreciate the opportunity to address this newly formed committee and your nation. As the Parmithian mission leader, my planet has given me responsibility over this first contact with Earth. Besides introducing ourselves, it is my duty to decide if Parmithia should provide our technology with Earth. In doing so, will it help or harm your planet? In this case, it is a difficult decision to make."

The faces of the subcommittee hardened at this news. By design, congressional investigatory meetings were meant to intimidate witnesses. It didn't seem to be working well on Darius. The Parmithian ambassador was aware of the reactions he was provoking but calmly continued his defense.

"The decision to not immediately provide you with dark-energy technology was made even before we arrived on your planet. Based on the constant unrest and violence we saw in your television broadcasts, it was clear Earth could not be trusted with a technology that can so easily be…weaponized." Darius said the last word distastefully, as if it was bitter to his tongue.

Phil shifted in his chair. If Darius was any indicator of his people, Parmithians spoke directly and to the point. Darius was not couching his remarks with compliments.

Darius continued, "In regard to production and utilizing planet resources, you are very advanced. In fact, the wealthy of your planet live far and above the highest living standards of our own citizenry. You have bigger houses, fancier transportation vehicles, more clothing, more jewelry, and more elaborate parties. You have the trappings of being civilized but not the moral standards required for such an advanced society. The fact that you do not prioritize the well-being of your next generation means to us that you are…still morally uncivilized."

Phil groaned audibly, hoping Darius would hear him. The words "still morally uncivilized" echoed off the chamber walls. Several of the committee, who had hunkered down expecting a long and windy apology by the Parmithian leader, were sitting up in shock. Had they heard him correctly? Didn't this alien understand his role as ambassador? He was here to be judged by *them*, not the other way around.

Darius paused for a moment to gather his thoughts. He had found a pair of red dice somewhere and was fiddling with them in his right hand, helping him divert some of his nervous energy.

"I have tasked the United Nations with finding an immediate solution to this issue. This is a global problem that requires a global solution. I hope the citizens of your world will realize the error of their ways and make changes."

Darius paused and Senator Croft took the opportunity to interrupt. "So," Croft summarized, "you have judged our planet and found it wanting."

The Parmithian shrugged and shook his head.

"Actually, you have interrupted us in the middle of our fact-finding. I have yet to make a final decision. You are correct that there are significant opportunities for our two planets to benefit from diplomatic relations and trade. Your planet could especially benefit from our food production and environmental sanitation capabilities."

The senator from Virginia considered this last point for a moment. Yes, in any planetary cooperation, Earth would certainly benefit more. However, five-year voyages from Parmithia to Earth would put a crimp on trade; only his grandchildren could expect to profit from it. But acquiring the dark-energy drive would assure his legacy and that his name would be noted in future history books.

Jumping to the point of the meeting, Senator Croft shot back, "Well then, Ambassador Darius, what does the United States have to do to merit an exchange of energy source technologies?"

Darius held the senator's eyes, speaking only to him but knowing the turmoil his next words would cause. Very deliberately, Darius outlined his expectations. "The United States is the technological and economic leader of Earth. Your country *must* be a part of the planetary agreement with Parmithia, or there will be no agreement. But your nation is torn apart by hundreds of tribes, ethnic groups, and special interests. Such instability is…unacceptable for a partner of Parmithian exchange. These petty conflicts distract your nation from working on the real problems that assault your planet. There is only one way to get your country on track to take the leadership role required of it."

Darius paused for a moment, adding to the drama of the moment. Everyone was holding their breath. Congressional committee meetings were normally not this exciting. Phil placed his hand over his microphone and leaned over to speak with Darius, but he was ignored. The Parmithian leader never broke eye contact with Senator Croft as he presented his demands.

"The United States must repeal all laws and regulations that provide entitlements, quotas, supplier preferences, tax deductions, and all other unearned advantages that are based on ethnicity, gender, religion, or lifestyle choice. Any group that seeks to promote such government and corporate bias will be disbanded. Congress must enact new laws to establish and enforce this new approach to removing the systemic biases in your society".

Gradually, the committee and everyone else in the room came to understand the intent of Darius's ultimatum. Multiple side conversations were initiated. Darius broke eye contact with Senator Croft. He leaned back in his chair and waited for the din to subside. Several committee members were petitioning for the floor, but Croft was not done with it yet. Obviously, this alien had no idea what he was requesting.

"Ambassador Darius, do you think you can force this country to change our government, culture, and society by dangling a new energy resource before us?"

Darius responded, "Senator, your list of technical problems is getting longer and more severe. Global warming has caused extreme weather, deforestation, desertification, and sea level rise resulting in the flooding of coastal cities. Soil infertility is leading to agricultural collapse and food shortages. Your freshwater sources are drying up. Instead of funding research to solve those problems, you waste your resources on social ills that should not even exist.

"If it is any consolation, Earth is not the first world to suffer such a problem with priorities. My people have studied many technically developed planets in the past century. As I mentioned in my remarks at the White House, all of these planets were civilized by human beings, identical to you and me. I have seen populations much like Earth's in various stages of self-destruction due to poor, short-sighted decisions of their governments. The most valuable thing that I can offer your country is not an energy resource. It is a view of your *future*. I am highly recommending that you make major changes to your policies. Otherwise, your country and planet will descend into chaos. Any efforts on our part to establish long-term alliances with Earth will end up being a colossal waste of my time!"

At this last comment, Senator Croft paled a bit. The meeting chamber quieted, broken only by the soft clicking of the dice Darius was rolling in his hand. Reactions were mixed between shock, anger, and fear. One committee member, forgetting to request the floor, blurted out the implications of this new information. "You mean other planets of humans have followed the same course we are on?"

Turning to face the questioner, Darius settled into his explanation of how Earth had arrived at its present situation.

"Congressman, in the early days of our respective evolutions, being part of a tribe meant security in a dangerous world. Our brains evolved to seek out family and friends who would cooperate in raising food, building shelters, and protecting each other from their enemies. But those days are long past for both of our planets. Tribal loyalties in a civilized world of millions do *not* unite a people. They tear them apart."

Like a war correspondent breaking bad news to his audience, Darius continued his explanation. "Humankind is competitive by nature, so every person believes that their tribe is better than all the others. One man will believe that only *his* tribe understands the nature of God, and he will wage war on anyone who disagrees. Another man will passionately believe that his ethnicity or wealth somehow makes his tribe superior and that it deserves special treatment. If such prejudices are not suppressed by law, the planet will eventually settle into wars of anarchy. The United States has more divisive tribalism than I ever witnessed. Its future is easily predictable."

Darius was getting emotional. Phil placed his hand on Darius's shoulder to calm him. Darius understood Phil's message. He visibly relaxed, resigned to the reality of what he was facing. In a calmer voice, he defined the logic behind his argument. "Ethnic clashes are so illogical. Why would anyone be proud of individual characteristics, which they had no part in choosing or developing? Your genetics, your parentage, and your birthplace are all random events."

Darius finally dropped the dice with which he had been rolling in his hand since before the meeting began. They clattered on the table for a moment, quieting the room.

"Being proud of unearned endowments of birth are like feeling superior to others for"—Darius looked down at his dice—"rolling a seven with this pair of dice. Neither is a noteworthy accomplishment."

Darius had given his speech. He turned his eyes up to the committee chair to ask one last question of his own. "Tell me, Senator Croft, when has the formation of special-interest groups based on ethnicity, religion, or politics ever helped bring your country together?"

The senator flushed in frustration, furiously trying to remember a time in history when diversity had brought peace to the land. There seemed no getting around the fact that the words *diverse* and *divisive* came from the same Latin root.

When no answer was forthcoming, Darius continued, "Sirs, I have read criticisms asking why our delegation has no one with darker skin, differing accents, or other evidence of diversity. You should understand that a Parmithian citizen would not even understand such a question. You can see there is a range of skin tones in our group, but such a characteristic is as unimportant to us as eye color, nose size, or left-handedness. On Parmithia, we have consciously worked for *decades* to eliminate the self-importance of distinctions of birth. Parmithians are recognized for their accomplishments in life—educational degrees, career success, charitable work, or scaling a mountain peak! Actual achievements form the legacies for which we are remembered."

Darius rubbed his forehead as if a headache was forming there. He had issued his challenge. He wrapped up his appeal with an ultimatum. "Congress is the lawmaking body for the United States. This is the *United* States of America, so be *united*. When you are successful at that, *then* maybe we can talk about providing energy technology."

Darius slid back his chair and started to stand up. It was apparent that he was leaving. Matthew and Allie both shot their hands out and placed them on Darius's shoulders, pushing him gently back down into his chair.

Seeing the encounter, Phil leaned forward and used his microphone for the first time. "Ladies and gentlemen of the committee, I would like to request a recess!"

Senator Croft, needing to regroup after this humiliating debacle, nodded in agreement. "We will take a thirty-minute break to consider this testimony."

When everyone returned to their seats, it was Matthew who sat behind the microphone next to Phil. Darius had left, complaining of light-headedness after the difficult and emotional speech he had made.

Senator Croft and the Extraterrestrial Affairs committee grilled Matthew for the next two hours, looking for ways around the newly established Parmithian requirement. Matthew repeatedly and patiently explained that his mission commander did indeed have the authority to judge Earth's capacity to solve its own problems. Darius was very experienced at first contacts. The Parmithian government would undoubtedly accept whatever recommendation he made.

Finally, the committee had asked all their questions and expressed all their outrage. Just before he declared the meeting over, Senator Croft warned the Parmithian team. "This discussion is not over. By a long shot, it is not over!"

Chapter 8

ESCAPE

Immediately after the thud of Senator Croft's gavel closed the meeting, most of the congressmen and their entourages stormed out of the auditorium. A few committee members and a fair share of the audience were able to deftly corner each member of the Parmithian team. Three women were talking to Amelia, apparently thinking that their shared gender would evoke sympathy for their situation. Matthew was surrounded by several senators, all interrupting one another with their objections. Even Newton and Friedrich had been engaged in conversations. Many people just wanted to meet an alien, but most everyone seemed desperate to communicate the impossibility of Darius's stipulation.

Phil managed to extract each member of the team, apologizing that they were late for lunch appointments that did not exist. With his security team diverting reporters and supplicants, Phil herded the Parmithians to the doors. Finally, they got everyone into the hallway and moving away from the meeting chamber.

Phil had sent three members of the team to retrieve their SUVs for a quick departure. The group passed into the Hart Building parking garage and started piling into their vehicles. Everyone froze when they heard angry shouts echoing off the parking garage walls. Suddenly several dozen armed protestors rounded the corner onto the garage ramp just behind and below them. Spotting their prey, the attackers howled like bloodhounds in a hunt and sprinted up the ramp toward them.

"Let's go, let's go, let's go!" shouted Phil.

Phil jumped into the driver's seat of the lead SUV, chastising his stupidity. The interview with the congressional committee had been scheduled for two days. It had been broadcasted live. It would have taken little effort to organize a riot, complete with a strategy to trap the alien team. Their assailants had come armed with clubs, handguns, and assault rifles. The implied safety of being on Capitol Hill in the middle of Washington, DC had lulled Phil's normally cautious mind. This attack should have been impossible.

"We can get out of this," Phil mumbled to himself as he cranked the steering wheel around. With tires squealing, Phil drove to the closest exit, his companion vehicles following close behind. As he arrived, he saw that two pickup trucks flying American and Confederate flags had blocked the exit. Two more trucks blocked the entrance ramp. Men with assault rifles stood in the truck beds, threatening security guards and anyone else who tried to get close. Other protestors waved their signs and encouraged one another with their chants.

"Resist the alien threat!"

"Nuke the mothership!"

When the three black SUV's with darkly tinted windows pulled up, the protestors immediately recognized their prey. Like paparazzi chasing a major film star, the rioters jostled one another as they sprinted toward the vehicles. Phil twirled his steering wheel, avoiding the exit. A few shots rang out, especially loud in the confines of the garage. Phil circled the spiraling ramp and drove to the next closest exit ramp that emptied out onto First Street and Constitution. But this exit was blocked just as the first one had been.

Phil didn't even slow down, again driving past the exit ramp and dropping deeper into the bowels of the parking garage. After a couple of fast turns, they unexpectedly found themselves clear of anyone who wanted to kill them. As the realization of what was happening finally hit him, Phil shouted into his headset, "They're driving us toward the bottom of the garage. We're driving into a trap!"

"Stop the cars!" came through his headphones but with an echoed quality that made it obvious it was not the voice of the security team driver who wore the headset. With no other good options before him, Phil obeyed the order and came to an abrupt halt. The other two vehicles screeched to a stop behind him. Phil quickly glanced at his two side mirrors to check for any pursuit.

Suddenly, Newton, the jovial Parmithian ship engineer, appeared from nowhere just outside of his side window. Newton had gotten out of the second SUV and sprinted to Phil's vehicle, balancing his briefcase on his left forearm. Phil jumped at Newton's sudden appearance and tried to open his door. Newton, a large man, slammed the door closed again and wagged his right index finger at Phil in the universal don't-do-that gesture. Newton dropped out of sight as he suddenly kneeled and laid his open briefcase on the ground.

The engineer appeared again, holding what looked like a thick square laptop computer in his hands. He placed the device against the car frame between the two car doors and pushed it, apparently activating a magnet that held the gadget securely in place. Picking up the briefcase, he ran to the front of the car and pressed a similar device to the front bumper. Finally, he ran to the passenger side of the car and attached a third device, leaving just enough space for him to open the back door and climb in beside Amelia. Phil noted that the beautiful ship's pilot had been in the back seat by herself. A small alarm went off in Phil's head at the realization, but much louder alarms drowned it out.

"What the hell, Newton!" Phil thundered.

Newton opened up his briefcase again, displaying a keyboard and small screen. He flipped a switch and typed in a few entries.

Newton folded his fingers together and watched his screen intently, brightening as three remote connection lights flashed.

"Major Casaverde, you're going to have to trust me! Um…you can drive now. Proceed to the nearest exit," he said matter-of-factly.

The major put the car into drive. Pulling his microphone to his mouth, he declared, "Follow me and stay close. We have a plan."

What an overstatement, Phil thought. Tires squealed as the vehicles made U-turns and headed back up toward the final garage exit.

As Phil had feared, the third exit was also blocked by parked trucks and over a hundred rioters. Again, Phil chastised himself for his incompetence. He had thought this a normal diplomatic protection assignment, and a protest march *inside a parking garage* made no sense. There was no press to publicize their turnout, no television cameras to record their demands. These ruffians weren't here to *protest* an alien presence; they were here to *eliminate* an alien threat. If the Parmithians were killed by angry rioters, there would be no single person to blame or prosecute.

As before, the rioters again ran toward the three Parmithian vehicles. Bullets started pinging off the car and bulletproof glass. Despite its hopelessness, Phil grabbed the gear shift to put the car in reverse.

"Wait!" cried Newton from the back seat. "Hang on!" He gently tapped a key on his laptop.

A gigantic WHUMP echoed off the walls. Phil watched as the first line of assailants suddenly all flew backward, as if a giant invisible hand had smacked into them. At the same time, in what felt like a head-on collision, the Suburban was shoved back. From the back seats, Amelia screamed, and Matthew shouted what might have been Parmithian profanities. Phil realized that the device Newton had put on the front bumper had caused the powerful repulsion of the protestor attack and the reactive jarring of his vehicle. Anticipating the next shock, Phil moved toward the center of the vehicle, straining against the restraint of his seat belt.

Sure enough, a second WHUMP, followed by a third, tossed the SUV around like a toy. Bouncing first left and then rebounding hard right, it felt as if the sturdy vehicle had been T-boned by two invisible compact cars on each side. The rear window shattered from the impact. Rioters who had advanced to the sides of the Suburban were flung into pillars and porcelain-tiled walls, several of them leaving large divots before crumpling to the floor.

The assault paused. The psychological effect of being attacked by an unknown force was almost as damaging as the physical attack itself. There had been no explosions. There was no smoke, no fire. The attackers realized that an alien weapon was being used against them. They didn't understand it, and thus, they feared it. Could it be deadly? Most of the mob stopped dead in their tracks.

Yet another WHUMP projected from the front of the SUV. Rioters who had staggered to their feet from the first attack, and a few who had wandered into the blast zone were again swept off their feet away from the vehicle. Most landed heavily against cement walls; some bounced off the low ceiling. The Suburban was a total wreck, but with the repeated blast, it seemed to declare, "I can keep this up all day!" The alien nature of the counterattack was too much for the rioters. They turned and sprinted toward the garage exit. The drivers of the pickup trucks blocking the exit jumped into their cabs and peeled away. In a few moments, the path out of the parking garage was clear.

Amazingly enough, the engine of Phil's Suburban was still running. The front bumper had protected the engine well enough to still be drivable. Phil thought it doubtful the attackers would return, but then again, he had been making poor conclusions all day. With the two other entourage vehicles behind him, Phil drove out onto Second Street. He activated his headset.

"I don't trust that the hotel can provide us acceptable security any longer. We're going straight to the Parmithian ship at Andrews Air Force Base." Phil hurt all over, and from the groans coming from the back seat, he knew his passengers were aching as well. "Is everyone all right back there?" he asked, looking into his rearview mirror.

Matthew and his bodyguard, who had been in the far back seat, assured him they had survived. Newton answered for himself and Amelia, "We are fine as well, thank you. Major, I'm sorry for the surprise buffeting. There was no time to explain my plan."

Phil glanced in the rearview mirror to look at the Parmithian engineer. "Newton, you saved all our lives back there. No apologies are necessary. What were those devices you put on the car?"

"They are small dark-energy projectors, similar to our ship engine, but on a much smaller scale of course. They create a stable repulsive force. They are handy for moving pallets and other heavy objects, lifting broken vehicles, and even for elevating myself to work on the exterior of the ship. I always carry a few in my ready bag, which was stored in the back of my vehicle. I set them to maximum repulsion and triggered them with their remote controls."

Phil nodded in appreciation. "Thanks for your quick thinking."

Newton smiled at him. "You are indeed welcome, Major. Again, I'm sorry about the pounding. The repulsive energy that knocked down our attackers had to push off from something...which was this automobile, of course."

As his adrenaline levels dropped, Phil relaxed a little, though he was still aching.

"Next time, could you maybe simply pull a phaser or a blaster out of that briefcase?"

Newton was looking curiously around the back of the vehicle as he replied, "Plots by *Star Trek* and *Star Wars* movies notwithstanding, Major, I'm afraid those weapons do not actually exist in this galaxy." Newton turned back around and asked offhandedly, "Say, where's Darius? Doesn't he usually ride in this vehicle?"

Phil groaned and realized that he had not seen Darius since he had excused himself from the congressional committee meeting. He activated his headset again. "Circle the wagons," he ordered tersely as he pulled into the parking lot of a Wendy's restaurant.

The two other Suburbans pulled in close behind him, forming a rough triangle. Everyone piled out into the center of the triangle. A quick headcount revealed that Darius was indeed missing.

"Who saw him last?" Phil looked at his security team and the Parmithians.

Two members of his team, Lieutenants Eleanor Stenson and Tyson Young, had been assigned to be on watch outside of the Senate meeting room. Lieutenant Young spoke up first, chagrin and embarrassment apparent in his voice. "Darius was sitting in one of the chairs in the hallway just outside of the meeting chamber. A large delegation of Asian diplomats walked between us. A few moments after they passed, I noticed Darius was gone. I thought he had gone to the restroom…but he never came back. I thought he had rejoined us as we left the building, but in the confusion, I never confirmed it. I take full responsibility for my oversight. I apologize."

Phil verbalized the question everyone was considering. "Why would Darius leave the group?" Phil asked.

He looked at Amelia, realizing that if anyone in the group would know, it would be her. She had traveled with the man for five years. Amelia was trying to diagnose a growing bruise on her left cheek. She stiffened when she noticed Phil looking at her. Her eyes darted back and forth as if looking for Darius behind the parked cars. Taking ahold of herself, she closed her eyes and thought for a moment.

Finally, she spoke, "Darius was very upset at how the hearing went. He lost his temper and felt he had ruined any chance of Congress attempting to solve the country's problems. Darius has become very emotional about this first contact. I think he decided his speech had doomed your planet to failure. But I have no idea where he would have gone."

The group was engulfed by the uncomfortable silence of not knowing what to do next. Seconds ticked away, no one able to strategize on how to find the lost Parmithian.

"Darius will be speaking on a radio talk show in about twenty minutes!" announced a clear feminine voice from the back of the group. Everyone turned to look at Major Heroux. Allie was gazing intently at her cell phone, slowly scrolling through the text.

"I Googled 'Darius,' and there is an announcement by *The Tom Blackstone Show* on KUTV that Darius will be a guest on their broadcast this afternoon… And before you ask, no, I did not set up this interview."

Phil looked at his counterpart. He had been about to call out a city-wide manhunt, but Allie had thought to use her cell phone to locate their missing alien. There was no doubt they had to recover Darius. The man was completely unstable and capable of doing much more harm to their mission. He needed a task force. Lieutenant Tyson Young appeared to be a man who spent a lot of time in the gym. His light-blond hair made him appear like a fresh recruit, but his uniform couldn't mask the muscular build of his torso. Young was staring intently at Phil, determined to recoup from his earlier failure, if given a chance.

"Lieutenant Young, Major Heroux, and Matthew, you're with me in vehicle three. We're going to find Darius. Everyone else get in the first two vehicles and head back to Andrews Air Force Base. Newton, get everyone back into the spaceship and lock it down."

As everyone sorted themselves out, Amelia approached Phil. She was visibly upset and physically leaned into him. He hugged her, wishing it could be extended but realizing he had to leave. During the chase in the parking garage, Amelia had smashed her face into a side window. A purple bruise was spreading into her left cheek. As they pulled apart, Amelia followed Phil's eyes as he inspected the damage.

"Is it bad?" she asked plaintively, cautiously touching her face.

Phil winced as he examined the bruise. "Yeah, it's bad. Half of your face will be purple and swollen in a few hours."

Amelia dropped her head, tears flowing freely now. Allie, standing to Phil's side, whacked him on the back of the head as she stepped around him. She muttered something about him being a lunkhead and stepped forward to engulf Amelia in a walking embrace.

"But…those kinds of bruises…they heal quickly!" Phil stammered at the retreating women. Phil fumed but decided this was not the right time for an apology. They had a runaway Parmithian to find.

Chapter 9

THE TOM BLACKSTONE SHOW

With Allie acting as navigator from the front passenger seat, Phil wound his way back through Washington traffic toward the radio station. For several minutes, everyone was content to remain silent, trying to recover their wits about them. From the back seat, Matthew shifted uncomfortably.

"Major Casaverde, why am I here?" he asked timidly.

Phil glanced at Matthew in his rearview mirror.

"Matthew, you are Darius's second-in-command. Darius may not know that this radio interview is dangerous for him. I doubt he will listen to me if I ask him to leave, but he may come with us if *you* ask him. I need you along to calm him down and get him to come with us."

Major Heroux, engrossed in her searches on her phone, removed her earpiece. She was visibly upset at what she had been viewing.

"Radio and television stations are replaying Darius's testimony to the congressional committee. They are calling his speech the Parmithian Judgment. Social media is blowing up. Special-interest groups, racial justice groups, and offended political leaders are railing against the Parmithians. Protests are being planned across the country all this week. Some are calling for violence. National Guard units are being called up in preparation for expected riots and looting."

FIRST JUDGMENT

Allie's phone played the first notes of Beethoven's *Fifth*, announcing the arrival of an important text. She glanced down and then looked up at Phil. "I have been texting updates to General Bart, keeping him apprised of our situation. He wants to know if we need any help."

For a moment, Phil's pride battled against his logic, but it quickly lost the argument. This situation was…deteriorating quickly.

"Tell him yes. We will need some help at the broadcast station."

Allie's thumbs flew across the keys of her phone. A few moments later, she announced, "The general says helicopter ETA is one hour."

With considerably less enthusiasm, she sighed. "And in other news, Darius's interview is beginning." Streaming the broadcast through the vehicle video system, she hugged herself and sat back in her car seat. On the screen, a middle-aged man appeared. Tom Blackstone's dark, slick-backed hair made him look rather like a used car salesman. His intense gaze, sharp features, and erect posture gave him the appearance of a dedicated journalist. He was built like someone who liked to run marathons. Blackstone stepped forward and clasped his hands in front of him.

"Ladies and gentlemen, welcome to *The Tom Blackstone Show*, broadcasting to you from KUTV studios. I am your host, Tom Blackstone, and we have a very controversial guest visiting us today. So we are going to dispense with our normal review of weekly politics and jump right into our interview. I'm sure our viewers want to hear from the alien commander Darius visiting us from a planet called Parmithia. Unless you've been living in a cave the past week, you already know about the visit and world tour of the Parmithian delegation."

Behind him a big-screen TV suddenly lit up, showing camera footage from outside the studio. About fifty people had already gathered, just outside the chain-link fence surrounding the KUTV building and parking lot. Some held signs declaring their outrage at the Parmithians. Blackstone looked up at the images with some concern.

"In fact, we have a number of viewers who seem to be protesting just outside of our gates. KUTV Studios would like to remind *everyone* that we *support* your protests of the harsh judgments that

Darius has rendered against our country," Blackstone continued. "We plan to uncover truth in this interview and ask that everyone remain peaceful." *So*, he thought, *there is no need to destroy the studio.*

Blackstone and Darius both sat on barstools in front of a couple of ferns and the large-screen television. Blackstone shifted uncomfortably in his chair. He knew the barstools were used to make the program appear edgier; the implication was that neither he nor his guests had time to sit down and get comfortable. But today, he regretted the posturing. He really couldn't get comfortable. The studio was in danger, and Blackstone couldn't shake the feeling of dread that things were going to go poorly today.

The television host's face darkened as the image on the screen behind him shifted to a drone camera flying over the studio. From all directions, more people were flocking to the broadcast studio. Blackstone knew they'd been advertising the upcoming interview with Darius for well over an hour. People were starting to pack around the gates and fencing. Chants arose and then gradually died out. The crowd was working itself up. Almost everyone out there was looking at their cell phones, curious as to what would be discussed on the show.

It was obvious to Tom that KUTV had no idea of what they'd gotten themselves into. But Darius had called *them* and asked *them* for the interview. It was too tempting an offer for the producers to turn down. The good news was that the broadcast would be watched by millions. The bad news was that there was a mob forming outside their very gates. The fact that this show might end up destroying the studio was an unexpected setback of the plan. Blackstone turned to the alien that was causing all the problems. Clipping the end of each word and in the harshest tones he could muster, Blackstone tried to initiate some damage control.

"Darius, as you know, you called *us* to request this interview today. Your testimony before the Committee of Extraterrestrial Affairs has caused a great deal of anger, not only in Washington but across the country. Protests are being planned starting tomorrow, and civic leaders fear that violence may accompany those protests! Did you expect any of this to result from your words? Was there something you wanted to tell our viewers today?"

Blackstone was fishing for an apology or anything to calm the mob displayed on the screen behind him. Darius looked uncertainly at the camera directly in front of him but then addressed his host directly.

"Mr. Blackstone, first I wish to thank you for having me on your program today. I requested to come on your show to appeal directly to the inhabitants of Earth and specifically to the citizens of the United States."

"Darius, what would you like to say to America?"

As he had seen Blackstone do, Darius turned toward the closest camera. "The United States is the most powerful nation on Earth. It leads the world in military strength, a strong economy, a large population, and a history of leadership. The United Nations is based here. From our studies of your planet, we believe that many countries will follow America's lead in whatever they choose to do. Thus, it is up to the United States to make good decisions to pull planet Earth from the brink of disaster."

Blackstone shifted uncomfortably on his barstool. Less than two minutes into the interview and it was not headed in a good direction. It was time to push back.

"Darius, you're being a bit melodramatic, don't you think?" Blackstone snorted. "Doomsayers have been predicting the end of the world for centuries. Is there really a need for such gloom and doom?"

"Mr. Blackstone, your fellow earthlings who predicted the end of the world were just guessing. During our journey here, my statistician, Friedrich, has downloaded terabytes of economic and social data from your Internet. He has built models around global warming, agricultural output, and the effects of armed conflicts. Friedrich compared those results to equivalent data from several dozen other inhabited worlds. Some of those planets had very stable societies, while some were in the final stages of collapse. The comparisons are valid."

Blackstone tried to interrupt, but Darius would not permit it. His words came faster, knowing the time for his appeal was short.

"In short, Mr. Blackstone, human species must either develop balanced and fair societies or they develop selfish, vain, and narcissistic cultures that eventually collapse. According to our models, you are less than a decade away from a massive breakdown of your global social structure."

Tom Blackstone had stopped looking at the gathering mob outside his building, totally absorbed by what Darius was saying. The Parmithians were not guessing about the downfall of Earth. Their statisticians had already *seen* Earth's future on other worlds. Tom felt like he had been punched in the gut. He realized he should have seen this coming.

In college, Blackstone had been an environmental activist. He had seen the difficulties that had become more serious each passing year. After graduation, his career had taken over his life. There was simply no time to keep saving the world. But his concern for the Earth and its health was never far from his mind. Many of his guests were certifiable crackpots, and it helped sooth his conscience that their charges were nonsense. But other of his guests were serious researchers who had data to show the Earth was in serious trouble. He, like most of the Washington politicians he had interviewed, had embraced a comfortable state of denial. Blackstone looked up at the TV monitor behind him, still showing the growing crowds outside the station. Suddenly, the mob didn't seem quite as important to him anymore.

*****

Phil, Allie, Matthew, and Tyson Young had gotten within five blocks of the KUTV building when traffic stopped. The protest had drawn several hundred participants and spectators. The gray day reflected the mood of the protestors. In a gesture of added defiance, many people had simply left their cars parked in the middle of the street. Traffic was at a standstill.

"Everybody out of the car. We run from here!" Phil instructed. He jumped out of the vehicle, lifted its back hatch, and grabbed the emergency backpack that he carried in the SUV. Everyone but Matthew was still in dress uniform from the congressional hearing. Phil started peeling off his shirt, drawing puzzled looks from his gathering team.

Phil opened his backpack and pulled out a couple of well-worn T-shirts. He threw them to Matthew and Tyson. "Put these on!" Meanwhile, Phil struggled into an old Washington Commanders sweatshirt.

Allie pulled off her military jacket but then looked at Phil and shrugged. If she did any further disrobing, it would draw more attention to the group, not detract from it. Phil smiled at her, shaking his head.

"I have an idea. Allie, leave your sidearm. Everyone, follow me and stay close. Use first names only, no one mention rank."

Lieutenant Young, now simply Tyson, slammed the hatch down as they set off for the broadcast station.

*****

Blackstone looked at his guest. Part of him desperately wanted the man to shut up. But the part of him that had been an environmental activist demanded he listen to the end to this story.

"Darius, what can we do to avoid this Armageddon you are describing?"

Darius had rather expected to have been dragged off the stage by now. The opportunity to continue delivering his message surprised him.

"Mr. Blackstone, Earth needs Parmithian help. You need our technology to remedy your environmental crises, reestablish healthy farmlands to bolster your food production systems. Climate change has made vast areas of your world unusable for growing crops. Food distribution channels have been blocked by rebellious factions trying to overthrow their governments."

Blackstone took a deep breath. He recognized this argument. Agronomists, soil scientists from the USDA, and several farmers had been on his program in the past, forewarning of this same catastrophic situation. There was nothing about Darius's statements that was a surprise. Yet Darius's declarations came with the authority of an outside source who had seen worlds similar to Earth fall to ruin. Tom knew he should be trying harder to placate the demonstrators outside, but their protests seemed childish right now. He continued his interview.

"Darius, I heard what you said to the Congressional Committee this morning. What can I and this show do to help us qualify for Parmithian aid?"

Darius knew this was the moment when he had to turn a country of millions against itself.

"Mr. Blackstone, the government of Parmithia will not take on a losing cause by trying to help planets that will squander our help. If a society is so divided as to be beyond redemption and refuses to change, then my superiors have ordered me to leave it to its fate. I have had to walk away from planets in conflict twice in my career. Those two decisions ..they resulted in the deaths of millions of people."

Roars and chants could be heard as the mob reacted to what they were hearing on their cell phones. Blackstone glanced up at the screen. Protestors were starting to climb over the chain-link fence. Darius continued, becoming more emotional, but unperturbed by the crowd.

"I don't want to have to make the decision to leave Earth without our assistance. Yet I can't lie to my government either. My political leaders are aware of the attacks on our delegation. They know about the armed conflicts and violent protests going on across this world and now apparently right outside your doors. This violence will disqualify Earth from Parmithian assistance. I don't want that to happen. I believe most of your listeners don't want it to happen either."

Blackstone made no move to speak. Obviously, Darius was ready to deliver the punchline. He was certain that neither he nor the crowd outside his gates were going to like it. Blackstone did not trust himself to say anything. Any statement he made would become an attempt to stop Darius from saying what must be said. This was too important of an opportunity for mankind. His career and this studio building be damned. He nodded to Darius, holding his gaze, giving him nonverbal permission to finish his appeal.

Darius plunged forward, knowing this would be his last opportunity to change the course of destruction Earth seemed intent on taking.

"Tom, I am convinced that the ills of your planet are due to leaders who refuse to carry out their responsibilities to care for this planet and provide for the next generation. Special-interest groups are a minority in this nation, but they are controlling its decisions. This vocal, sometimes violent minority will determine the fate of this planet if nothing changes. But it must change. If your nation wants Earth to have a future, its majority must step forward and change its course."

Darius motioned to the television screen showing images of a protest now becoming a riot. Hundreds had climbed the fences. A pickup truck with monster wheels had pushed down the gate and was driving over it.

"Conflicts like this must be stopped. Your country—and planet—must find a way to evolve from this dog-eat-dog world to a higher law of empathy and caring for one another. This is not a new concept for Earth! A man who called himself a son of God taught these principles in Israel over two thousand years ago. Religions created to teach these truths were once numerous. What has happened to your world, that such beliefs have been lost? This people must step forward and stop the violence and social disruption. If not... my Parmithian team and I must leave, and we won't be allowed to return."

Blackstone swallowed, aware of the fact that this broadcast would go down in the history books if anyone was left to write them. Darius had just looked into the eyes of the mob outside as well as all agitators and anarchists around the world and did not blink. Instead, he had predicted their downfall.

For a moment, Blackstone's world was silent as he contemplated the ultimatum Darius had just delivered. The silence was broken by a roar of rage and wrath from the throats of a thousand people as they broke through the gates of the security fence and flooded toward the building.

*****

Allie could just make out the words "KUTV Broadcasting" on the front of their destination. She was winded; Phil had led an all-out sprint for five blocks, dodging gawkers watching the protest. Suddenly, Phil broke off his sprint and jogged to a WTEL television van, where cameramen were recording the protest outside the gates of their competitor station. Phil flashed his military ID and asked to speak to the person in charge. A lead reporter stepped forward. What began as an animated discussion quickly escalated into a heated argument. There was a pause in the shouting as the combatants glared at one another. Allie approached the two men, ready to give Phil any backup he required.

Phil purposefully dropped his hand to rest on his sidearm. He slowly and emphatically said, "I need a camera, and I need it now," in a tone that promised any further delay meant things were going to get ugly.

The reporter finally raised both his hands in a defeated motion. It wasn't his camera. One of the camera crew hustled a large WTEL News camera over to Phil. Phil motioned for Matthew to join them and take the camera.

"Matthew, you are now our cameraman. Learn how to point this thing and turn it on."

Phil then grabbed a large black microphone from another crew member. He handed it to Allie. "Allie, you are now our lead WTEL field correspondent. Congratulations."

Chapter 10

RESCUE OPERATION

A thousand angry rioters bent on murder separated Phil and his team from Darius. The sheer numbers of the mob were making it hard for them to even approach the front door of the building. Phil and Tyson took the lead, throwing attackers out of the way to create a space for their group. Tyson kept bellowing, "Make room for the press!" though his command didn't seem to make much of an impression. Matthew, lugging the large camera on his shoulder, and Allie, pretending to be a hard-charging news correspondent, followed closely behind in his wake. No one impeded their progress for long. To all appearances, this was just an overly aggressive female reporter with a couple of muscle-bound thugs handling the crowd for her.

Finally, they arrived at the front door, jammed with people. Tyson wedged himself between two big, hairy rioters who were clogging up the center of the crowd and pushed them apart, forming a small gap. Allie and Matthew squeezed through the hole just before one of the two thugs turned and took a swing at the trained Army man. Tyson ducked the blow and caught the man with two swift counterpunches. The rioter dropped to his hands and knees, so Phil stepped on him, forcing him down and creating a larger hole in the crowded doorway. He took the lead, and Tyson took up rear guard.

As they cleared the front door, the crowd loosened up as rioters dispersed in all directions, looking for aliens or something valuable to steal. Allie glanced at a map on the countertop of the abandoned reception desk.

"*The Tom Blackstone Show* is in studio B, second floor!" she yelled.

Phil charged up the stairs, followed by Allie, her cameraman Matthew, and Tyson. Studio B was at the top of the stairs and packed with shouting rioters. In the center of the mob stood one of the largest men Phil had ever seen. He wore a pair of overalls over a worn T-shirt stenciled with *These Colors Don't Run*. A battered *America First* trucker's hat sat atop his bald head. This giant of a man was clutching Darius with one hand by the front of his shirt and jacket. He had just used the other hand to pummel Darius with a punch and then a backhand. Darius was dazed and barely standing. His nose was bleeding freely, and his left eye was already beginning to swell. Three fellow henchmen formed an honor guard around their leader, pushing back the crowd. But the beating had just begun, and the attacker's hand was rising for yet another blow.

"Stop!" thundered Phil. His hand dropped to his sidearm, but there were a number of handguns in this horde. Hammers clicked, and pistols were raised. It looked like the studio would become the scene of a shootout. Phil froze, leaving his sidearm in its holster.

"Wait!" screamed Allie. Amazingly, everyone stopped and looked at her. Allie was still in a white blouse and dress skirt, decidedly overdressed for the occasion. Between that and the microphone she was waving in front of her, the crowd parted to let her pass. Not hesitating, she thrust the microphone in the face of the giant assailant and asked the most distracting question she could think of.

"Sir, what is your name?"

Matthew had seen enough Earth news videos to understand his job. He hovered just over Allie's shoulder, his eye pressed into the viewfinder and pointing the camera directly at the large man in overalls. The man appeared confused and stared into the camera lens. He looked at his hand, streaked red with Darius's blood. Guilt, fear, and stage fright washed over his face. Obviously, he was not expecting an interview in the middle of giving a beating.

Allie gave Mr. Overalls just a few seconds to answer. He was not forthcoming, so not wanting to lose the moment, Allie turned toward the camera and moved the microphone back to her mouth. In her loudest reporting voice, she nearly shouted into the camera.

"This is Allison Heroux reporting to you from the KUTV broadcasting station, where the man behind me is *beating* the leader of the Parmithian delegation that has come to Earth on a goodwill mission! Because of this assault, it seems highly likely that Parmithia will send spaceships to attack the United States in retribution for *this man's* violent actions! Americans deserve to know the name of the man who may have just destroyed our homes, children, and way of life."

Turning toward the attacker, she attacked, "So, sir, I ask you again. WHAT IS YOUR NAME?"

Allie pushed the microphone back in front of the aggressor's mouth and raised her eyebrows in her best answer-the-damn-question expression.

The assailant, certainly not the smartest man in the world, recognized that he did not want to be here any longer. Being responsible for the destruction of Earth probably carried some serious jail time. Besides, assaulting someone on camera was never a good idea. Mr. Overalls dropped Darius, pushed through his minions, and lumbered out the door. Without external support, Darius fell to his knees.

The three henchmen looked at one another, completely flummoxed by the loss of their leader. Allie turned toward the closest of the three and purposefully moved toward him, extending the microphone. Matthew swiveled the video camera toward the lackey and drew closer. It was too much for the bewildered man. Before Allie could ask another question, all three men fled in panic, pushing their way through the door.

Phil and Tyson appeared beside Darius, took him by his arms, and gently raised him from the floor.

Phil looked up at Allie, continuing his hired muscle impersonation. "Ms. Heroux, Ambassador Darius is in need of medical attention. We should go." They practically carried the dazed Darius to a fire exit behind them that led to a concrete stairwell.

Allie turned toward the confused protesters standing around her. She knew they needed to continue standing there for a few moments longer. Matthew now had the camera pointed at her. Allie straightened her blouse, raised her chin, and took on the self-confident air of an investigative reporter.

"Reporting from the KUTV broadcast center, this is Allie Heroux from WTEL, signing off."

Allie lowered the microphone from her mouth. Maintaining the charade another few moments, she announced, "Okay, Matt, that's a wrap. Let's go see if we can get an interview."

Walking quickly but not running, Allie and Matthew followed their companions out the emergency exit. As they entered the stairwell, Matthew pointed up at Phil, Tyson, and Darius, who had paused to wait for the camera team one flight above them. Allie was exhausted, and going up these stairs did not offer much hope for an escape from this madness.

"We need to go *down*!" Allie yelled, protesting the logic of the chosen direction.

"We need to go *up*!" Phil yelled back. "No one commits murder on television, but look at the mob down there! They won't just let us make it to the gate. We go up to the roof!"

The trio disappeared around a turn of the staircase. Allie and Matthew followed. The team trudged up five more floors and burst through a door onto the roof. Phil spotted some large HVAC fans in a far corner of the roof and, still holding Darius upright, pointed at them. The five fugitives hustled along, crouching in the awkward running position required to keep their profiles hidden from those on the ground. Once they had arrived, Phil and Tyson carefully lowered Darius to the floor, drew their handguns, and took up defensive positions. Matthew bent down to care for his fallen leader, and Allie, feeling only a little ridiculous, pulled out her cell phone.

A few minutes later, as Phil had predicted, rioters exited from the stairwell onto the roof. Apparently, word of the news team deception and escape had gotten out. Enough of the mob had been milling around the bottom of the stairwell to report that the alien and his collaborators had not come down the stairs. Many of the protest group were headed home, some laden with computers and other electronics they had looted. The remaining hardcore dissidents still wanted to dispose of the alien and escape before the police arrived. Time was getting short, but the hunt had just begun.

With guns drawn, a couple dozen hunters filed onto the roof, looking right and then left as they came through the door. Though many wore bulletproof vests, Phil saw little evidence of military or police training. In fact, most of these misfits appeared to be acting out their favorite combat video game. Yet the guns and bullets were real. Phil remained quiet, not wanting to begin a shootout if it could be avoided. Sirens could now be heard, but it would take a large police contingent to evacuate the area. The hunting party spread out over the rooftop, ignoring the wailing alarms.

Darius had regained consciousness, but as he tried to rise, he stumbled and fell against the side of a large HVAC duct. The thin sheet metal bent inward, booming with the impact. As Darius quickly pulled back, the metal boomed again as it regained its shape. The insurgents reacted like sharks to a wounded fish, converging quickly on the group's position.

One attacker called out an ultimatum in a thick Southern drawl, "We just want the alien, so send him out! No need for any real humans to die tonight!"

Phil shouted back, "Gentlemen, I assure you that unless you withdraw, humans will die tonight! Lieutenant Tyson, Major Heroux, and I will be shooting to kill! Everyone needs to call it a day and go home!"

Phil hoped that the mention of three defending military personnel would discourage the mob. Granted, it was a bit of an exaggeration since Allie was not carrying her firearm.

Shots started plinking into the fans from all different angles. The fans were built on a foot-high concrete base, so Phil and his team flattened themselves behind it. The roof smelled like asphalt on a hot summer day. Phil and Tyson started returning fire when they could, but the barrage of bullets was nearly continuous. The attackers were rapid-firing their handguns and assault rifles, pausing only to eject old magazines and slam in new ones. These men had each brought an arsenal, hoping that the chaos of the protests would allow them an opportunity to use their weapons. In their minds, they were protecting their country from an alien invasion. Their favorite extremist websites had told them so.

"Sixty seconds!" Allie screamed above the sound of the gunfire. Two rioters broke away from their cover and started a kamikaze attack run, wildly shooting ahead of them. Phil peered above a large steel pipe that was providing him some protection. The firing had slowed as the two attackers got in the way of their comrades' line of fire. With a three-shot barrage of his own, Phil dropped the two point men. Phil heard volleys of gunshots coming from his flank, but Tyson was covering his back. Then he heard a cry of pain. Tyson had been hit, but he kept firing, dropping two snipers who had crawled up unto the base of a small radio tower. Several men were now firing from the roof of the stairwell, improving their shooting angles with the additional height. Phil inserted the last clip he had into his handgun. Sometimes, he thought, sixty seconds could be an eternity.

Suddenly, the sound of gunshots was drowned out by the cyclic thunder of approaching helicopters. In the fading light of the day, Phil saw two UH-90 Blackhawks approaching their position. General Bart had followed through on his promise. Phil watched as the small arms fire was further interrupted by a nearly perfect line of 7 mm bullets spattered tar and concrete between the attackers and their prey. These were warning shots only. The general did not want a military-civilian conflict to further incite an angry nation. But once again, the bullets and message were real. Cross the line just laid down and you will be shot. The two Blackhawks formed a defensive perimeter above the HVAC fans, each with an M-340 machine gun aimed directly at the scattering mob. The downdraft was overwhelming. One attacker started firing his assault rifle at the helicopter as he sprinted to the door. Army sharpshooters brought him down. The rest of the rioters realized they were heavily outgunned. There was no doubt how this encounter would end. The attackers dropped their weapons and bolted through the stairwell door.

One of the Blackhawks slowly descended to the roof surface, and Army Rangers jumped down to help Phil and his group into the choppers. Matthew supported Darius, who appeared to have recovered somewhat. Tyson was attempting to jog over, but he was limping badly. A growing bloodstain marked the hip where he'd been hit. Phil and Allie ran over to guide his unsteady path to the Blackhawk. As they reached him, Tyson smiled weakly, shook his head, and waved them off. Then his eyes crossed, and he passed out into their arms.

Chapter 11

RECOVERY

Allie awoke the next morning in a bed that was not hers and in a room that she did not recognize. She felt a moment of panic and took a deep breath, which she released slowly. She closed her eyes again and let the details of the night before work their way through her mind. Had this been reality, a nightmare, or buried memories of an action movie? Had they really survived two attacks by rioters bent on killing the Parmithian delegation? The congressional hearing, which had seemed so intimidating early yesterday, paled in comparison to the events that had occurred afterward.

Allie vaguely remembered the helicopter ride. They had been packed into jump seats in the back of the Blackhawk. Tyson was given emergency medical attention on a stretcher at her feet. She remembered they gave him fluids and had asked her to hold the IV bag. Then her legs started shaking as her adrenaline subsided. She couldn't stop the trembling, which she remembered was very upsetting to her. One of the medics had given her a mild sedative, and her mind had gotten foggy. She vaguely remembered being helped off the helicopter and escorted into an unfamiliar room… Where the hell was she?

She glanced at her nightstand. With relief, she spotted her cell phone on top of a notepad with the letterhead "Andrews Air Force

Base" stamped on the top. She heard a soft knock on the door, and a female Army Ranger poked her head through the door.

"Good morning, Major Heroux. General Bart would like to speak with you and Major Casaverde as soon as possible. I'll be back in thirty minutes to escort you to our conference room."

The Ranger reached her arm into the room and hung a new uniform on the doorknob as she closed the door. Allie had to force herself to hold back tears of gratitude. She didn't think she could face clothes covered in broken glass, dirt, and roof tar. After yesterday's events, Allie's emotions were hovering very close to the surface. Nevertheless, crying in front of the general and Phil was simply not going to be acceptable.

Thirty minutes later, showered, with her hair pulled up and a cup of hot coffee in her hand, Allie entered the conference room. Phil and General Bart were already there waiting for her. Allie caught Phil's eyes for a long moment…and felt a wave of affection for this man run through her. He had, after all, pulled her through two threats to her life. Only the hot coffee in her hand prevented her from hugging him.

Phil looked at her and smiled. "And how are you on this fine morning? You look considerably better than you did last night."

"I am happy to be alive. Thank you for asking." She took a seat and with it a long swig of coffee to clear her head.

General Bart looked concerned, apparently trying to determine if Major Heroux was as recovered as she was acting. As was his habit, the general initiated the discussion, keeping an eye on Allie for any signs of breakdown.

"Well, you two certainly had an interesting day yesterday. Fleeing from mobs in the parking garage of the Hart Senate Building. Rescuing Darius from a talk show where he called on the silent majority to step up and save Earth from itself. It's amazing you made it out alive with only one wounded soldier."

Phil and Allie both jerked their eyes away from their coffee and looked at the general with the same concerned look in their eyes. The general saw the concern and dismissively waived a hand in front of him.

"Lieutenant Young is fine and resting in the infirmary upstairs. He keeps asking the medical staff for his clothes and a cane. The nurse finally gave him a sedative just to shut him up. He's a very dedicated soldier. I will be recommending him for a commendation for his actions yesterday."

Major Casaverde interrupted, "Thank you, General. Lieutenant Young intentionally drew fire upon himself to protect Darius and Matthew. He deserves as many commendations as you can find for him."

Allie nodded and just managed to say, "Absolutely!" Then she choked up again with relief that Tyson was okay. Hoping the Styrofoam would cover up the tears welling in her eyes, she slowly drained her coffee cup. *Got to get...ahold of myself...,* she thought, chiding herself for her emotions.

The general continued, "As for you two, I can't decide whether to give you medals or pull you from the Parmithian assignment. However, I don't see how you could have foreseen an attack in a parking garage on Capitol Hill or Darius's sudden decision to appear on a talk show. The president still hopes that the Parmithians will decide to provide us with their technologies. He wants to leave the world tour in place for now."

General Bart sat forward in his chair. Concern showed on his face. In hushed tones, he continued, "I need to warn you that Darius has made a lot of powerful enemies in his short time here. His speech to the Congressional Committee of Extraterrestrial Affairs humiliated most of its members. Lobbyists are becoming especially active. It seems many careers are based on strengthening the divisions in our country, not eliminating them. Darius's talk show appearance is being cast as nothing less than a call to civil war. Long story short, your job just got harder."

Neither Phil nor Allie spoke. It appeared they might get through this meeting without being verbally pummeled by a distraught General Bart. There was no use in pushing their luck with a comment. Their commander continued, "According to the official itinerary, you and the Parmithian team are scheduled to be in Rome in a couple of days."

"Yes, General," Phil and Allie said in unison.

"Well, the timing couldn't be better. We're going to see large, possibly violent protests across the country over the next several days. Getting the Parmithians out of the way is a great idea. In fact, if you can find a way to stay in Europe for a week or two, I wouldn't object."

Phil and Allie both nodded and started shifting forward in their chairs to stand up.

General Bart shifted in his seat as if to rise but then smacked his open hand on the table instead. Allie jumped and dropped her empty coffee cup.

"And, Majors, do *not* let Darius out of your sight again! Do I make myself clear?"

"Yes, sir!" Phil and Allie had both stood and, out of conditioned reflex learned during their days as cadets, snapped to attention at the roar of their superior officer.

The general looked them over to see if there would be any response or excuse. Phil and Allie remained quiet. They had been *so* close to making it to the end of this meeting without the general yelling. General Bart stood slowly. He fully realized that goodbyes in the military were often unexpectedly permanent. His voice softened, "Be careful out there and take precautions. No repeats of yesterday's antics."

Phil quipped, "Oh, don't worry, sir. We're much too creative to repeat a performance. We'll do something much more novel."

Allie closed her eyes and shook her head slightly. How could such a capable man speak without thinking? Before the general could respond, she hurried to assure her commanding general. "Sir, I will continue to keep you informed."

Chapter 12

LOST WORLDS

Later that day, Darius invited Phil and Allie to join them on the spaceship for the flight to Rome. Phil accepted for them both, excited to finally ride in a star craft right out of his favorite science-fiction books. A day off in a secured location had been a welcome break from the stress of the past two weeks. Everyone felt rested enough to return to their duties. Phil had met with Tyson's replacement for his orientation. Tyson had pleaded to go with them, but his doctor had denied the request out of hand.

Late the next morning, Matthew showed them to their rooms, where they could stow their gear. Allie noted that the sleeping quarters were on the floor just below a cozy central gathering area with a large table and chairs. The Parmithians had invited Phil, Allie, and the rest of the security team for lunch, which would apparently be provided here. Friedrich was setting a large table with square plates, forks, and mugs.

As they gathered, Phil saw Amelia enter the room, having piloted the liftoff of the ship and engaged the ship's autopilot. He approached her slowly and a little apprehensively.

"So…how's your face?"

Amelia smiled but raised her hand to cover the bruise. "Well, Major, I know you to be quite honest. Why don't you tell me?"

FIRST JUDGMENT

Phil responded with a groan and a slight blush, "I'm so sorry about my crude diagnosis yesterday. Usually, I take time to think about things I say to…a woman. My only excuse is that I was preoccupied. Your face looks much better. Really, it does seem to be quite improved and…beautiful again."

Amelia blushed and arched her eyes in pleasant surprise. "Why, Major Casaverde, what a sweet apology. Thank you."

Phil's slight blush deepened dramatically. He quickly changed the subject. "So what's for lunch?"

"Well, in English, the best translation would be Justorium rooster. It is a fowl somewhat like Earth's chicken, though quite a bit larger. A full-grown Justorium could almost look you straight in the eyes. We think you'll like it, and the proteins should be easy for you to digest. Oh, and we're also serving a delicious side dish of slices of a deep-fried starchy vegetable."

"Really, what do you call them?"

"Lay's potato chips. We got them from the dining hall at Fort Andrews."

Amelia started giggling at her own joke and put her hand on Phil's arm. Phil laughed with her. After the week's strain, it felt good to laugh…and Amelia's hand on his arm was a pleasant addition.

The meat did have a unique tanginess to it that Phil had never tasted before. He was about to mention it to Amelia, who was sitting next to him. Then he realized that neither he nor anyone else on Earth had ever tasted this dish before. Of course it was unique. In any case, lunch was great, with plenty of discussion between the Parmithian crew and the security team. Potato chips were a comfort food for Phil, and he had eaten far more than his fair share.

Darius had two black eyes, and his face was still puffy from his beating, but he seemed relaxed and conversational with Allie and Friedrich, who sat next to him.

As lunch ended, most of the crew filtered out to attend to their duties. Newton, as ship engineer, offered to give Phil's security team a tour of the vessel, which they all accepted. Finally, only Darius, Amelia, Matthew, Phil, and Allie remained at the head of the long table. Phil realized this was the perfect time for a conversation they needed to have.

"Darius, I don't want to offend you, I really don't. But yesterday you left our group during the congressional committee meeting. That decision put several of us at risk, and we barely made it out alive. I respect you enough to know that your action was not some spurious, unnecessary act on your part. You seem…desperate…to convince Earth to make the changes needed for your planet to provide aid. However, appearing on a talk show program was a long shot at best."

The Parmithian commander bowed his head and seemed to be inspecting his plate. When he did not look up or move to speak, Allie took up the plea. "Darius, Major Casaverde and I need to understand the rules of engagement. To help you, we need to know how the Parmithian selection process works and what is driving you personally. It will help us to assist you in your quest. The United States has a personal interest in helping you. Having the whole story will help us to know how to best do that."

Darius looked at Matthew and Amelia, who both nodded their heads in agreement. Darius raised his hands in surrender. Haltingly, he said, "I appreciate your heroic efforts yesterday, saving us as you did. I owe you much. You deserve to better understand our mission…and my compulsion. It appears we have some time during our flight, and I have a couple stories I should share with you."

Allie picked up her cell phone and showed it to Darius. "If you don't mind, we may want to share this story with others."

Darius nodded, and Allie tapped the voice record button on her phone. She placed it back on the table, and the group settled into their chairs to hear the story. Darius took a deep breath and launched into his story of lost worlds.

Chapter 13

THE LOST WORLD OF KARUL

"Earth is the sixth first-contact visit of my career. I have been the commander for the last three of them. Turnover of first-contact crews is rather high. There are dangers in space travel. There are even more dangers in contacting alien populations. You never know what to expect. I have been lucky…but I have lost people too."

Considering the events of the last couple of days, this first point was easy enough to believe. Darius's voice slipped into a storyteller's tone, expressive and anxious to be understood.

"My first couple of first contacts were relatively easy and successful. The first planet had little arable land and was well along in its overpopulation. Resources were stretched to the breaking point, so the population welcomed us and our intervention. On the second planet, a quickly mutating virus was threatening to depopulate an entire continent. Its inhabitants also readily accepted our help with little argument. We left them with needed technology and, from what we know, the situations on the two planets have stabilized." Darius sounded happy about these successes; what they were doing was important.

"We were too late to help the third planet we visited. An asteroid belt had shifted into the orbit of the planet. Meteor showers had caused immense destruction and climate change. We responded to their distress signal as quickly as we could. By the time we got there, civilization had collapsed. The people had returned to living as hunter-gatherers in the wilderness. Small tribes were already at war with one another. They had lost the technology and culture they had once possessed. We couldn't help them."

Darius's voice now turned even more solemn. "The visit to the fourth planet was the first under my command. The planet was called Karul, which contained three large continents. Each of them had its own separate and distinct population. The Alphinians were the most advanced culture, with plentiful power and technology. They controlled their population growth and were an industrious people. By developing significant automation in their agriculture and manufacturing tasks, the Alphinians lived in relative luxury with ample leisure time, even compared to Earth standards.

"The second people, who we called the Betas, was an agrarian society. Theirs was the largest continent on the planet, but the population was spread thinly over that land mass. With only a few cities, the Betas had developed considerably less technology than Alphinia. After centuries of use, their arable land was losing its ability to support crops. The Betas were beginning to strain their resources. They looked at the luxury and plenty the Alphinians enjoyed and started to covet what they saw there.

"The Omegas were the least technically developed people on Karul. They, too, were a society based on agriculture, but the Omegas had a very strong spiritual base as well. Their religion taught fairness for all and love for their land, their environment, and other people. They were a happy people who endeavored to communicate with their gods through meditation and prayer. For centuries, these three societies had lived in peace and harmony, conducting trade that was of mutual benefit to all three countries."

Allie could tell where this story was going. It had been a story repeated countless times in Earth's own history. The outcome was nearly inevitable. Allie looked at Darius, who shifted uncomfortably in his chair. He was entering into the sadder part of his narration.

"With their agricultural difficulties, the Betas had become more and more discontented with their lives. The existence of their

Alphinian neighbors continually reminded the Betas that their lives could be easier. Their envy and discontent grew. The Betas increasingly found reasons to become offended by actions of the Alphinians. Betas leaders, sensing their people's frustrations, spoke out against Alphinian greed, inciting their people to violence. Eventually, they blew a simple border dispute out of proportion, claiming it to be a major offensive by the Alphinians. War was declared."

Darius now shifted forward in his chair, the emotions of his memories demanding a more forceful speaking position.

"When we arrived, Karul was in the middle of a full-blown world war. The Alphinians and Betas were locked in combat. The Omegas had been drawn into the conflict as well. Warlords of small, ethnically separate regions had declared independence from their nations and were also in armed conflict with their neighbors.

"When we arrived, manufacturing and agricultural production operations were shutting down due to disruptions of war. Food was in short supply, and large cities were experiencing the early stages of famine. Yet we knew we still had time to save the planet! We offered to help the Alphinians to rebuild their cities. We offered soil remediation technology to the Betas to recover their agricultural output. We explained to the Omegas that an end to the hostilities would allow them to return to their search for spiritual truth. Our help rested only on the requirement that they stop warring. "However, all three peoples were past feeling and without principle. Atrocities committed by all three factions did not allow them to trust one another enough to gather for peace talks. Even the Omegas, who sorely missed their lost spiritual lives, would not agree to a ceasefire. Revenge for what was lost would not allow them to find forgiveness in their hearts."

Darius turned in his chair, physically uncomfortable in reviewing these harsh and sad memories. His voice turned wistful.

"After several weeks of flying back and forth between the Alphinian capital, several Beta towns, and smaller Omega villages, we admitted defeat. There was nothing we could do, so we left. The planet had been the home to sixty-seven million people. Since then, other Parmithian ships have passed close to the planet. There are no electronic communications coming from the planet's surface. My failure to get a few people to talk to one another and make peace caused the deaths of…millions of souls.

"I do not want the mistakes that destroyed Karul to be repeated on Earth. Eight *billion* people live on this planet. To explain my sudden departure yesterday is difficult. My speech at the congressional committee hearing went very poorly. I was desperate for the American people to listen to me, hoping they would make different decisions than their leaders. During our voyage to Earth, I had listened to *The Tom Blackstone Show* frequently. I knew he had a large following, and I decided to take a chance in trying to communicate with his audience. I'm sorry I put you in danger. My efforts were in vain."

Darius shook his head, pushing back the memories that were overwhelming him. He looked up at his audience, all of whom were silent. Darius arose from his chair.

"But now I have duties to perform, and Amelia needs to land the ship soon. I suggest we leave the rest of our discussion for tonight after dinner. If you will excuse me."

Amelia arose and followed Darius out the door leading to the bridge.

Chapter 14

THE LOST WORLD OF MARSHON

Phil and Amelia spent the rest of the afternoon meeting with the security team and writing reports. Phil was a bit disappointed that flight on a spaceship was quite similar to that of a commercial airliner flight. They saw little of the Parmithian crew. Allie searched through news reports to assess the violence of today's demonstrations against Darius.

"Demonstrations in Los Angeles today led to angry riots and violence. Fires are raging in multiple locations throughout the city. Spokesmen from numerous protest groups are calling for the arrest and prosecution of the entire Parmithian delegation..."

"Riots have broken out in Portland, Denver, and Chicago. The National Guard has been called up to maintain order..."

"Police and private security have armed themselves and formed barricades to prevent rioters from storming Microsoft headquarters."

News stations broadcast videos from the demonstrations. The scenes were typical of such protests—lots of placards and angry people shouting through bullhorns. The protestors included a wide variety of special interest groups. Ultraconservatives marched alongside ultraliberals. Numerous ethnic groups were represented, though they marched separately. The protests were aimed at Darius's demand that laws be established so all people would be treated equally. The protestors did not want equal treatment and were willingly to resort to violence to prove their point. Parked cars had been turned over and set afire. At a few locations, looters could be seen lugging armloads of clothes snatched from nearby stores. Phil watched the scenes play out on Allie's laptop. Finally, he stood and paced the floor.

"Can't these people see they are proving the point that protests are tearing the nation apart? They're rioting to protect their right to riot…"

Shortly thereafter, Allie felt a soft bump, indicating the ship had landed at the NSA Gaeta Navy Base outside of Rome. Phil and Allie disembarked to coordinate the around-the-clock security details in guarding the ship. Allie had made all arrangements previously; there was little to do besides meet the base commander and sign a few forms.

Dinner that evening was another Parmithian dish—a white fish similar in appearance and taste to tilapia. Side dishes included an angel hair pasta and a purple fruit that tasted like a mixture of avocado and apple.

Phil had snagged the chair next to Amelia for the meal. However, Allie and Teresa were sitting across from her, and the three women were deep in discussion about Rome, fashion, and Italian phrases. Phil was torn as to whether he would be welcome to the conversation. The women were butchering Italian pronunciations, and the linguist in him begged to correct them. Phil listened to the conversation for a while and decided his corrections would not be welcome. He sighed and turned to Ship Engineer Newton to discuss the structural architecture of the ship.

After dinner, the security team excused themselves and retired to their rooms as Phil had instructed them. The Parmithian crew, except for Amelia, also excused themselves to attend to their duties. Darius had to tell the rest of his story.

A very nice white wine had been served with the fish. Darius perused his goblet, already lost in thought. Everyone knew why they were still gathered together, but Darius seemed hesitant to begin the discussion.

"Darius, may we hear the rest of your story now?" Phil invited softly.

Repeating her earlier actions, Allie glanced at Darius, hit the record button on her phone, and placed it on the table in front of Darius.

Darius nodded, understanding that those at the table needed to hear and understand his story. He sat forward in his chair and folded his hands in front of him.

"Before recounting the next story, I want you to understand that planets that refuse our aid do so because of the shared weaknesses that human beings possess. We are a complex, yet flawed species. The development of our greater intellect brings with it ego and self-interest. Both of these traits help in our survival even as they cause problems in interacting with others. We learn to cherish our loved ones and develop fears they might be lost to us. We develop imagination, which often causes us to see threats where none exist. Fear leads us to desire for more control over our surroundings, so we quest for power.

"Civilizations are built to overcome the basic, selfish instincts of our species. So are religions. If fear and greed triumph over civilization and religion, as they did in Karul, then you get war and, often, self-extinction." Darius paused. His references to selfish instincts overcoming civilization were obviously applicable to Earth. He slipped into his storytellers' tone and continued his recounting.

"After our failure at Karul, we visited a planet called Marshon. It was a world that had developed its own impressive technologies but had not yet achieved space flight. It was a simple task to follow the planet's electronic chatter to their capital city. As we learned how to translate those broadcasts, we came to understand that Marshon was a world in trouble. Most of the planet was covered by oceans, and Marshon had only two large landmasses. Each continent was home to its own nation and people. Like Karul, these two continents had enjoyed stable diplomatic relations and trade with each other. Immigration and emigration between the two countries was allowed, but rare. The larger of the two nations, Sivillon, was highly skilled in technical pursuits—electronics, communications, and manufacturing. The smaller nation of Gaia was more skilled in biology, chemistry, organic synthesis, and microbiology."

"After a change in their president, Sivillon started to ramp up its development of military technology. When Gaia learned of this emphasis on weapons development, it naturally objected. Toward what other country would this military engine be directed if not Gaia? Sivillon denied any such plan, claiming they were merely developing technologies for planetary defense.

Darius leaned forward, resting his arms on the table. He took a deep breath and continued, resigned to the sadness of the narration. "The people of Sivillon were not warlike. Their leader, however, had become drunk with the power of their technologies and their capacity to destroy. A few months after his election, missile explosions were reported in isolated, unpopulated areas of northern and eastern Gaia. Of course, Gaia publicly condemned Sivillon missile strikes within their borders. Sivillon contested the objections, pointing out the areas were uninhabited. However, a few weeks later, a missile left Sivillon airspace and struck a town on the western coast of Gaia, killing nine hundred of its inhabitants. Sivillon claimed a prototype missile had gone off course, and it was all just a terrible accident. They even contributed supplies and relief workers to help in the cleanup. Gaia was uncharacteristically silent about the whole incident. Construction of missile sites on the coasts of Sivillon continued unabated. Gaia did not have the defensive armaments to protect their cities. They were defenseless and desperate.

"A few months after the attack, a new product called RageMints appeared in Sivillon markets. RageMints was marketed as an after-dinner mint, a simple candy. It was quite expensive for a sweet, but it soon became enormously popular. Their motto was 'A candy that's all the rage.' The taste was exquisite, and eating one led to the desire for another…and another. Stores started selling out their supply within a few hours of receiving new shipments. At first, customers laughed even as they called the candy addictive. It was just a mint after all.

"After a few more months, users stopped laughing. They realized they could think of nothing but enjoying their next RageMint. They were hooked, and it was a nasty dependency. If addicts went a day without mints, they got itchy and irritable. Before long, stores and warehouses were being looted of any RageMints they had in stock. A black market developed for the candy, making it available for one hundred times the normal cost of the mint. The Sivillon government, which had been distracted by its military preparations, finally took notice. RageMints were pulled from store shelves, and black marketeers were arrested. Yet these actions were too little, too late. Over half of the Sivillon population was addicted."

Darius leaned back in his chair, his emotions too overwhelming to find a comfortable position.

"We learned later that RageMints contained a replica of a neurochemical required for the nerve center of the brain to function normally. The hormone provided mental stimulus and emotional lift. Its harm came from the fact that even the little amount of chemical consumed with the candy caused the brain to stop producing its own natural version of the neurochemical. Addicts who ran out of RageMints suffered enormous pain and could not control their rage at that pain. Hospitals were overwhelmed by patients, many of whom physically attacked doctors and nurses when RageMints were not provided to them. Riots erupted throughout the country. The most severely addicted users died. Their brains had forgotten how to produce the needed neurochemical and simply shut down from the chemical imbalance.

"Inevitably, Sivillon traced the production of RageMints to manufacturing plants in Gaia. Biology was Gaia's strength, and its scientists had used their knowledge of chemical synthesis to defend itself against Sivillon aggression. Proclaiming Gaia's biological attack to be an act of war, Sivillon unleashed all its missiles against Gaian cities. It appeared that Sivillon had been planning this missile attack on Gaia for months."

Phil realized he had been holding his breath. Earth's history was filled with similar stories. Countries had utilized new technologies for military advantage ever since the invention of archery and then gunpowder. It was unnerving to hear that the same practices existed on other worlds.

Darius continued his story slowly and precisely, wanting his audience to understand the challenges of the situation. "By the time we arrived on the planet, Sivillon was being torn apart by its own citizens. Guarded barricades surrounded all government buildings and military production plants. The government was shooting any citizens who were rampaging to find RageMints. Gaia was in even worse shape as uncontrolled fires caused by missile strikes swept through its cities. Most of the leaders of the two nations were solidly against any attempts at peace. Millions had died.

"Finally, we convinced President Sashi Guresh of Gaia that we could broker a peace. However, he had to be willing to negotiate that truce in Sivillon. My crew scheduled the peace conference, and we flew President Guresh to Sivillon's capital. As we entered the presidential palace, we were attacked by a contingent of the Gaian government that opposed peace. President Guresh was killed, as were two of my crew, including Amelia's husband."

Phil and Allie were both startled and straightened in their chairs. What had he said? As one, they turned to face Amelia. Silent tears were streaming down her face, confirming what they had heard. Allie was sitting next to Amelia, and immediately she reached over and embraced her friend.

Allie managed to gasp, "I'm *so* sorry... I didn't know."

After an uncomfortable minute, Amelia wiped the tears from her face and smiled her gratitude to Allie. "Thank you for your concern, Allie. He has been gone for over five years now, but I still miss him." Allie scooted her chair closer to Amelia and took her hand.

Phil managed to catch Amelia's eye, and the concern on his face brought tears to her eyes again. She tilted her head and directed her words toward him.

"Drake, my husband, was our security officer. On Marshon, he had stayed behind to cover our retreat to the safety of the ship. You... rather remind me of him."

Phil caught his breath, his mind and emotions swirling. "Thank you. Such a compliment means a lot."

Amelia turned back to Darius, her face imploring him to continue with his story. Darius picked up from where he had left off.

"Well, we left Marshon shortly thereafter. The Gaian president was dead, and Gaia had no interest in sending another ambassador into danger. Sivillon's government was busy quelling its own populace as well as managing a ground war. Neither side would listen to us. The planet Marshon had been home to two hundred million human beings. We have received reports that this planet, too, has gone silent. It appears Sivillon and Gaia destroyed each other."

Darius's face hardened with resolve to finish the story and state his conclusions.

"In summary, I am responsible for the deaths of almost three hundred million people. The planet Karul destroyed itself with covetousness, greed, and fear. Marshon destroyed itself due to aggression, pursuit of power, and treachery. Upon our arrival at the two planets, it was *not* too late for them. We were prepared to provide them with technology to reverse the damage to their planets and escape from the consequences of their conflicts. No one from either planet was willing to make the changes to their societies that would bring peace. Despite our efforts, both planets rejected our aid. Simply put, no side on either planet was willing to feel remorse for their actions. They rejected any suggestion that they should reform and make reparations."

Darius concluded with the summary of why he had told the two stories in the first place. "I think about those failures every day. I don't want to include Earth on my list of failures." Finished with his story, Darius connected the past with the present. "Tomorrow, we are visiting the leader of one of the largest religious organizations on Earth. The Catholic Church preaches repentance to every corner of this world. We are visiting the Vatican tomorrow to ask if they believe that Earth can feel enough remorse to save their civilization."

Chapter 15

A VISIT TO THE VATICAN

Obtaining an audience with the Pope can be a difficult meeting to schedule, but there was far too much curiosity in the Vatican about the alien visitors to delay their introduction. Allie had arranged for this meeting with little difficulty. The proceedings would be recorded but not broadcasted, pending the church's decision. Pope John Paul III would attend the meeting, though he was not expected to speak. The meeting would be held in English, with translations available via wireless headphones. The church decided that Cardinal John Cappellion, a senior cardinal based in Boston, would conduct the meeting. Cardinal Cappellion had been raised in one of the rougher neighborhoods in New Jersey. He was known for his imposing personality and unyielding defense of the church. No man, woman, or alien could intimidate him, and he would certainly not tolerate sacrilege from anyone in attendance.

The meeting was being held in the Papal Audience Hall. A few Roman government officials had been invited, but the rest of the audience was made up of church leadership. Surprisingly, Phil, Allie, and their security team were given permission to attend the meeting. The Vatican understood the need for security. Though tourists did not have access to this part of the Vatican, there were always thousands of sightseers nearby.

FIRST JUDGMENT

As Pope John Paul and his attending cardinals entered the room, everyone rose in respect. The Parmithian men were dressed in their formal suits, white shirts, and conservative ties. The two women wore long, modest dresses and had again braided their hair. Phil had to credit Darius's team for doing their homework and, probably with help from Allie, looked very appropriate for this meeting.

The Pope sat down in the middle of the raised stage, underneath a massive metal sculpture. The Parmithian team sat behind a table in front of him and to his left. Cardinal Cappellion and several other Vatican officials sat to his right. The normal pomp and circumstance of such meetings was observed. After everyone was seated, a prayer was offered in Latin by Cardinal Anthony del Torres. At the prayer's conclusion, Cardinal Cappellion rose from his chair and addressed the assembly.

"Good morning, fellow priests and cardinals of the holy Catholic Church and honored guests. Welcome to the Vatican and your special audience with the bishop of Rome and vicar, Pope John Paul III. I am Cardinal John Cappellion."

If Cardinal Cappellion had not become a priest, he would have made a great mafia boss, thought Phil. His stocky frame, flat nose, and an accent that combined a nasally Boston accent with the singsong accent of his native Italy sounded like something right out of the mob movies.

Phil and Allie sat in the audience but as near to the Parmithians as possible. As the cardinal continued his greetings and recognition of attending dignitaries, Phil thought how Cappellion's nasally English was at odds with a sanctuary where Italian or Latin was the norm. However, Phil found that he was quite relaxed; this was as safe a place as they could ever hope to be. If Darius would behave himself, they might make it through another day. Allie appeared...a bit overwhelmed. Her eyes were wide, and she kept looking around the room in awe. Cardinal Cappellion continued to address the Parmithians.

"Your visit to Earth has raised quite a stir in the Christian world. For centuries, we have wondered whether God had children on other planets besides our own. We have many questions to ask of you. But we must start with the most obvious question of all which will form the foundation for any further discussions." The cardinal looked at the faces of the Parmithian team and asked, "Ambassadors from the planet Parmithia, do you believe in God?"

Cardinal Cappellion sat down in his chair, purposefully leaving the open question open. Matthew slowly rose to speak. Phil had expected Darius to take the lead again and was mildly surprised at the change. He then realized that Matthew was the specialist for religion and culture. Given the sensitivity of humans to religious affronts, it made sense to have their religion specialist lead a discussion about God.

Matthew seemed calm in the face of such a blunt question. He gave something between a nod and a bow to acknowledge the religious leaders around him.

"Your Eminence Cardinal Cappellion and Pope John Paul, we wish to express appreciation for accepting our request for this audience. My name is Matthew. We appreciate the hospitality you have shown us. The history and sacredness of these buildings and their priceless artifacts are very inspiring. We have come to discuss the religious and spiritual aspects of your planet. I have read much about the history of Earth's religions. In essence, we wish to understand the level of religion observance that exists in your world today. Your first question is fair, and the appropriate place to begin our dialogue. Please forgive me for taking a moment to set the stage for my answer."

When the cardinal smiled and nodded, Matthew began his presentation. "As you know, yours and our home galaxy is a spiral galaxy called the Milky Way. Your sun is located on the inner edge of what you call the Orion-Cygnus Arm of that galaxy. Our sun is in the same arm. In a map of the galaxy, our sun would appear to be insignificantly closer to the galaxy center. But it is still a vast distance away. I have spent my entire adult life as an ambassador of Parmithia, traveling between the stars at speeds somewhat beyond the speed of light. We have visited numerous inhabited planets populated by humanoids much like you and me.

"You would be interested to know that the majority of these civilizations believe in gods. The religions they have been developed to worship those gods are remarkably similar. It seems to be a deep-seated need in humanoid species to find and worship God. We always assess the religious activity of societies we visit. It is a vitally important characteristic of any culture."

Matthew hesitated and then proceeded a little more warily, "However, in all of our wanderings through space, you should know that we have never encountered...a god. We have found no evidence of a god's power, no relics containing power to heal or artifacts with the power to kill. We have found worlds in the earliest phases of creation, but we have never found a god overseeing that evolution."

Matthew paused to allow his audience to consider his statement. Cardinal Cappellion voiced his own conclusion. "So since you have not found physical evidence of Him, you do *not* believe in God?"

"Actually, Your Eminence, we do believe in God," Matthew countered. "As first mentioned by Darius in his speech in Washington, we believe that a Higher Power has directed the evolution of mankind on hundreds of planets throughout the galaxy. While animal species differ greatly between planets, humans are essentially identical. The only explanation of such a phenomenon is that a deity is directing our evolution. Though we look for God in our corner of the galaxy, we realize that we are searching in the wrong places. God exists in the spiritual realm of our existence, a place where our spaceships cannot go."

Matthew collected his thoughts. His next question had to worded very carefully.

"Parmithians believe that *faith* in God is a very personal characteristic. Your belief in God depends on spiritual moments you have experienced, whether you recognize blessings from His hand or if you blame Him for your disappointments. On the other hand, *religion* is a measurement of the beliefs of entire populations. Most all religions stress kindness to others, empathy, charity, and teaching these virtues to the young. Church members meet to worship God and to encourage one another to do good throughout the week. The strength of religious worship in a world gives us a measure of the generosity and concern a people has for one another."

Cardinal Cappellion was sitting on the edge of his seat, anxious to understand Matthew's point. He could not help himself as he interrupted with his own question. "Matthew, the Catholic Church has taught these concepts for centuries. Our critics argue that one can be kind and generous with others without a belief in God. How do you answer such attacks?"

Matthew responded immediately, "Can a man be good without God? Yes, obviously one can do good things without having a belief in a deity who is watching you. It rather depends on whether you think that man by nature is selfish or generous. Is mankind naturally concerned for his neighbors or just for himself and his family?

"We have found in our travels that mankind's nature is to be selfish and self-justifying. We love and care for our family or tribe but generally not for those outside of our sphere. Normally, men and women gratify their own self-image by diminishing others and surrounding themselves with proof of their wealth. Many religions teach that God observes and judges those actions."

Matthew paused in case there were further questions. No one moved, eager to understand Parmithian theology. Matthew took a deep breath and continued his address, "If a society has a strong religious base, its people will try to care for one another, even in hard times. If a world is weak in its religion observance, it will not care for its distressed people, *especially* in hard times. If the disparity becomes acute in very hard times, masses of starving people eventually riot. Thus, religion affects how quickly a civilization will collapse. It also influences the decisions the society makes.

"For example, with our development of space travel, Parmithia had a choice to make. We could have decided to live like kings, using our technologies to exploit less technically advanced planets. The influence of our religion caused us to choose a more spiritual way or the higher path, as you call it. To ever hope to find God and spiritual truth, we had no other choice.

"We have read that some of your religions have warred over the nature of—God and who He loves more. While possibly interesting discussions, such questions matter little to us. I don't know if God listens to my prayers, but it makes me a better man to say them. Obviously, I don't know if God will judge me in the end. But expecting that eventual judgment encourages me to be a better husband, a better father, and a better man."

Matthew stopped to take a breath. Cardinal Cappellion was raising his hand in an effort to insert his own comment.

"In our scriptures we read, 'But if we hope for that we see not, then do we with patience wait for it.' I believe that you, Matthew, will someday know that God exists, for you shall see Him."

Matthew smiled. "I hope so, Cardinal. But please know that if there is no afterlife and God does not exist, it will make no difference to me. My belief in God will have caused me to strive to be a moral person who has lived the best life possible. I can ask no more of a way of life than that."

It was apparent that Matthew was finishing up, but it was just as apparent that he had one more point to make. "Please know that as a planet, Parmithians have varying success in spiritual pursuits. We still have crime, and we have jails to keep lawbreakers from further damaging our society. While most all of us believe in God, our people are very diverse in their religious observance. Many people meditate and pray daily. Some regularly visit our temples for contemplation and study. Many do nothing at all." Turning toward Teresa, who sat beside him, Matthew asked, "Teresa, could you please stand?"

Teresa self-consciously arose from her chair. She wore long light-blue dress with a loose brown robe over it. Teresa folded her arms around her waist and slowly bowed to the pontiff. When she straightened, she gave him a smile of perfect joy. Obviously, Teresa was experiencing her own spiritual and emotional enlightenment she would never forget.

Matthew continued, "Teresa is one of the best examples I know of a person who lives a truly spiritual life. She is a nun in the Parmithian church of God. She has taken her earthly name from Mother Teresa, a valiant nun of your church who Teresa wishes to emulate. She is our spiritual counselor as well as my apprentice."

John Paul made the sign of the cross and then whispered, "Bless you, my child."

Teresa sat down as tears streamed down her cheeks. It appeared that followers of God could come from any planet. Matthew expressed his appreciation for everyone's time and attention and took his seat.

With that, Cardinal Cappellion called for a short recess. Everyone seemed to need a break. Major Casaverde used the time to check in on his security team. Several of his team seemed to be quite emotional; Matthew's speech had affected them deeply. The Parmithians were in discussions among themselves, so Phil returned to talk with Allie.

"Major Heroux, what did you think about Matthew's speech?" Phil asked casually. Allie looked up at him, and Phil was taken aback. Allie was crying, her eyes red and brimming with tears. Embarrassed, Allie removed her glasses and brushed away the evidence of her emotions.

"I thought...," Allie quietly responded, her voice shaking a bit, "that Matthew's was the best approach to believing in God that I have ever heard." Phil never knew what to say to a crying woman, so he remained silent. Fortunately, Allie seemed to need to talk. Softly she explained, "I'm sorry, Phil. I was raised Catholic, so maybe being in the Vatican is affecting me. I have not gone to mass for years...ever since I was a teenager trying to figure my life out. Like most idealists, I knew I wanted to help people without having a clue as to what that meant. But unless someone could show me God, I decided religion was certainly not the way to do it. My parents, my born-again sister, and religious friends have tried to prove to me that God is in a heaven somewhere. But they could never get Him to make an appearance. It never occurred to me that believing in God *was a choice* to motivate you to be a better person, and you put the question of His existence on hold..."

"Phil, Parmithians hold themselves to a higher standard than any group of people I have ever met. Could earthlings ever do that? Can I be like Theresa and never speak an unkind word to anyone? Could I be like Matthew and seek the wisdom of understanding people?"

Phil didn't know what to say; matters of the spirit were well outside his understanding. Yet he wondered if he, too, should correct this oversight. Fortunately, the recess was ending. He would have to think about this later.

FIRST JUDGMENT

Cardinal Cappellion cleared his throat and invited everyone back to their chairs. Phil placed a hand on Allie's shoulder in a gesture of support and comfort. She glanced at him appreciatively. Pope John Paul, who had gotten up to stretch his legs, was assisted back to his chair. When he had sat down, everyone but the cardinal took their seats as well. When everyone was settled, the cardinal turned toward the visitors.

"Matthew, thank you for the answer to our question and your explanation of Parmithian beliefs. We are gratified to know of your continued search for spiritual direction and that an entire planet of God's children continues in their search for Him. This is wonderful news. Is there any way that we can help you in your efforts?"

Matthew arose once again. "Your Eminence, our delegation has come to Earth on a fact-finding mission. We wish to learn about the state of your world. Across the planet, we have found there is a great range of personal wealth—from distressingly poor to fabulously wealthy. We've endeavored to understand your economies, politics, and social tensions. However, through simple observation, we cannot accurately assess the spiritual dedication of a planet's people. The Roman Catholic church extends to all corners of this globe. We thought that your leadership might be best able to best answer our question. Compared to your church history and the expectations you have of your people, what is the spiritual condition of Earth?"

Matthew turned to check the position of his chair and sat down. Church leadership had been informed about this question several days ago, so it was not a surprise. The query was not meant to simply give the Vatican an opportunity to make a pronouncement. Matthew had made it clear that the Parmithian delegation felt it vital that they receive a clear and honest answer to their question. They were asking the Pope to give his opinion on the religious state of affairs of the entire world. Matthew had even suggested that this part of the meeting be kept confidential and unrecorded. But the Pontiff had turned down the suggestion. John Paul wanted his answer to be recorded for posterity, knowing this recording might be revealed to the entire world.

With papers in hand, Cardinal Cappellion rose from his chair. "At the request of His Holiness, I have been asked to read his response to your question." Cappellion adjusted his glasses and began to read a response that was, indeed, clear and honest. "In the book of Matthew chapter 24, the Savior describes the state of the world shortly before His second coming. In verse 10, we read, 'And then shall many be offended and shall betray one another and shall hate one another.' It is our opinion that we live in the days of offense the Savior tells us that would come. The world has divided itself into uncounted clusters, each offending the other. Offenses become protests, and protests become violent brawls. Brawls then become battles, and battles become wars. Too few people are willing to compromise. Too few are willing to forgive.

"This Parmithian delegation has reassured us that a people can make significant *technological* progress without diminishing their *spiritual* progress. Many church members have come to believe that the world has moved on from the religious traditions of our ancestors. Church attendance continues to drop each year. Our holy churches are vandalized and defaced with graffiti. Belief in God, prayer, church donations, and charitable works have decreased alarmingly. The love of men for God and their fellow man waxes cold."

Cardinal Cappellion took a moment to take a sip of water but also to compose himself. These admissions were not easy. The religions of Earth were struggling. Confessing those struggles to an outside observer and judge was difficult. With a resigned tone, Cappellion continued. "Our dear Parmithian brothers, we know that none of you are gods nor are you angels. Your people has surpassed us in technology development…and it appears you surpass us in spiritual development as well. You are making demands of our Earth governments that the church has sought for decades. Many of our membership believe that God has sent you here to judge us or to give us a standard against which we should judge ourselves. Thank you for your visit with us today. We have learned much. You have traveled a very long distance to learn of us and judge us as a planet. I wish we could give you a better report."

The cardinal placed his papers on a nearby desk, turned to the television camera, and concluded, "We thank you all for watching today's broadcast. The time set aside for this recording has passed, and we must now conclude." The cardinal made the sign of the cross and said, "May God bless you." He then stepped back, and the television camera lights turned off.

Cameramen and technicians started gathering cables and moving cameras out of the way. John Paul arose. Followed closely by Cardinal Cappellion, he shook hands with each Parmithian in turn. Thanks were expressed all around. Other church leaders also filed past, determined to shake hands with God's children from another planet. It would be a fitting ending to a story they would relate to congregations for years to come.

Chapter 16

ROME

After saying farewell to the Pope and numerous cardinals, Phil, Allie, the security team, and the Parmithians were led out of the Vatican via guarded, private hallways. They climbed into their black SUVs and drove toward the Marriott Grand Hotel. Darius had explained that he would need the afternoon to confer privately with his team and to send out a few emails. He was hoping they could meet for dinner that evening in a private dining room.

During the drive to the hotel, Amelia managed to catch Phil's eye in the rearview mirror again. She flashed him a smile. "Hi, Phil. Is it still against the rules to call you Phil? Still not allowed?" She raised her eyebrows in a questioning glance. "We haven't really spoken since Darius told you our mission history." Suddenly, her bravado crumbled a bit, and she glanced out the window. "I wanted to ask you. Does it change your opinion of me to know that I am…a widow?"

Phil turned in his seat so he could, as best as possible, look directly at Amelia. "It doesn't change a thing. I'm glad to learn that you had a companion for your long flights to new planets. Since I heard the story, I wanted to ask you. What was your husband, Drake, like?"

Amelia looked sideways in confusion, both surprised by the question and pleased by it. She gave Phil the kind of smile one has when recalling a dear memory. "Drake was caring, funny, handsome, and very dedicated to protecting those he cared about. His principles were not open to debate. He never knew what to say to a woman. I used to tease him just to see him blush, which was very easy to do."

Amelia looked out the window, remembering days past. Phil looked at Amelia without attempting to respond. She could have just described him. She returned his look, confirming that she understood that too. They held each other's eyes too long to end it comfortably. Phil snapped out of his trance and blushed. Though this… flirtation…was enjoyable, it was unprofessional. The Parmithians would be leaving in a couple of weeks, and he already had to answer for a number of infractions in this assignment. Phil turned back toward the front of the car.

"You still should probably call me Major Casaverde, certainly in public." Inwardly, Casaverde grimaced. That had come out harsher than he had planned.

Amelia considered his request for moment, trying to read his face in the small mirror. "Hmm… Okay, Phil, I will try to keep that in mind."

After arriving at the hotel and exiting the cars, Phil thought he might have time to chat with Amelia on the walk to the elevators. But it was not to be. Major Heroux cut him off even as he approached the entrance.

"General Bart would like to have a video chat with us immediately."

Phil winced. "A chat with the general. Major, you make that sound so homey and fun. Please, lead the way." As they separated from the main group, Phil gave his security team their assignments and then walked beside Allie as they sought an available conference room. "By the way, Allie, you are the worst wingman in the history of wingmen."

Allie smiled. "Phil, ignoring the inaccurate gender reference, of all the many threats you are facing that might damage your career, I am most worried about Amelia. Flirting must be a very ingrained cultural trait on Parmithia because Amelia is very good at it. That is not an insult by the way. She's becoming a good friend of mine."

They arrived at an open conference room and soon had the image of General Bart on Allie's laptop screen. Phil reported of the day's events, hoping the general would be soothed by the fact that nothing bad or unexpected had occurred.

"Presently, the Parmithians are holed up in their rooms to meet and send out a few emails," Phil summarized.

General Bart glowered. "No, Major, not just a *few* emails. Darius and his team have sent out *hundreds* of emails. We gave them secure channels to use for their correspondence. But *we* can read their emails, as I'm sure they're aware. The emails are being sent to various corporate, government, and research leaders, but the list also includes farmers, construction engineers, and a few small-town mayors."

The general looked at Phil and Allie as if they should be able to explain what was going on. Dumbfounded, they looked back at him. The general took a slightly exasperated breath and continued his report.

"We don't know what to make of it. Our people are looking for patterns, but they really haven't discovered anything yet. Every email is simply an invitation to meet with them at a certain place and time. Using your photographs and identifications, we confirmed that those they invited to New York met with them there. They have meetings set up there in Rome today, in Paris in two days, and in San Francisco later this week. So far, recipients have respected the confidentiality of this correspondence and meetings. However, the press has heard rumors that Darius is sending secret emails to select people all over the world. By tomorrow, we think news agencies will confirm the rumors and break the story."

Something stirred inside of Phil's brain. There was something significant in the fact that recipients had respected the confidentiality of the Parmithian requests. How…unexpected. But he couldn't make the connection as to what that might be.

The general looked at Phil's image on his computer screen. "So before I am besieged by questions from the president and his staff, Major, do you have any additional conclusions that you'd like to report?"

Phil's mind froze. He realized the word *no* was certainly not a good answer. The general was frustrated by the lack of good intelligence on Darius's intentions. Phil's brain finally stumbled back to its latest thoughts, "General, did you ever see the television series *V?* It's an old science-fiction program, first broadcast in 2010. It only lasted for two seasons."

General Bart paused, caught off guard by the sudden shift in the conversation.

Phil didn't wait for an answer, speaking quickly to avoid interruption. "In the first episode, aliens arrive in giant spaceships that hover over major cities around Earth. The aliens look just like human beings—actually, incredibly *attractive* human beings. Their leader announces to the world that they had come in peace. They offer them access to their advanced technology and medical knowledge in exchange for just a few of Earth's resources. It seems too good to be true, and it is. But by the end of the first episode, we learn that the *V* visitors are *not* human. They are reptiles living inside a covering of human skin and muscle, and they were set on conquering Earth!"

Phil paused to take a breath. Allie was looking at him as if he had lost his mind. General Bart, obviously confused, blurted, "Major, why are you telling me—"

Phil interrupted, knowing he had only a few moments to make his point. "Sir, since the day I met Darius, Amelia, and the other Parmithians, I have been expecting their skins to split open at any moment and see reptiles crawling out to attack us. For the first few days, the image gave me nightmares. But I'm not having nightmares anymore..."

General Bart and Allie were both looking at Phil quizzically. Neither said a word, waiting for Phil to make his point.

"General, I *like* the Parmithians, and I respect them. At NASA, they were genuinely grieved to not be able to share dark-energy technology with their fellow scientists and engineers. At the United Nations, Darius wasn't chastising the ambassadors. He was pushing them to change global law to provide two parents for our *children*. He is demanding the United States put an end to government programs that divide our people. I've stopped expecting to see reptiles anymore because the Parmithians are human beings, and they're good, conscientious humans at that."

Phil paused to draw a breath, and Allie jumped into the conversation before the general could get a word in edgewise. "General, I don't have as graphic an explanation as Major Casaverde, but I agree with him. We have neither heard nor seen anything that would make us suspect the Parmithians of planning to overthrow our government. If they want to conquer Earth, they are going about it all wrong. It seems they are truly an open and caring people."

The general considered their words for a few moments. "Well, if they are so open, then find out what those emails are all about!" General Bart hit a key on his keyboard and broke the connection.

As Allie closed her laptop, she looked sideways at Phil. "Reptiles, Phil? Did your dreams include Amelia crawling out of her skin to attack you?"

Phil rubbed his face. "Yep, and it freaked me out. First, I dream Amelia is sitting in my room, coyly laughing at one of my jokes, and then she opens her mouth, and it's full of sharp fangs,. "

Allie held up her hand and interrupted, "Stop, please." She gasped. "I'm quite certain I don't want to hear any more."

Phil sighed and then nodded in agreement. "Yeah, that's probably for the best."

Chapter 17

PARIS PRESS CONFERENCE

That evening, everyone had dinner in a private room of a Rome restaurant near their hotel. Allie had decided a relaxed meal of authentic Italian cuisine was needed. The Parmithians had spent the day in private meetings at the hotel as planned. Everyone was tired from a busy, but thankfully peaceful day.

As the meal was winding up and the Parmithians were appreciating the novel taste of tiramisu, Darius arose to address the party. "Tomorrow is our travel day to Paris. Saturday, we were planning to have one-on-one meetings at the hotel. I would like to amend that plan. Saturday morning, we would like to ask Major Heroux to schedule a..." Darius glanced down at his notes. "Press conference. Rumors about some of our decisions and plans must be addressed. We need to make an announcement to end the confusion and would like to do so in a broadcast as soon as possible. In the afternoon, we will conduct the private meetings already scheduled. Major Heroux, could you please organize such an event?"

Allie looked over at Phil in bewilderment. Phil had buried his face in his hands, so he was no help. Allie looked up at the Parmithian leader. She stammered, "Darius, the hotel rooms and conference rooms are reserved, of course. But a press conference? To announce what exactly? Why Paris? Where do you want to hold it?"

"I believe it appropriate that we hold the press conference in one of the halls of the Louvre Museum."

Phil slid his hands down off his face and looked up at the Parmithian. Just when things seemed to be settling down…

"In the Louvre? Darius, I'd like to remind you that both of your last two public appearances almost got us killed. You and your team are now the target of violence by a number of alien hate groups throughout the world. You'll forgive me, but I must strongly protest this plan. Why does it have to be made in the Louvre? What announcement must you make from there?"

Darius looked at Phil and held his gaze for a moment. "Major Casaverde, I expect that General Bart has asked you about our numerous emails and the private meetings we are having with select individuals at each of our destinations."

Phil glanced up, mildly surprised. Was that just a good guess, or did Darius have his own surveillance of their communications with the general? The man had purposefully not answered his question, misdirecting his response to offer Phil something he knew the general wanted to know.

Darius continued with his diversion, "We are aware that those emails and our meetings will not remain confidential much longer. I want to get ahead of the discovery of our plans and announce them to the world as soon as possible. There is no need for further secrecy about the matter. You will see on Saturday morning why the Louvre is the most appropriate place for this announcement."

"Darius, I'm not going to try to detail for you the security problems of holding a press conference at a museum visited by thousands of tourists every day. We can't just—"

"Major, after discussing this issue with my team, it is our conclusion that this press conference is overdue. We accept whatever security risks that you can't control, but this event must happen, and it must happen Saturday morning at the Louvre." Darius smiled appreciatively, obviously considering this discussion to be over. He continued, "Thank you all for your efforts today. The visit with the Pope was very beneficial in making our decisions. But I am weary from the day and must bid you all good night." Darius gathered his papers and, followed by the security man assigned to him, left the room.

Early the next day, the *We Come in Peace* landed in France's Villacoublay Air Base just outside of Paris. Allie had made special arrangements for French security forces to secure the spacecraft. With the authority of General Bart and the uniqueness of the requests, approvals to land at the French air base were easily attained. Making the arrangements for a press conference at the Louvre Museum had not been quite so simple. However, the press conference was finally scheduled, and news agencies were alerted.

Early Saturday morning, everyone boarded one of their convoy vehicles and rode to the famous glass pyramid that covered the entrance to the museum. Allie had arranged for the Parmithian team to tour the museum before the press conference. For two hours, the team strolled through the displays. Darius and Matthew wanted to tour the religious history section, while Newton wanted to visit the industrial revolution section. Phil's security team was scrambling just to keep up with their charges.

Just before nine o'clock, the group headed to the second floor of the Sully wing of the museum, which had been closed to the public for the press conference. The Parmithian team had been very relaxed during their tour, acting like typical tourists.

Allie found herself standing next to Friedrich and Teresa and decided to mention her observation, "You know, Phil and I are rather nervous about Darius's announcement in a few minutes. The last couple of public announcements have gone…well, rather poorly. Yet all of you seem to be quite calm. I'm glad you are enjoying your tour of the museum. Really, I am. Why don't you look more worried?"

Allie was expecting Friedrich to answer and was surprised when the normally timid Teresa spoke up first. "I'm so sorry we've had to keep things from you!" she blurted out. Teresa looked like a teenage girl admitting a dark secret to her best friend. She took a deep breath and plunged ahead with her confession.

"You've been so nice to us. You deserve to know everything, but Darius told us that we cannot show favoritism to the United States, or the rest of the world would take it badly. You…and your nation…have to be as surprised as the rest of the world at our announcement."

Allie nodded. "Well, we will surely be surprised. And surprises can be nice surprises, can't they?" she said with a please-agree-with-me nod and half smile.

Teresa returned both her nod and her half smile. "Well, yes, some surprises can be nice, but I'm not sure how this one will be accepted…"

At that moment, Darius cleared his throat and made the gather-together motion to his team. The press was about to arrive. Darius had insisted the Parmithian team be seated in a secure area where Phil and his security team could block any attempts by the press to get a preconference interview with an alien.

Teresa walked away to comply with the request, but Friedrich hesitated. He turned back toward Allie. "Major Heroux, Darius and I have gone over this announcement word by word several times. Darius believes that this decision is a good thing for planet Earth. You might also think of it as an insurance policy if things go badly in the next couple of weeks." Friedrich started to leave and turned back yet again to make one last comment. Holding up a finger to make his point, he added, "As you listen to the announcement, think about what it will communicate to the world about their actions so far… and their deadline." Then he left to join the others and allow Allie time to wonder and worry.

A small speaker's platform and podium had been set up in a room next to the Hall of Egyptian Treasures. A couple hundred padded conference chairs had been arranged in neat rows, and they were filling rapidly. Attendance was limited to official invitation only. Though they had been given very short notice, no television network or news outlet was going to pass up *this* opportunity. History would be made in Paris today, and the world would be watching.

Reporters had positioned their television cameras to the sides and behind the chairs, jockeying for optimal angles. At nine o'clock, a man stepped to the microphone. He rapped his knuckles on the podium as if he were a judge calling his court to order. In French, he welcomed his visitors, "*Mesdames et Messieurs du Corps de la presse, si vous pouviez vous asseoir, nous sommes prêts à commencer. Par respect pour nos invités parmithiens, le reste de cette réunion se déroulera en anglais.*"

He then switched to English. "I am Monsieur Jacques Dimont, director of the Musée du Louvre, and I have been asked to open this press conference with a welcome and introductions. The Parmithian delegation has requested this press conference be held here in the museum, and we were glad to accommodate them. Messieurs Darius, Matthew, Siegfried, and Newton and Madams Amelia and Teresa have captivated the world with their visit. Their visit has been… controversial, and our visitors have been subjected to armed attack." Dimont shrugged. "They can, of course, expect much better treatment here in France."

The museum director knew that the press was waiting for the main event to unfold and wanted to get to it as quickly as possible. Taking his cue, Dimont finished up his introduction of Darius.

"In consideration of our Parmithian guests, we will conduct this meeting in English. Interruptions of any kind will not be tolerated. With no more ado, I would like to introduce Ambassador Darius of Parmithia to update Paris, France, and the rest of the world on his progress."

One could feel both anticipation and animosity fill the room. Most of the reporters looked stone-faced and suspicious. What were the aliens going to demand of Earth now? What aspect of Earth culture would they criticize? They had taken their shots at the United Nations and the United States. Were they going to complain about Europe now?

Darius stepped to the podium. Phil and Allie, sitting next to each other on the front row, both focused on steadying their breathing. Allie had recounted her conversation with Friedrich. Phil checked the exit points from the hallway and the position of his security team. Nothing had yet happened to comfort him about his premonition that something would go wrong today.

In his most diplomatic voice, Darius began, "Ladies and gentlemen of the press, merci beaucoup for your attendance today. In my travels throughout the galaxy, my favorite places to visit are always museums. In all my travels, I have never seen an equal to the Louvre. Museums are sanctuaries for the most magnificent art, sculpture, literature, and other treasures of your world. The valuables in this museum document the finest moments of your history and witness to the artistic accomplishments of great men and women who have lived in it. Whatever may happen in your future, Earth has been the birthplace of billions of people and the home for masters of great art and accomplishment. The government of Parmithia would like to help Earth to preserve both its rich heritage and its people."

Darius hesitated. He had labored to keep the next statements secret. Revealing their activities to the public would make their future work more difficult and dangerous. However, this was not the time to second-guess himself. Their efforts would be revealed soon anyway. He plunged ahead.

"I would like to announce today that at my request, Parmithia is sending three large transport ships to Earth. First-contact teams like mine are sent out in specific search patterns and our transport ships trail behind them to be available for required emigrations. We wish to offer transportation to select citizens of your world to voyage to another world very similar to Earth. There they will colonize the planet and build a civilization. This is a one-way trip for these colonists. There will be no return."

Though the reporters were all videotaping this event, many were taking notes, perhaps to document their own reactions to this news.

Darius continued, "Since before our arrival, my team and I have been actively searching through your Internet for those people who meet our specifications for new colonists. Those who are candidates for this colonization have been invited to meet with us for interviews. Those people we choose to offer passage will be selected based on their unique capabilities, accomplishments, and demonstrated virtue."

"A total of five hundred people will be chosen and invited to join the colonization team. Each of the five hundred who pass their interview may bring up to five family members or friends with them. These companions must also pass a background check, of course. This group, a total of approximately three thousand people, will be given supplies and assistance to colonize this New Earth. The three transport ships are already on their way here. One ship will land in Washington, DC, one in Paris, and one in New Delhi. Those who have been chosen for this emigration must travel to one of those three locations to board their ship. One thousand passengers will fit into each spaceship."

Darius had offered all the assurances he could and started winding down his announcement. He continued, "Once they have arrived on New Earth, a few of our people will remain to assist in the colonization efforts. Eventually, however, New Earthlings will be left to form their own society. Once again, this emigration is by invitation. We are not kidnapping these people. We are giving them a ride to a new planet and a fresh beginning."

Darius turned to speak to the director of the museum in which they stood. "Director Dimont, we chose the Louvre Museum to make our announcement because we want you to know that we have room on the ship for a limited number of masterpieces of art and history that you might want to send with this group. We can only preserve a fraction of the treasures you have in your museums, but what you entrust to us will be safely preserved on New Earth for millennia to come."

Darius concluded, again trying to be reassuring, "Whatever happens to Earth—and that has yet to be determined—at least you can be assured that your species and a small part of your culture will be preserved. The ships will be arriving two weeks from tomorrow." Darius tapped his papers on the podium and then looked up. "So that is all I have for you in my prepared statement. Are there any questions?"

For a few moments, almost a hundred reporters sat dumbfounded and at a complete loss for words. Were there any questions? Earth's first-contact alien ambassador has just made the most important announcement in modern history. Of course, there were questions! After a second of stunned silence, the halls reverberated with questions shouted in French, English, and several other languages. Darius waved both hands to dismiss all the shouting and pointed to young female reporter. Ladies first.

"Does the arrival of your transport ships mean that you have decided *not* to help Earth with our energy and food crises?"

Darius had expected this question. Indeed, he had hoped for it. "That decision has not been made yet. Earth still has two weeks to show they are willing to make changes that we have requested. As of yet, it appears there has been no executive action on our appeals."

Darius pointed to another female reporter.

"What criteria did you use to choose the three thousand people invited onto the transport ships?"

Darius paused, realizing the importance of this question. "People were chosen based on their expertise, their accomplishments...and on their virtue and integrity."

"Virtue and integrity?"

Darius shrugged as if the answer was obvious. He asked, "Has the candidate lived a clean, charitable, and honest life? Have they obeyed the laws of their land? Have they given service and been charitable? These attributes are, by far, the hardest to research and judge. But they are critically important characteristics for colonists. We don't want New Earth to continue to...make the same mistakes as Old Earth. We want to start it out with the most virtuous people we can find."

Darius pointed to an earnest young man, who had been quietly and continuously holding up his hand like a student in class. From his accent, it was apparent the journalist was from Great Britain.

"Ambassador Darius, for those of us who are staying on Old Earth, does Europe pass your qualification requirements for sharing your technologies here?"

Darius paused, wondering why he was always giving bad news to people who had done nothing to deserve it.

"I realize this is disappointing, but none of the individual countries in Europe is large enough to take the lead on bringing Parmithian technology to Earth. If we gave dark energy to a member of the European Union, we believe it would soon be taken away by a nation of greater power. Qualification of a nation to receive our technology is based on the values of their culture. However, the strength of the nation to hold onto the technology must also be considered.

We hope that France and the rest of Europe can actively help the planet in meeting those requirements."

Questions were being shouted, as reporters talked over one another. But Darius was apparently ready to end the meeting and stepped back from the podium. Monsieur Dimont stepped forward. "Ambassador Darius, thank you for your address and your offer to help Earth and the Louvre Museum. I would like to thank the press for their attendance on such short notice. This press conference is now ended."

Phil's security team moved in and deflected a few ambitious reporters pushing forward to get one last quote from the Parmithian team. Phil and Allie attended to the social necessities of wrapping up the press conference, thanking Dimont and his staff for their hospitality. The museum director walked them to the door of the museum, obviously deep in thought. However, as he bid farewell, Dimont stopped in front of Darius.

"Ambassador, thank you for your offer to take some of the treasures of the Louvre Museum to New Earth. Given the state of our world… I accept your offer. The increasing threat of terrorist actions or anarchy in our streets plague me. Our board of directors will have to approve my decision…but I believe we will send as many crates as you will allow us on your ships. Retaining Earth's treasures is the purpose of the museum. I would be remiss if I did not take this opportunity to assure the safety of some of our masterpieces. These items will also help those who migrate to New Earth a way to remember their origins. Thank you…and goodbye. Safe travels, my friend."

A few minutes later, the caravan of three Chevy Suburbans was on its way back to Villacoublay Air Base. It seemed like it had been a long day, yet it was only noon. Phil's driver was following his GPS, trying to avoid French traffic and the crazy traffic circles with no lane markers. Road construction workers had just set up detour signs and were impatiently signaling their vehicle to turn right. Car horns were blaring behind him, but even as his driver began making the turn, alarms in Phil's head started screaming for attention. Unexpected detours could be dangerous.

Sure enough, after his convoy of three vehicles had made the turn, the detour signs were moved again, this time to block traffic from the street onto which they had turned. Suddenly, two large cargo vans pulled behind them from a side alley, blocking escape and any visibility from the street behind them. Just as quickly, two Mercedes GLS SUVs pulled in front of them, blocking escape ahead. A fifth and sixth gray SUV pulled in from opposing side streets, making the blockade complete. The trap had been sprung, and there was nowhere to flee. Phil's first thought, wedging its way to the front of his mind ahead of the panic, was how well executed this enemy operation had been. One must admire such excellent work…

Doors of the cargo vans and SUVs opened, and a dozen armed men poured out onto the street. They were all dressed in the medium-gray jumpsuits of warehouse dockworkers. However, these were elite, well-trained soldiers, now aiming assault rifles and sidearms at the Parmithian vehicles. Three of the men held shoulder-fired rocket launchers, each trained on one of Phil's three vehicles. Phil realized this was not a ragtag group of protestors ready to do violence to an alien invasion force. Phil noticed that all the agents were, heaven help him, Chinese.

Phil spoke slowly into his headset, enunciating each word clearly, "Security team, roll down your windows a few inches and slowly drop your weapons onto the street. Do *not* open your doors. Then just sit tight!"

Phil checked his mirrors and assured that everyone obeyed his order. Then he waited. The rear door of the lead enemy vehicle was opened by its driver. A small but athletically built Chinese man, dressed in a pin-striped black suit over a white shirt, emerged from the car. He sported a distinct military haircut, wrap-around sunglasses, and the bearing of a man familiar with authority. He walked forward and calmly stopped a couple of car lengths in front of Phil's vehicle. He removed his sunglasses and folded his hands in front of him. No bodyguards accompanied him; it appeared no one believed they were necessary. Phil felt like he was in a James Bond movie and the bad guy had just made his grand entrance. With a start, Phil realized he recognized this man.

"Colonel Alex Xi," Phil whispered. The man's identity explained a lot about this operation.

Xi had been the lead security man for a couple of Chinese delegation visits to which Phil had been assigned. From reports, Xi was now the commander of the special operations division of the Chinese Army. Xi knew that Phil was leading the security detail for the Parmithian delegation. He knew about the press conference and that Phil's group would be passing this street when it was over. Arranging this ambush would have been complex, but… Xi was more than capable enough. Xi knew in which vehicle Phil sat and that Phil would eventually recognize him. Not anxious to provoke an unnecessary conflict, Xi was waiting for Phil to get out of the car to talk.

Very slowly, Phil opened his passenger side door and, with his hands held high, stepped out. He showed his empty hands to the soldiers around him and then slowly dropped them to his side. He casually approached the leader of the Chinese special ops team, positioning himself to allow each of them plenty of personal space. Phil kept repeating to himself, "Cool and calm." It seemed appropriate that he should initiate this conversation.

"Hello, Alex. We haven't seen each other…since the Nuclear Disarmament Summit in Washington last November, isn't that right? Well, it's good to see you again, though I must fervently protest this military action against us. What exactly can we do for you?"

Commander Xi remained nonplussed. He gave Phil a broad smile for his nonchalance and answered in kind. "Hello, Phil, it's good to see you as well. Yes, we last saw each other in Washington in November. I believe mobs burnt down a large part of Chinatown there to protest our presence. In response to your accusation, let me be clear. This is not a military operation. We are here simply to… invite the Parmithian delegation to accompany us to Beijing. They have visited the United States, Italy, and France. China is feeling… left out. My leaders would like the honor of meeting the members of the first extraterrestrial delegation to visit Earth. From our news reports, the United States severely botched its first contact with our visitors from space. Obviously, it was a poor first choice on the part of the aliens, but what's done is done. China would like to have its turn in meeting our guests."

Phil was both relieved and alarmed. It appeared that despite the abundant weaponry, there were no plans for immediate violence. But it also seemed that the Chinese were intent on taking his Parmithian charges to China.

"Colonel, you could have just requested an audience through official channels."

Xi laughed aloud and replied, "We *have* been making requests through official channels ever since the aliens arrived. We have been denied for numerous reasons, but I can recognize General Bart's heavy-handed diplomacy behind those denials. We finally decided to take the matter into our own hands."

Phil asserted, "This might be considered an act of war."

"Major Casaverde, you misunderstand," Xi said soothingly. "You and your security team are welcome to leave. A few of you may be allowed to accompany the Parmithians to Beijing but only if you wish to do so. We are not detaining you, and the Parmithians are *not* citizens of the United States. They have no recognizable diplomatic immunity. You have no claim on them simply because they visited Washington first. By any definition, this is *not* an act of war."

Phil hesitated as he considered his next move. Alex Xi was not a man to be trifled with. He was outgunned, and any defensive move on his part would only get someone shot. But he had to try something. "And if we resist?"

Recognizing the question as the last resort of a desperate man, Xi ignored it.

"Major, could you please advise the Parmithian commander, pilot, and engineer that we will be taking them back to their ship so they can fly it to the Beijing Xijiao Airport? My superiors are anxious to tour a starship as are our engineers. The other half of the delegation is invited to fly to Beijing with me in our presidential jet. They will be shown every courtesy. When we are done with our discussions, the Parmithians will be released to go wherever they wish. You have my word. As long as they are cooperative in our talks, no one will be harmed."

Phil didn't like the proviso of the last statement, but he recognized any further objections would be a waste of time.

"My security team will accompany—"

Commander Xi interrupted Phil's dictate with one of his own, "Major Casaverde, only you and Major Heroux are invited to accompany our extraterrestrial visitors to Beijing. We hope your presence will help keep both them and the United States calm and cooperative. You will help shuttle the spaceship to Beijing. Major Heroux is invited to join us on our government jet. I suggest you go now to inform your team of the new plans."

Phil had to admire Xi's plan. Half of the Parmithian team would be held hostage so the other half would shuttle the spaceship to Beijing. So far, he had heard no police sirens, which was probably a good thing. Police interference could be catastrophic in such a standoff. There was no good reason to delay the inevitable. He walked back to each vehicle and explained the reasons behind the ambush.

When he finished, Allie put on her bravest smile and commented, "I have always wanted to visit Beijing. I'm sure our time there will be less frightening than the invitation has been." She gathered up her computer case. In a voice she might use to get everyone out the door to go to lunch, she exclaimed, "So let's go. Okay, everyone?"

Friedrich, Matthew, Teresa, and Allie all got out of their vehicles and walked toward the Chinese and their guns. Seeing them, Alex Xi spoke a sharp command in Chinese. As one, guns were lowered, and the soldiers holding them shuffled in lockstep back to their own vehicles. Xi fell in stride with Allie and Friedrich, expressing his gratitude that they had agreed to visit his capital. Allie, playing the diplomat, held back several stinging retorts that came to mind. There was no benefit in offending their captor, and there was no turning back.

During the drive to the airport, Allie decided to test out Commander Xi's assurances they would not be held or prevented from attending to their duties. She pulled out her cell phone and started typing away. Xi appraised her, a smile playing across his lips.

"Who are you texting, Major Heroux?" he finally asked.

"General Theodore Bart" she responded, fully expecting to be relieved of her phone.

"How nice. Give him my regards, won't you?" Xi replied dryly.

Chapter 18

BEIJING

The drive to Charles de Gaulle Airport was uneventful. The group was driven directly to the Chinese private jet, a luxurious aircraft with a dozen first-class seats, a small kitchen, and a stocked bar. Chinese stewardesses helped them find seats and offered them food and drink. Within a few minutes, the jet took off. Minutes later a delicious lunch of rice, shrimp, and dumplings was served. Allie closed her eyes, fairly certain that she was dreaming and needed to wake up. A special press conference in the Louvre Museum, a heavily armed kidnapping, and then a gourmet lunch in a private jet bound for China. It was simply too much for one day.

Allie found herself sitting beside Friedrich…yet again. Considering there were six Parmithians, it seemed she was spending a lot of time with the statistician/cook. She realized that she had not asked how the Parmithians were handling this violent interruption of their mission. Did kidnappings happen on a planet like Parmithia?

"Friedrich, I don't know what I can tell you about the Chinese intentions, but I can try to answer any questions you have about the country."

Friedrich turned toward her, pleasantly surprised by her offer. He seemed calm about their situation. He leaned closer to her and spoke softly, "Actually, we studied China as a possible starting point for our first contact. As you know, China has an authoritarian, communist government. Complaints against political leaders are rather forcefully discouraged. Thus, there are few protest marches or riots so prevalent in the United States. Social obedience is forced upon the Chinese. This is not the government or message that Parmithia wishes to support. We would rather the people be allowed to choose to follow their political leaders. Consequently, China was not chosen."

Friedrich leaned even closer and whispered, "There is no cause for worry. Darius will explain to Chinese leadership the changes that we would require to give them access to our technology. We think it unlikely that the government will accept those prerequisites. They will have no further use for us and will let us go."

Allie did not know if the outcome would be all that simple, but she felt better with Friedrich's assurances. He was calming *her*, and it was working. Suddenly, without thinking, she blurted, "Friedrich, are you married?"

Friedrich tilted his head back in surprise and then smiled. "No, Major, I am not married. I knew as a child that I wanted to explore space. It takes an average of ten years for a round trip to planets close enough to Parmithia to visit. With the time dilation effect of traveling at the speed of light, a young spouse on Parmithia would be an old woman before I could return from even one mission. It's impossible. Only if a husband and wife travel together like Amelia and her husband, Drake, could a marriage work in the exploration of space."

Friedrich looked into Allie's eyes and held her gaze. Allie maintained a passive expression and smiled her understanding, dropping eye contact. Inside her head, she was screaming at herself. Kidnapped by Chinese operatives, on a jet bound for Beijing, and she was talking about Parmithian marriage to a man she barely knew! Wrong time, wrong place, wrong subject!

Not trusting herself to say anything appropriate, Allie closed her eyes and laid her head back on the seat cushion. After a few moments of staring at her face, Friedrich did the same.

The plane landed just after midnight. A white Escalade stretch limo pulled up beside the jet. Allie, Friedrich, Matthew, Teresa, and Commander Xi loaded into the vehicle. The Cadillac was set up as a conversation pit style for its passengers. Allie realized that this trip would include nothing but the best. The Chinese were out to impress, the first step in any negotiation.

Inside the vehicle, an attractive young Chinese woman sat waiting as everyone boarded the limousine. Recognizing his duties as host, Commander Xi made introductions, "I would like to introduce you to JinJing Soon. She will be coordinating your stay while you are here. If you have a question, Ms. Soon will answer it. If you need anything, she will provide it."

Xi's job done, he turned to his cell phone to check messages. JinJing smiled her broadest smile and bowed toward her guests. With only a slight but charming Chinese accent, she welcomed them. "First, please call me Jin. Welcome to Beijing. We are bound for the hotel *JEN Beijing by Shangri-La* in our central business district. There will be a late dinner at the hotel, but attendance is not mandatory. You may order room service if you wish. I'm sure you are very fatigued after such an eventful day."

Allie noted that JinJing sounded like an accomplished diplomat. Her English was perfect, and her welcome was worded to put everyone at ease. She decided to test her conclusion. Disarmingly, she asked, "Jin, your English is very precise. Did you study outside of China?"

Jin smiled and, in the confined space of the limousine, gave a slight head bow. "Major Allison Heroux, it is so nice to meet you. Yes, I studied at Wellesley College in the United States for four years, obtaining my degree in political science and government."

Allie smiled and nodded in understanding. Nothing but the best.

Jin chatted with each Parmithian, calling each by name and title. Allie had to admit, their new hostess was delightful. By the time they reached the hotel, the group had visibly relaxed. Jin led them directly to the elevators, two of which were being held for them. They ascended to the twentieth floor. Walking down the hallway, JinJing indicated which room belonged to whom, handing each person a key card. One might have mistaken this for the beginning of a wonderful vacation had it not been for the three armed Chinese guards posted in the hallway outside their rooms.

It was now well after midnight. Allie was exhausted, and their visit to the Louvre seemed to have been days ago. As she walked to the bedroom, she dimly noted the spectacular view of Beijing and the large bouquet of fresh flowers before she dropped onto the bed.

The next morning, Allie wondered if she could get her clothes laundered. She opened the closet to find several new outfits hanging there. She checked and found that yes, everything in the closet was her size. Matching pairs of stylish shoes sat on a shelf in front of her! She knew the Chinese were trying to impress, but this was officially above and beyond all expectations. Allie fought back her admiration of the Chinese reception. Would the Parmithians be swayed by this level of attention? How could they *not* be awed? Compared to being attacked as a part of their greeting by the United States, China was already making a good case for itself.

At precisely 9:00 a.m., her phone rang. A pleasant Chinese voice advised her that breakfast would be ready in thirty minutes. Ms. JinJing Soon would come by and escort the group to the dining room, and a tour of Beijing would begin immediately after the meal.

When Allie and her companions walked into the dining room, Phil, Darius, Amelia, and Friedrich were all waiting for them. Hugs and handshakes were shared all around. Allie felt herself tear up as she gave Phil a very nonmilitary hug. She pulled him away from the group.

"So, Phil, did you get picked up by a limousine when you landed?

"Yep."

"Do you like your room and the clothes provided for today's activities?"

"Yes, the room is beautiful, and the clothes are comfortable. How *did* they know my shoe size?"

"We can probably discuss that later… Apparently, the Chinese have decided to awe and impress their guests before negotiations." Allie looked down at her new shoes. "One has to admire the strategy. How does Darius seem to be handling the attention?"

Phil shrugged and took a deep breath. "Darius was resigned to this meeting from the moment we were ambushed. He admitted during the flight here that he had been worried about the Chinese response to being snubbed. He is pleased with the reception, but I think he will see through the luxury treatment. Courtesy toward one's guests is rooted in Chinese culture. And of course, they do want dark-energy technology, a resource they know they probably won't get through sheer force. So for the moment at least, Alex Xi is offering the Parmithians first-class treatment and a respectful request that Parmithia provide its technology to Earth through China. I don't know what Darius will do."

Phil started to move away but then stopped himself. "Have you been in communication with General Bart?"

"Yes, I have. Commander Xi knows I am submitting reports and has made no move to stop me."

"Great. Did the general relay any orders?"

"Just two, be careful and don't start a world war."

That day, the Parmithian team, Phil, and Allie were given a tour of Beijing. They visited Tiananmen Square, the National Museum of China, and the Forbidden City. The tour bus drove past the headquarters for Alibaba, Baidu, and Zhongguancun Software Park. Jin was the perfect tour guide, threading the ancient Chinese cultures of the past with the technical abilities of the present to showcase a country on the rise to world leadership. They returned to the hotel by midafternoon to rest up and dress for a black-tie reception dinner to be held that evening.

By the time Phil arrived at the hotel dining room, the festivities were well underway. Phil sported a tuxedo with a Mandarin collar that he had found waiting in his closet upon their return from the tour. About one hundred people were in attendance, many of whom Phil recognized from past security assignments. Phil noticed that Commander Alex Xi was personally escorting Darius and Matthew, introducing them to industrial CEOs, government leaders, and even a couple of military generals. Friedrich and Newton were talking to leaders of Chinese engineering and power conglomerates. Teresa had entered into a deep conversation with a Buddhist monk, and Amelia was chatting with the head of the Chinese space program. Handshakes and bows of respect were abundant.

Allie spotted Phil at the door and broke of her own conversation to talk to him. She wore a blue gown with oriental patterns stitched throughout. Phil could not help but be impressed.

"May I say you look quite stunning, Major Heroux. Did I pull you away from talking to one of the many VIPs in the room?"

"Oh, I was actually chatting with the designer of my gown. She is the head of the leading clothes designer in all of Asia. She designed Amelia's and Teresa's gowns as well."

"Well then, she is much more talented and probably much more interesting than I am. She is obviously incredible at her job."

Phil had noticed Amelia as soon as he had entered the room. How could he not? She wore a white gown that looked as if it had been tailor-made for her. The glistening fabric perfectly accentuated the most interesting curves of Amelia's figure. Her hair had been professionally styled. She looked relaxed and very much at home at this party, effortlessly charming the six gentlemen who now surrounded her. Her smile was dazzling…

Phil sobered, consigning himself to reality.

"You know, Allie, those guys standing around Amelia are probably all billionaires. She is a beautiful woman from another planet, and she could probably get any one of those schmucks to marry her with little effort. She could live in luxury the rest of her life."

Allie was about to chide Phil for being so distracted, but he looked so miserable she couldn't do it.

"Phil… I don't think that Amelia came to Earth just to marry big money. It's *really* not her style. Can we perhaps focus on the problem at hand? Should we be doing something to impede the Chinese in their seduction of the Parmithians? We're wearing the clothes they gave us and going on limousine tours of their capital. I keep thinking if dark energy were mine, *I* would give it to the Chinese. Shouldn't we be objecting somehow?"

Phil shook his head and shrugged again. "Allie, first, to what treatment could we possibly object? Secondly, if we object too much, Commander Xi will put us on the first flight out of China. I think that Darius appreciates us being here, but he can handle the negotiations without us. He won't suspend the negotiations if we are suddenly uninvited. At the very least, our presence reminds the Parmithians of the concern and wishes of the United States. After the pitiful reception they received in Washington, someone has to remind them of our better efforts."

Allie considered the logic of Phil's reasoning and found it sound. They were here at the benevolence of the Chinese government. Any infraction would just get them sent home. She sighed.

"Well, today was a nice break from the craziness of the past few weeks. But the break is over after tonight. A technical review is scheduled for tomorrow at 10:00 a.m. Like the seminar at NASA, Newton will present. Tours of the *We Come in Peace* spaceship will occur over the lunch break. It is expected that serious negotiations will begin in the early afternoon."

A bell chimed to request that everyone make their way to the dining tables. Seats were assigned, with name cards printed out in beautiful Asian calligraphy. A five-course meal was then served, with crab meat and morel mushrooms as the main entrée. As she ate her first bite, Allie closed her eyes at the exquisite taste. *I can die now,* she thought. *My taste buds will never be this happy again.* The dissonance of this place was nearly unbearable. It was like being in a wonderful dream and a nightmare at the same time.

To her chagrin, Allie saw that that Darius and the Parmithian team were obviously delighted with the delicacies and discussions of the evening. They realized they were being honored by the most important people the Chinese government could assemble. How could the alien delegation *not* be persuaded by this attention and recognition?

*****

After dinner, the party continued well into the night. After-dinner drinks included baijiu, sake, snow beer, and green tea. Allie had excused herself and gone to bed, but Phil waited by the door, nursing his mineral water. He realized with a start that he was waiting to ambush Amelia. They hadn't had two minutes alone since Paris, though that was probably no excuse for stalking her now. He admitted to himself that he was jealous at the attention Amelia had been receiving all evening. He realized this was probably unprofessional, but he wanted to at least say good night.

As the festivities were finally ending, when oversight of Amelia was being passed from her party hosts back to JinJing, Phil saw his opportunity. As Jin turned to summon the elevator, Phil came up from behind Amelia, put his hand on her waist, and quickly ushered her around a corner.

Amelia seemed pleasantly surprised by the detour. "Phil, I haven't seen you all night. What a party... Why didn't you come talk to me?" Amelia's speech was a bit slurred. Too many admirers had encouraged her to drink too many of Earth's signature alcoholic beverages.

Phil stammered, "Amelia, I just wanted to say good night. You were so occupied it would have looked brutish of me to barge in...to your rescue. Also, I wanted to tell you that you look stunning...and that I have missed you."

Jin had noticed that Amelia had disappeared, and her questioning voice came from around the corner. "Ms. Amelia? Are you back here?"

The increasing volume of her voice indicated she was headed their way. Amelia smiled at Phil, her eyes took on a wistful look... and she threw her arms around his neck and kissed him. It was a short kiss, but it was a kiss. She broke it off and hurried back around the corner to intercept JinJing, apologizing repeatedly for getting lost while looking around the beautiful hotel. Their voices drifted away as they returned to the elevators. Phil leaned against a wall, recovering his wits. He realized that Amelia had been perceptive in leaving him as quickly as she had. Being found alone with Amelia would have almost certainly earned him a plane ticket home. But it might have been worth it. He wondered about the possibility of trying to visit her room tonight, finally deciding that getting past the armed Chinese guards might be too difficult.

Chapter 19

NEGOTIATIONS WITH CHINA

The next morning began with a technical seminar at the China National Space Administration in the Haidian District of Beijing. Phil and Amelia had been in the same limousine but obviously did not have enough privacy to talk. Phil caught Amelia's eyes once, and she did not look away. After a moment, she smiled and *winked* at him. Phil flushed with pleasure and felt like a schoolboy flirting with the prettiest girl in the class. His phone dinged, indicating the arrival of a text. It was from Allie, and just said, "Stop it!" He glanced at her, saw her mean-teacher face, and casually looked out at the window at the passing city streets. Did that woman miss anything?

As Chinese scientists and engineers filled the auditorium, Phil could not avoid feeling déjà vu of a very similar meeting at NASA just a couple of weeks ago. There was a mood of general anticipation among the participants, and he could hear the excitement in the conversations in Chinese that filled the room. Phil understood most of what he heard. From what he could tell, there was no subterfuge or villainous planning going on. The discussions were much like he had heard at NASA. Scientists were interested in advancing science, not in politics. For a moment, his eyes locked with those of Alex Xi, but the commander did not feel the need to speak with him and turned away.

Newton presented the same PowerPoint slides that he had shown at NASA. Many of the attendees wore headphones to hear the Chinese translation of the presentation. When it was time for questions, hands shot into the air. The translator chose which scientists were allowed to ask a question. The questions were designed to push Newton for as much information as possible about dark-energy drive and associated technologies. Everyone in the room knew what had been revealed at NASA and realized the Parmithian engineer couldn't provide operational details about the space drive. But they were still intent on discovering the potential of this alien science and knowledge.

Just knowing that dark-energy technology was attainable and *not* an inevitable dead-end research project meant much to the Chinese engineers. It would become an undertaking that would be funded and researched for years to come. There was none of the despair felt at NASA about the continued defunding of their programs. The mood was unquestionably optimistic. There were several questions about the possibility of opening the dark-energy drive. Newton repeated his warnings about an orbit-shifting explosion, but apparently the possibility remained on the table.

Lunch was served, during which Newton again took groups of twenty engineers and scientists on tours of his ship, which rested in the main parking lot of the Space Administration building. The technical exchange was spirited. Newton's spirits were high. He had not had to break the bad news about not being able to share dark-energy technology. He decided to stay on the ship for the rest of the day. Amelia, Friedrich, and Teresa were invited to tour of the Space Administration facility. Only Darius and Matthew had been invited to attend the negotiation meetings after lunch.

*****

The negotiation meeting was to be held in a much smaller but more elegant room of the building. Only five Chinese officials attended, all of whom sat on one end of the conference table. Alex Xi had scheduled this meeting, but it was apparent the commander held the lowest rank of the five Chinese leaders. Darius and Matthew sat at the other end of the conference table. Phil and Allie had found seats in the back of the conference room, not invited to take a seat at the table. As they sat down, Commander Xi gave Phil a look that assured him that if he tried to interrupt the proceedings in any way, he would be forcibly removed.

The Chinese diplomat closest to Darius rose from his chair. The man was older, thin, and balding, almost a stereotype of the venerable Chinese grandfather. He smiled warmly at his audience, obviously hoping to get the meeting off to an amiable start. In perfect but heavily accented English, he announced, "We would like to get started with our meeting, if we may. I am Liao Haoran, director of the China National Space Administration. I am your host today and will conduct this meeting. Sitting beside me is Zhang Chow Kai, vice-chairman of the Chinese Communist Party. Next to him is Chung Guowei, secretary of technology to Premier Pan Qiang Tao, our nation's supreme leader. Finally, at the end of the table is Commander Alex Xi of the Ministry of State Security, whom I believe you have met. Ambassador Darius, I wish to welcome you and Matthew to this discussion. Your introductions are not necessary. We have studied your files in detail."

Zhang Chow Kai and Chung Guowei sat without expression. Both appeared to be lifetime politicians, unwilling to communicate any emotions they might be feeling. Both were heavier-set men who apparently enjoyed the luxuries of fine food and old age.

Director Liao continued, "Ambassador, I hope you can forgive us for the way we brought you to Beijing. The technology you bring to our planet could radically change the balance of power on Earth. We deemed it imperative that we meet, and we were forced to take somewhat unconventional means to get you here... I have been told that you have studied the cultures and societies of our planet. You met with our United Nations and challenged the world to provide two parents for every child. We wish you to know that this practice is not a problem in China. Our honor and tradition strongly discourage single-parent homes."

It was apparent that Director Liao was starting to build his case. His tone remained respectful, but he was making his point.

"You have met with the political leaders of the United States and have challenged them to put a stop to laws and policies that support divisions throughout their nation. Very few discriminations still exist in our country, but the government is actively working to eliminate them. Violent protests are simply not allowed.

"You have visited France and announced that nations of the European Union are too small to administer the development of dark-energy technology. We agree with your conclusion. However, I believe you will recognize that China is a world leader in both economic and military power. We have research and development capabilities that are second to none. While NASA is on the decline, the China Space Administration receives full funding for the development of space travel.

"With that being said, we are here to discuss your willingness to provide China with Parmithian technology. We admit that our country needs help to address environmental, agricultural, and clean energy issues. We are, however, willing to share that help with the rest of the world. But China feels it can provide you the best primary Earth contact for our partnership. What say you, Ambassador Darius?"

Liao Haoran sat back down in his chair, his speech ended. Phil had to admit that it had been a very good speech. Liao had painted Darius into a corner, using his own words and announcements to prove that China was the best choice to be Parmithia's partner on Earth. Phil didn't see how Darius could argue otherwise. Already this meeting was going poorly for the United States, and there was absolutely nothing Phil could do about it.

*****

Darius slowly sat forward in his chair. He knew that what he would say in the next few minutes could seal the fate of his mission on Earth. He cleared his throat. It was the first time that Allie had ever seen Darius nervous, which made her anxious as well. Darius had been the definitive leader and spokesman who had provided a clear definition of Parmithia's policy and expectations. But the pushback against those policies had increased.

"Director Liao, you have made some excellent points, and your logic is irrefutable. As I have previously explained, mankind—or Homo sapiens—is the final result of evolution on a number of planets. In every case where men and women have peopled a planet, they have claimed its resources as their own. They have relegated all other species to lands they do not want. As men conquer their world, they establish governments to rule over their people. These governments are established to meet the needs of the people being governed."

Darius continued to develop his argument, "All men have two forces working within them. One is social. We enjoy forming tribes of friends and family who are like us. Tribes are strong influencers upon its people, and most would gladly give their lives for the survival of their tribe. Men do not rebel against their government as individuals. They only rebel against their government as groups."

Darius was making his own case, and he was taking his time to establish his arguments. The Chinese leadership did not interrupt. They would allow Darius his time. Darius continued, sounding a bit like an attorney making his case to a jury, "But having tribes continually at war with one another for food, resources, and land only results in chaos and anarchy. At one time in its history, China was ruled by warlords of multiple tribes within your nation. Your own history witnesses to the chaos inherent in such government. Any ruler who establishes a government to tax its people and work for the public good must be able to control the tribes within his borders. On Earth today, you have two approaches to such government. The United States and other nations allow their tribes to gather, organize, and fight against the government through protests and riots. Special interest groups are allowed to lobby and garner favor with politicians to gain government concessions for themselves. As one might expect, the United States is weakened by such tribal competition. This instability makes them a poor choice to receive dark-energy technology. We have challenged America to repair their society and halt divisive efforts. For their own good, this destabilization must stop."

So far, Darius's comments had been good news for the Chinese officials. Now it would be time for the bad news.

"On the other extreme, we have China and its communist government. Yours is an authoritative government that controls its population more strictly, often using police and armed forces. Such strict oversight has existed throughout Earth's history. Ironically, the three largest such governments—Nazi Germany, the Russian Communist Party, and the Chinese Communist Party—all began at the same point in your history about one century ago. Though you have a rich history as a country, your form of government is still young."

Darius shift in his chair. He knew he was heading into the most dangerous part of his speech.

"Parmithia's main expectation of governments is that they remain stable, and it is a high expectation. Director Liao, my round trip from Parmithia will take a total of ten Earth years of my life. Due to time dilation caused by traveling at the speed of light, when I return to my home planet about, one hundred Earth years will have passed there. Indeed, due to my chosen career of traveling through space, over five hundred years have passed in Parmithia since I first left it."

The alien commander continued, "During those centuries, my government has been stable. Of course, there are changes in dress, speech, and even philosophy. But the people are content, and the government remains stable. There are no revolutions to destabilize our world. There are no attempts to use dark energy to conquer other worlds. I say this not to brag about my home planet but to set it as a benchmark and example of the stability that governments can enjoy. The United States government is 258 years old. The government of the People's Republic of China is 85 years old. From our social models, neither will be stable in the turbulent years to come.

"The philosophy of the Parmithian government lies somewhere between the ideologies of China and the United States. The United States allows *too much* latitude of its citizens, who are loyal to their tribe but not to their nation. These divisions are to the detriment of the entire country. China does not allow its citizens *enough* latitude to express their individuality, which is the source of its instability."

It was apparent that Darius was shifting his tactic from providing evidence to stating his demands. His voice became more sincere, but there was no apology in his tone. Phil shifted forward in his chair, resting his elbows on his knees. Neither the United Nations nor Congress had been happy with Darius's injunctions to get their house in order. How was China going to react to theirs?

"We call upon China to allow its citizens more freedoms. We suggest you start with unlimited freedom of religion. Seeking for spiritual strength from gods, whoever they may be, leads people to continually try to improve themselves and help others. Religion provides cultural stability. The population is happier, seeking for a higher purpose in life than mere survival. Thus, governments are more stable. Why would a government give up such a potential source of stability?"

The question was rhetorical, so Darius continued, "Your world is on the brink of a food crisis. Many Earth governments are so oppressive, weak, or distracted by the wealth of leadership that they are failing to provide for their citizens. Global warming is affecting your weather patterns. Infrastructures are being allowed to deteriorate. As a nation, China is probably best prepared to defend itself from the chaos. But our social models of your world predict that your efforts will not be enough. Your borders will be attacked. Like your ancient Roman Empire, China's fall will be brought about by the attacks of modern-day peoples seeking food and refuge."

"In summary, China is a country that we admire for its people and accomplishments. We invite you to take a leading role in making the needed social changes required for Earth's long-term stability. Only then can we hope to transition our technology to your planet."

Phil looked at the Chinese leadership at the head of the conference table. These men were experienced negotiators. Darius had just offered Parmithian energy technology to them. But there was a catch to the proposal that required major changes to governing policy that had existed for nearly a century.

Director Liao voiced what everyone in the room was wondering, "Ambassador Darius, besides allowing religious freedoms, what more must China do to receive dark-energy technology?"

Darius took a deep breath. Here was the point in the sales pitch when he must tell China the total cost of Parmithian technology and of saving their planet. "Director Liao, let me be frank about what has happened in our decision process. As you may know, our interview with the congressional committee of the United States did not go well." Darius reached up to his face and touched the healing but apparent bruises to his face that had resulted from his beating. "The resulting protests came close to killing my team…and then me," he said reflectively.

"Our presentation to the United Nations and our visit with the Pope in Rome were equally discouraging. I decided that the likelihood of success on Earth is low. As we announced in Paris, we have three ships heading here to provide lifeboats for three thousand people. Then your government rather firmly invited us to Beijing. During the flight here, Engineer Newton and I revised our social models but now with China working *in concert* with our efforts. The results were actually…much more hopeful."

Darius started talking faster, excited about the potential of his proposal, "The United States and China are the two leading superpowers on Earth. If your two governments take the lead in saving the planet, then there is a significant possibility that your planet can make its transition to a sustainable world. One country alone could not accomplish the task. However, if the two most powerful nations on Earth form an alliance and *work together*, then the probability of success more than doubles. Both countries would hold each other accountable for the changes they must make. Your two governments must work as partners, following new governing principles that implement more religious freedom for the Chinese and more constraints on division in America."

Darius moved into his closing argument. "As the Parmithian authority, my job is to coax planets away from self-destruction. This is not a task that you can rework if you get it wrong the first time. We have indicated the paths that the United Nations and the United States must take to receive our help. They may or may not choose to take those paths. China may or may not accept what we have told you today. If not, Parmithia will not share our dark energy or any other technology with you. As I have said before, there would be no point. If you refuse our recommendations, your world is doomed."

Darius did not look down at a cell phone or any other communication device. It was a surprise when, without dropping the amiable smile on his face, he announced, "However, our alliance doesn't seem to be off to a very good start. My ship engineer tells me that your soldiers have just broken into our spacecraft and your engineers are tearing apart the ship to try to figure out its operation."

Phil decided it was time to throw caution to the wind. He stood up from his back corner of the conference room and announced, "Commander Xi, you have heard the Parmithian proposal. I think this is the point in time when I hold you to your guarantee that the Parmithian team will be set free."

Xi stood as well, but he remained unruffled. "Major Casaverde, your request is premature. We still have questions that must be answered. Our engineers are inspecting the Parmithian ship to determine if we can reverse-engineer their technology without having to restructure our government! We have *not* learned all that we require!"

Phil realized he would shortly be escorted out of the room, so he had nothing more to lose. "You plan to tear apart the dark-energy drive? You are aware that opening the drive will cause an explosion that will destroy Beijing, are you not?"

As one, the three Chinese political leaders stood, gathered their belongings, and walked toward the door. This was not their argument.

Darius interrupted their departure, "Director Liao, Vice-Chairman Zhang, and Advisor Chung, could we meet together again tomorrow? Within twenty-four hours, I think there will be more information to discuss and new decisions to be made."

The three men looked at one another and nodded. They appeared slightly embarrassed at the heavy-handedness of the spaceship invasion, so agreeing to another meeting was acceptable. No one thought to ask what new information might be available.

*****

The limousine ride back to the hotel was understandably tense. Newton had not rejoined the group. Apparently, he had been detained in the spaceship. Darius demanded to see the ship engineer but was denied by Commander Xi.

"He will not be harmed," Xi sighed dismissively.

Phil, sitting by Allie, leaned forward to object, but Allie grabbed his arm, digging her fingernails into his sleeve. Her eyes told him the rest. Any token resistance would be futile and just get him removed from the negotiation. She needed him close, and argument was pointless now.

Everyone was emotionally exhausted. The reversal of courtesies extended by the Chinese was unexpected. Was the *We Come in Peace* being torn apart? The rules of the negotiation had changed. Everyone had been relieved of their cell phones and laptops before they boarded the shuttle. Apparently, no more reports to General Bart were going out anytime soon. It didn't matter. They were in China's capital city. The US military would not risk a world war by attempting an ill-fated rescue mission.

It was early evening when they all arrived at their hotel. Allie was not surprised when room service called to confirm that Commander Xi had ordered that everyone take dinner in their rooms tonight. What would she like to eat? Allie was not hungry but, knowing she had to keep up her energy, ordered fish and quinoa.

As the room service cart was pushed into her room, she looked at the server and realized it was JinJing Soon! She started to greet her, but Jin caught her eye and shook her head. Allie swallowed her exclamation.

As she was closing the door on the two guards in the hall, Jin cheerfully offered, "Now just let me get this set up for you."

But like her statement, her gaiety was for the benefit of the guards only. Tears came to her eyes. In hushed tones, Jin explained, "I'm so sorry this happened. Things were not meant to turn out like this. Commander Xi is very angry. No one is allowed to leave their rooms."

Allie nodded. "How is everyone else? Have you seen them?"

"Teresa is distraught. The others seem to be handling it well. I am going to drop off Major Casaverde's dinner now. Would you like me to tell him anything?"

FIRST JUDGMENT

Jin was noisily uncovering dishes and moving cutlery around to maintain the appearance of preparing the table. Allie thought for a moment.

"Please tell him not to get himself kicked out of the country. His speech today might be overlooked, but any more resistance and I won't have a partner any longer. And tell him to trust in Darius. I think he has a plan."

Jin nodded her head, pointed to the food, and whispered, "You must eat to keep up your strength… Besides, the fish and quinoa are delicious." Then she let herself out the door.

Chapter 20

DO YOU THINK US WEAK?

The next morning, a room-service breakfast arrived that included a note to be ready to depart at 10:00 a.m. At precisely that time, JinJing Soon arrived to escort everyone to their transportation. As they bordered the limousine, Commander Xi greeted each person by name. His face could have been etched in stone. With the downward turn in the negotiations, Phil expected some tension in his Chinese counterpart. Yet Xi had the appearance of a man being led from death row to his execution. Something else was going on here, and it could not be good. Newton was still nowhere to be seen, which was concerning. Phil had to guess that he had spent the night on the ship, possibly under intense questioning.

As soon as they arrived at the Space Administration building, the Parmithian delegation was escorted back to their same conference room and, surprisingly, left alone there. Amelia turned to their young apprentice Teresa and took her by the shoulders. Teresa was the wallflower of the group, quietly learning what first contact meant so she could someday assume Matthew's role as a culture and religion expert.

"Teresa, are you doing all right? I'm sorry this is happening to you on your first mission. Generally, things aren't this…exciting."

Teresa threw her arms around the ship pilot, crying softly. She was a student of religion, not really built for the stresses of being in the middle of a military operation. Amelia returned the hug, stroking Teresa's hair. Matthew came up and placed a hand on Teresa's shoulder.

"Teresa, there is no reason for the Chinese to harm us," he stated calmly. "And I'm sure that Newton is fine. He's a very smart man."

Phil looked at Darius, who had already taken his seat at the conference table. Darius was understandably alert, but more relaxed than Phil had expected. Again, he knew that something was going on behind the scenes. Phil was not used to being out of the loop in a security operation, and he didn't like it. Even his allies were keeping secrets. He looked up at the ceiling, searching for the cameras he knew were trained on him now.

Phil ventured a question to see what he could learn. Feigning a hopefulness that he did not feel, he asked, "What do you think, Darius? Can we wrap up these meetings today?"

Darius folded his fingers together and placed his hands behind his head. It was a deliberately casual move, perhaps done to reassure Teresa and everyone else that the situation was under control. He smiled and responded, "Yes, Major Casaverde, I think everything will resolve itself shortly. It will be a busy day. For now, perhaps everyone can sit down and make themselves comfortable?"

Everyone took their seats, with only Darius, Matthew, and Amelia sitting at the conference table. After thirty minutes of small talk, Commander Xi entered the room. Two guards attended him and took their position at the door. Phil was intrigued. Xi was genuinely agitated, and the two guards were there as a show of power. *What was going on?*

Xi dropped a file of papers on the table in front of Darius.

"Ambassador Darius, thirty minutes ago, Director Liao, Vice-Chairman Zhang, several other directors, and I received emails warning us to evacuate the Chinese aerospace building, which so happens to be that building right there," Xi exclaimed, pointing out the window.

Xi had indicated an older-style stone building that stood across the street. The six-story structure appeared to have been built well before the turn of the twentieth century. There were gables off the top floor in each corner of the building. The gray stone made the building look like a fortress that had weathered one century and could easily weather the next few as well. Both national and provincial flags flew above the canopy over the entrance.

Xi continued his accusation, "The email states that at twelve o'clock noon, the building will be destroyed. It was signed 'Diedre Parth, Parmithian High Command.'"

Darius's face broke out in a huge grin, highly inappropriate for such a dire situation. Matthew sat up in his chair, looked at his commander, also smiled in surprise, and shook his head thoughtfully. Xi's face turned a mottled red.

"Ambassador Darius, did you send us this email? Your spaceship is in no position to launch an attack, I assure you."

Darius folded his hands in front of him and responded, "Commander Xi, you already know that I could not have sent out this email. I was confined to my room with no communication devices. Has the building been evacuated? I happen to know Diedre Parth, and she is extremely punctual. That building will be destroyed at exactly at twelve o'clock."

Xi countered, "It has been suggested that we move you and your team over to the aerospace building and see if your confederates will still try to destroy the building."

Darius shrugged and responded, "Commander, you are welcome to do that. I assure you the building will still be leveled."

Xi shook his head and nearly shouted, "Ambassador Darius, should we be preparing for an attack? Is the rest of the city in danger?"

Darius responded calmly, "Sir, the Parmithian people do exactly what they say they are going to do. The rest of the city is not in danger, for now at least. Preparations will be wasted effort. Only the Aerospace building will be harmed. However, I do request that you make sure no Chinese aircraft are flying above the aerospace building at noon. They, too, would be destroyed." Despite his treatment, Darius was still concerned about casualties.

Phil looked at his watch. It was already 11:45 a.m. He looked through the window at the aerospace building. People were streaming out the front doors, groups chatting about the mystery of their evacuation and the vacation day they had been gifted. Everyone hurried to cars and bus stops, apparently under orders to depart immediately.

Xi turned to leave but stopped himself and turned. "The ancient Chinese general Sun Tzu taught one should 'know your enemy.' Who is this Diedre Parth? What kind of commander is she?"

Despite the tense situation, Matthew chuckled. He could contain himself no longer. He exclaimed, "Commander, Diedre Parth is Darius Parth's sister! She is his older, *overly protective* sister, I might add. She is one of the most decorated admirals of the Parmithian fleet and, I assure you…a most formidable opponent."

Darius glanced at Matthew and couldn't contain a chuckle of his own. Tears of joy or mirth or love for his sibling welled up in his eyes, and he wiped them away. "We haven't seen each other in many years. It will be…good to see her."

Xi huffed out of the room, taking his guards with him.

Allie was both bewildered and concerned about this unexpected turn of events. Darius's sister was coming to their rescue! Did they know that the Chinese military was a formidable threat?

"Darius, aren't you worried about your sister going into battle? The Chinese have a strong military with technology of their own."

Darius was lost in thought, so Matthew volunteered a response, "Major Heroux, the transport ships are now just eleven days out. Diedre is probably passing Saturn about now. Do not be concerned. China does not have the technology to attack or defend itself at that great a distance. When the *We Come in Peace* was captured, an automated distress call was sent out in a faster-than-light dark-energy beam."

Allie still looked confused, so Matthew continued, "Remember that dark energy is not affected by distance. Our ships don't carry weapons, but the dark-energy *drive* can be focused into a very thin, very tight beam. For two days now, Admiral Parth has been slowing her speed by aiming the dark-energy drive at your sun. She will soon shift the aim of the drive from the sun to the aerospace building and tighten the beam significantly."

Allie glanced over at the target of imminent destruction just across the street from their own location. "Is it possible that Admiral

Parth might miss her target? We are sitting uncomfortably close to that building."

Darius, who had been following the conversation, scoffed, obviously both proud and confident in his sibling. He looked at Allie, smiled, and reassured her, "Don't worry, Major Heroux. Diedre does not miss."

At 11:55 a.m., Commander Xi, Director Liao, Vice-Chairman Zhang, and Advisor Chung all entered the conference room and took their seats at the head of the table.

Xi took the lead, addressing the entire group, "My colleagues and I have discussed what we should do with you. Our premier has been advised of the situation. He and other party leaders are now sitting in an underground bomb shelter. Our military is on full alert. Jets are being sent to patrol our borders and circle our location. Is Parmithia declaring war on China?"

"Commander Xi," Darius explained, "this is not a declaration of war. It is merely a demonstration of power. My sister commands the flagship of the three transport ships that were already on their way here. When your men captured my ship, it sent out a distress call on a very fast dark-energy beam. My sister is following a standard Parmithian protocol toward worlds whose leaders…do not understand our power. Diedre knows exactly where I am due to a microchip implanted in my left buttock when I was just a boy. The Aerospace Building was obviously chosen to be destroyed first so we could all have a front-row seat of the display. After that, protocol dictates that you will be given another two hours to evacuate another building or a large bridge or a power station before it, too, will be destroyed."

Darius felt his emotions clouding his mind, but he didn't care. Since their arrival on Earth, he and his team had been threatened, abused, and shot at. His team was as much a family to him as Diedre, and Xi was threatening that family. His rage, held back since the first attack in Washington, was finally being allowed to vent. Darius had too much emotional energy to stay seated. He arose from his chair and stood behind it, throttling its neck rest.

"There is nothing you can do now to save your aerospace building," Darius growled, nodding toward the window. "You can only put a stop to the continued destruction of Beijing's infrastructure by allowing all of us, including Majors Casaverde and Heroux, to return to our ship and depart. I will then send a message to my sister, and the assault on your capital city will end. If you decide to take your chances and kill us, Diedre will know. You will be given two hours to evacuate whole blocks of your inner city for the rest of the week! The destruction of your capital will continue until my sister's rage is spent!"

Darius's anger was that of a man who had been bullied long enough. Phil found he was holding his breath at this unexpected display of emotion. Darius had a superpower, and it was no longer a secret superpower.

"We are a peaceful people, not a violent people. We visit planets in small exploration teams to offer our counsel and technical assistance. This attitude causes some planetary leaders to underestimate us, to think that we can be bent to their purposes, and to think that we are weak.

Do you think us weak, Commander Xi?" Darius shouted.

The question was impeccably timed. As if on cue, the floor started shaking, and a rumbling reverberated through the building. It felt like a sustained, low-magnitude earthquake. Xi, who had been so red-faced a few minutes earlier, turned several shades paler. Everyone arose from their seats and looked out the window. Phil confirmed the location of the nearest exit, ready to lead his companions out of the building.

The conference room felt like it was being pressurized, though the aerospace building looked unaffected for the first few seconds. Then the air around the building shimmered, like heat waves coming off pavement on a hot summer day. There were no explosions, just a sustained earthquake. The four gables at the top of the building crumbled first, looking like overly dried sandcastles falling in on themselves. The noise of bending steel, breaking stone, and shattering glass assailed the onlookers. Stonework cracked and then broke apart, sending shards of rock hurtling to all sides of the building. Iron beams behind the stone became visible just before they bent sharply under the unseen force, pulling support columns reluctantly into the center of the destruction. Floors collapsed one upon another, each creating an ongoing explosion of concrete, drywall dust, and shattered glass. Like a tidal wave, a cloud of debris and dust rolled across the street, creating a staccato of dirt, rocks, and other small rubble against the conference room window. Everyone in the room reflexively turned their faces away, hoping the window would sustain the blast. The dust cloud covered the collapsing building, completely obstructing their view of the demolition.

Suddenly the rumbling gave way to silence. The floor stopped shaking. No one said anything. The experience had been too raw, too loud, and too destructive to mentally process what had just happened. Allie realized she was still holding her breath and willed herself to exhale. Everyone waited, wanting to confirm the results of what they had just seen. The dust hovered, blocking their view. Then like a cloth being removed from a piece of art, a breeze pushed the dust away. The building had completely collapsed. Steel girders stuck up at all angles. Ruined stonework covered the ground. Several fires were raging from broken gas lines, and water from broken plumbing was spurting up in numerous locations.

Commander Xi's cell phone dinged, signaling the arrival of a priority email. He stared numbly at the message for several moments and then looked up at the other Chinese leaders in the room. He reported, "It is another message from Diedre Parth of the Parmithian High Command. It says, 'Please evacuate the Beijing South Power Station. It will be destroyed in two hours.'"

*****

The destruction of the power station never occurred. Within the hour, the Parmithians, Phil, and Allie were entering the *We Come in Peace*. After witnessing the destruction of their aeronautics building, Commander Xi and the Chinese leaders had excused themselves to meet and make a phone call. Xi returned, hustled them all into the limousine, and escorted them to the door of the spaceship. As it turned out, the decision was simple. How do you fight an enemy that can destroy buildings from a million miles away in space?

Xi pulled Phil and Darius aside as they approached the stairs to the spaceship. His demeanor was calm and humble. Xi bowed deeply.

"Gentlemen, I humbly apologize for the decisions of my government in the past couple of days. Your requirements of China appeared impossible, and our leadership responded emotionally. We did not understand that your arrival signaled a new paradigm for Earth. China does not handle change well, but we cannot solve today's problems with solutions from the past. We hope that your offer of Chinese involvement in Parmithian technical assistance is still open despite our actions of the past twenty-four hours."

Xi bowed deeply again, turned, and walked back to the limousine.

As they entered the ship, Newton gave hugs to his returning comrades. His joy at their arrival was evident on his face. He was unharmed but unable to contain his relief.

As he ushered them in, he gave his report, "The Chinese asked me about every detail of the ship. When I started repeating myself for the fourth time, they finally confined me to my quarters. I heard them methodically tear apart nearly every system of the ship all night long. They inspected the dark-energy drive but didn't try to break the seals. Apparently, they believed our warnings. A few minutes before noon, they packed up all their tools and left. Then I felt the earthquake. One of the transport ships demonstrated its dark-energy drive, didn't it? Is that why the Chinese changed their minds about holding us here?"

"Newton, we will have to postpone your update," Darius interrupted. "When can we lift off?"

Newton sighed. "Every system of the ship was torn apart, photographed, and left scattered on the floor. It will take Friedrich and me at least ten to twelve hours to reassemble the mess."

It was Darius's turn to sigh. "Seal the hatch. I think it will be safe for us to stay here overnight. We will plan to leave at first light tomorrow. I will come to assist you in the repair after I send a message to my sister to cancel the destruction of a power plant."

Later that evening, Darius asked Phil and Allie to join him in the common room for a meeting. As soon as they arrived, he handed them each a list, which read:

> *Johannesburg, South Africa*
> *New Delhi, India*
> *Sydney, Australia*
> *San Francisco, United States*
> *São Paulo, Brazil*

"Our detour to Beijing has put us behind schedule in our visits to nominees for the transport ships. Those ships will be here in ten days. We need to visit these cities before then. Major Heroux, we will need a place to land and secure the *We Come in Peace*, ground transportation, and hotels with conference rooms for our meetings. Could you please make the arrangements?"

Allie looked up from her list. "Yes, Darius, I can. It will feel good to be of some help to the team again. I will need some help from General Bart and my department, but we can get this done."

Darius nodded appreciatively and turned to Phil. "Major Casaverde, will you make arrangements for security? Our visits will not be made public. Word might get out, but all nominees have been told to keep their meetings with us strictly confidential."

Phil looked at the list of cities again. Security in a suite of conference rooms in a major hotel was a relatively low-risk operation. Despite the short prep time provided, this should be relatively straightforward task.

Phil looked up from his list and said, "Of course, Darius. I'll be happy to arrange security."

Darius sighed. "Thank you both. I have a few hundred invitations for interviews yet to send out. If you will excuse me, good night." Darius arose from his chair and walked toward his office.

Seeing the meeting was over, Phil started to get up as well. Without looking at him, Allie reached out and grabbed his arm, holding him in place. She tapped a few keys on her laptop. She announced, "General Bart would like to talk with us now."

Phil groaned and dropped his head onto the dining room table. He moaned pathetically, "No." *Bang.* "No." *Bang.* "No." *Bang.* With his head still resting on the table, he whined, "Allie, it has been a long day. Must we really do this now?"

A voice came from Allie's laptop speaker, the deep voice of General Bart. With it, his stern image appeared on the screen. "Yes, Major Casaverde, you really *do* have to do this now!"

Phil sat up straight. "Um...of course, General. I didn't know Major Heroux had already made the connection... She should probably tell me that stuff. I was just thinking that I should go help Newton fix the ship."

"That's a noble thought, Major, but maybe you can spare me a few moments of your time to catch me up," General Bart answered.

Allie proceeded to give a report on the occurrences of the past few days. Phil tried to look interested and nod at the appropriate times. Despite Phil's protests, the call was well-timed. Both Phil and Allie made their requests for assistance from their divisions to safely continue the Parmithian world tour.

As they closed the meeting, General Bart added, "First, the United States thanks you for avoiding a world war with China. The Parmithian invitation to China to share leadership with the US in receiving Parmithian technology is a wrinkle we didn't expect. It may upset a few people here in Washington... I will make some contacts to see if the Chinese are actually considering making the changes Darius demanded of them. Their normal reaction to world disruptions is to hunker down and close their borders. I wonder what they'll do now."

Phil thought back to his last conversation with Alex Xi. He had said something about recognizing new paradigms and solving today's problems with new solutions. Maybe he had meant it...

General Bart concluded, "Secondly, you need to know what has been happening here in the States. A movement is gaining some traction here that offers me some hope that the United States will meet Parmithian demands. I want you both to view this video that

I am sending you now. That is all. I will expect a full written report tomorrow morning. Have a good night. Stay safe."

The general signed off. Phil waited until he was sure the connection had closed. Again, he dropped his head onto the table.

"Allie, couldn't you have warned me?"

"Phil, I'm sorry, I thought you would understand the statement, 'General Bart would like to talk with us *now*.' But apparently not." She smiled at him to soften the sarcasm. "Besides, he gave you an attaboy at the end. So good job! Let's watch the video the general sent, shall we?"

She clicked on a link and sat back in her chair. It was obvious to Phil that Allie was happy to be back in her coordinator role. In fact, she was nearly giddy.

Phil grumbled. "Fine, but you're writing the final report…" The video began, and Phil settled back to watch… *The Tom Blackstone Show?*

Chapter 21

THE SILENT MAJORITY

The set for *The Tom Blackstone Show* looked much the same as it had when Phil and Allie had run through it on their way to rescue Darius. Blackstone was talking with Senator Douglas Croft, the same man who presided over the Committee of Extraterrestrial Affairs and had prompted Darius's tirade at the congressional hearing. The video clip the general had sent was taken from the middle of the show, so the two men were already well immersed in their debate.

Using his hands to emphasize his points, Blackstone crisply summarized, "Senator Croft, the Parmithians are asking Earth to do things that *we know we should be doing anyway.* They asked the United Nations to provide two parents and financial support to our children. Everyone knows it's the right thing to do. But all we hear is whining and complaining about how difficult such a program would be to implement. Darius asked that we eliminate policies that support divisions in our country based on ethnicity, gender, lifestyle, or other characteristics of birth. Again, we all realize that equal rights for everyone is the right thing to do.

"Our own Declaration of Independence reads, 'We hold these truths to be self-evident, that all men are created equal…' Our current response to Thomas Jefferson's statement is to allow special-interest groups to create organizations and hire lobbyists to battle one another for federal funding, government contracts, and other monies. Unless we change this paradigm, special treatment of special interest groups will continue…well, forever. Doesn't it seem like *now* would be a good time to make the changes that should be made anyway?"

Senator Croft cleared his throat. Since the disastrous congressional investigatory meeting with the Parmithians, Croft had received much abuse from the press and angry constituents. His popularity rating had plunged in a few days' time. His hope in appearing on Blackstone's television show was to reverse that trend. Tom Blackstone had generally been a friend to the politicians in Washington; his show would never have lasted so long otherwise. But Blackstone had become outspoken in his support of the Parmithians. The entire country was in chaos.

A bit more defensively than he wished, Croft replied, "Mr. Blackstone, this country was built by great Americans of the past. Each person's heritage is an important part of their self-worth and an understanding of who they are. I will not tell the American people that they must sacrifice their heritage or their associations with others with that same heritage. America is a diverse nation, and we are proud of that diversity."

Blackstone immediately responded, "Senator, no one is saying that Americans must sacrifice their heritage. They can be as proud of their forebearers as they wish. However, no citizen should expect to profit from or receive special favors because of their ancestry. Such entitlements are a constant irritation to everyone else in the nation. Darius is correct. Until we remove all such considerations, we will never have a society that is at peace with itself."

"Mr. Blackstone, these are admirable sentiments, but I don't believe the American people are ready to give up a cornerstone of our culture that has existed for centuries. The so-called Equal Rights Amendment or ERA was debated but *not* ratified by this nation way back in the 1970s. I don't see any reason why it should be debated yet again. Americans are proud of their ethnicity, and nothing you or the Parmithians can do will change that."

"Mr. Croft, I'm glad you brought up the ERA. Most scholars agree that, though the concept was sound, the Equal Rights

Amendment of the 1970s was poorly written. Having had over sixty years to review it, a much-improved ERA document could be written today. In the nine days since the assault on our broadcasting station, we have been overwhelmed with phone calls from our listeners. They want Congress to draft and pass a new Equal Rights Amendment. We finally placed a sign-up sheet on our website. We asked callers to provide their contact information if they would support a new constitutional amendment. On the first day, we had ten thousand respondents. Social media outlets announced the existence of our little poll, and we are now receiving over *one hundred thousand* responses a day in support. Google provided additional servers just to handle our web traffic. How do you respond to these numbers, Senator?"

Senator Croft huffed, "I don't know anything about your polls, but…"

Blackstone was angry and decidedly *not* finished with his attack. "Senator, from the very chair in which you are sitting, Darius called upon the silent majority in America to step forward and drive this country toward meeting Parmithian requirements. To do what we know to be right. This is not only so we can receive the benefits of their technology, but so that our society can establish enough stability to work on our real problems. It appears that tide of public opinion is turning against you. Are you with the silent majority or not?"

The video ended abruptly. Apparently General Bart did not think it necessary for Phil and Allie to listen to Senator Croft's continued defense of an outdated system of governance. For a few moments, they sat in silence, contemplating what they had just heard.

Allie finally broke the revery. "What do you think, Phil? Can our country actually make the changes Darius demanded? I never would have believed it possible."

Phil looked at his counterpart. "I love my country, but I didn't believe it possible we could change either. I was furious with Darius for putting himself at risk to make his plea on Blackstone's show. Could it be making a difference? To tell you the truth, I don't know how the US will respond. But we'll find out soon enough. The Parmithian transport ships arrive in ten days, and Darius's offer will expire."

Chapter 22

GATHER MY SAINTS TOGETHER

Johannesburg, South Africa

In the dead of night, the *We Come in Peace* landed in US Air Force Base Swartkop just outside of Johannesburg, South Africa. Everyone caught a few hours of sleep but had to arise early the next morning. The US Embassy in Pretoria provided three standard-issue black Suburbans with tinted windows for the drive to the Royal Elephant Hotel. Conference rooms had been reserved for the day and hotel rooms for that night.

At the hotel, Phil was reunited with his security team, including Lieutenant Young. Tyson was using a cane but had his medical clearance in hand. After the salutes, hugs, and handshakes, Phil reviewed the floorplans of the conference rooms and made individual assignments. He was starting to feel in control of his assignment again.

The day brought a continuous stream of people from South Africa and surrounding countries. Phil recognized a few of them. Some came alone, but there were a number of couples and a few families. Phil was still not allowed to attend the meetings. But he could read the faces of everyone who had been invited for interviews. Their doubt, uncertainty, and anxiety were obvious. These people were trying to decide if they should leave their homes, family, and careers to settle a new planet. Which was more dangerous, staying on a planet that was on the verge of collapse or traveling to a world that had no established civilization or infrastructure? These people had accepted Darius's invitation for interviews because they were searching for a lifeline out of the chaos of their homelands. Was this opportunity too good to pass up? Should they trust these Parmithians, a race of aliens who had just come to Earth four weeks ago?

One young couple stopped Phil as he was escorting them back to the hotel lobby after their interview. The husband reached out to shake Phil's hand, politely introducing himself. "Sir, I am Lubanzi Khumalo. This is my wife, Amahle." Lubanzi was a young black man with close-cropped hair and a ready smile. His hands were rough and his physique that of a man accustomed to outside labor. His wife was equally fit, with dark-brown eyes that mirrored the anxiety and turmoil of her soul.

"It's very nice to meet you, Mr. Khumalo. I am Major Phil Casaverde."

"Major Casaverde, please excuse me, but I have seen you in several of the news films about Darius and the other Parmithians, have I not?"

"Yes," responded Phil, "I have directed the security efforts for our guests since their arrival."

"Yes, I thought I recognized you. I lead a cooperative of small farms north of Pretoria. We have been blessed with successful harvests in the past few years. This is why, I think, I was invited for an interview. I was told that farmers will be needed for the new colony to survive. The Par…mithians just told me that my family is approved to board the transport ship in New Delhi in nine days."

"Yes," said Phil, looking over his shoulder as a few new arrivals headed toward the conference center.

"Sir," Amahle interrupted her husband, seeing that Phil was thinking of escaping to attend to other duties. She put her hand on his arm, dropping her eyes at her boldness, and then looked back up at him.

"We think that perhaps…in the last few weeks…you have gotten to know the Parmithians. Newton seemed very nice in our interview. But a few minutes is much too short a time to learn to trust someone with the future of our family. You may have come to know these visitors. Can we trust them? Should we go with them?"

"Well, that is, of course, totally up to…"

Phil had started to offer the normal, patented it's-up-to-you speech that communicated nothing. But this couple was desperately seeking counsel. There were simply too many factors in this choice to make a well-informed decision. It was an impossible task, though everyone on the colonization list was being asked to make it. Looking at them, Phil was almost certain this couple would take his advice. They would radically change their lives at his word. The time had come for him to decide. Did he believe in the Parmithians, or didn't he? Phil realized that he had actually made this decision days ago. He had seen the Parmithians…his friends…in good times and bad. They had risked their lives to deliver their message. They had been true to their word. His eyes brimmed with tears at his epiphany. He cleared his throat of some of the emotion he was feeling.

"Look, I know that your country…and all of Africa…has been especially hard hit by the collapses of economies and food supplies. I know moving to a new planet is a life-changing decision, but I think the Parmithians are good people who want to give you the opportunity to start over again in a safe environment. Homesteading a new planet will be a lot of work. But I think this New Earth will be a safer place to raise your family. You are the first people to have asked me. I think you can trust them," Phil confided sincerely.

Lubanzi and Amahle looked at each other and, in that look, made their decision. Amahle started to cry at the relief of the end of her anxiety. She impulsively gave Phil a hug and then backed away. Grinning broadly, Lubanzi shook Phil's hand vigorously.

"Thank you, Major Casaverde! Thank you! We will go. Yes, it is time to leave our homeland for our future and for that of our children. Maybe we will see you on the transport ship, yes?" The couple was still thanking him and waving as they walked away.

Phil turned to return to his post outside the conference rooms but then stopped in his tracks. Maybe they would see him on the transport ship? Was that even possible?

*****

In a short time, social media and network news reported that the transport ship interviews had resumed after an unexplained delay. One news pundit called the trip the Parmithian Gathering of Saints, a sarcastic reference to a Bible verse in Psalms. World reaction was mixed. Speculating on the important people they could lose (and with them, the tax revenue they generated), several governments quickly passed legislation making emigration illegal for its citizens. Borders were closed, and international flights were cancelled.

As they finished the day, Phil realized that there was only one advantage to visiting five countries in ten days. By the time protestors realized the Parmithians were in their city, they were ready to leave it. Opposition did not have time to organize before the delegation was gone again. Late-night landings masked their arrival. Two days of interviews and a quick departure kept them safe. The downside was that it was an exhausting routine.

New Delhi, India

The arrival in New Delhi had been uneventful. Interviews proceeded on schedule, with one exception. Phil had just allowed a particularly large man to enter his interview with Darius when he came out again smelling strongly of burnt electronics and melted plastic. Phil and his team routinely collected all cell phones before anyone could enter their interview, so this was unexpected. Phil politely stopped the man. "Excuse me, sir?"

The man was large, with dark skin and tiny eyes that glared at him from behind an even darker beard. He moved to walk around Phil. Tyson and another security team member stepped up behind their leader, filling any gaps the man may have been considering. The dark man stepped back and glared menacingly at the security team.

Following his nose, Phil reached into the burly man's suit coat pocket and retrieved a partially melted cell phone. Examining it, Phil turned to Tyson.

"Please have our guest wait here for a couple of minutes." Phil walked around the big man and into Darius's conference room. He stepped inside and closed the door behind him. Darius looked up, only mildly annoyed by the interruption.

"Did you know about this?" he asked, holding the ruined cell phone in front of him for inspection.

Darius stopped writing on his tablet and looked up. "Oh yes, the smell was quite unpleasant…and has not improved. Can you please remove it from the room?"

Phil waited patiently, holding the stinking cell phone, still looking at Darius. There *was* going to be an explanation. Darius glanced up and sighed resignedly.

"Major, do you see my little paperweight here?" He held up a black object that looked like a hockey puck. All his team carried one of these into their meetings and had indeed used them to hold down files and paperwork. Darius studied the object as he explained.

"This little gadget emits a strong signal in a very specific wavelength of the electromagnetic spectrum that causes lithium batteries in the room to…overheat to the point of exploding. Despite explicit instructions, my last candidate decided to record our conversation. I have informed him that his invitation to board the transport ship has been revoked."

Phil nodded thoughtfully. "Okay, then." He returned to the hallway, threw the ruined cell phone into a trash bin, and asked Tyson to escort the man to the front door. Phil hated surprises. What other technology was being used by the Parmithians of which he was unaware?

Sydney, Australia

The interviews in Sydney were going smoothly. Around midafternoon on the second day, a group of about fifty people entered the hotel and approached the conference rooms. No one was carrying a weapon. In fact, everyone was very polite and quiet as they approached the conference rooms. Phil and Allie stepped out to meet the apparent leader, an older man who wore a simple white frock over his white shirt and tie. He stepped forward to introduce himself.

"Brother, I am Pastor Taylor of the Church of the Good Shepherd here in Sydney. We do not want to cause you any trouble, but may we please speak to Ambassador Darius? We have an appointment."

Phil checked his list. He had heard nothing about the Church of the Good Shepherd, and they had no appointment. The Parmithians weren't even doing group interviews. But how did Pastor Taylor know they were here in Sydney? Phil saw no threat in the old man or his group. If this was an assassination attempt, there were easier ways to do it than politely requesting an audience. Phil caught Tyson's eye and nodded toward the pastor.

Tyson approached the man and said softly, "Um, excuse me, sir." Tyson ran a quick pat down search, stood up, and shook his head at Phil.

Phil sighed, "Please wait here," and disappeared into the hallway leading to the conference rooms. A short minute later, he emerged with Darius in tow.

Darius smiled broadly at the pastor. He shook the old man's hand, a handshake that was vigorously returned.

"Pastor Taylor, I am honored to meet you. I am Darius. You had requested an audience for you and your congregation. What can I do for you?"

The minister smiled nervously, as if overwhelmed to be in the presence of such an important figure. "Thank you for agreeing to see me and some of my fellow believers."

Phil looked up from his notepad. Thousands of people, many from churches, had sought interviews with Darius but had been turned down. Why was this request any different?

"Darius, did you invite a whole church to interview?" Phil whispered under his breath.

Darius ignored him, focusing his attention on Pastor Taylor. Several people were taking video of the meeting with their cell phones. Undoubtedly, this discussion would be shared across the world within the hour—which, Phil realized, was probably the reason for the unscheduled meeting in the first place. Darius wanted to send a message to the world again, unofficially yet through popular media channels.

The pastor gathered himself to ask the one question he was here to ask, "Ambassador Darius, we have a story in our ancient scriptures that tells of a holy man named Abraham, who was a prophet of his time. God tells Abraham that two wicked cities named Sodom and Gomorrah had been judged and were going to be destroyed. Abraham has a righteous nephew named Lot, who lived in Sodom with his family. To protect his nephew, Abraham asks God, *'Wilt thou also destroy the righteous with the wicked?'*

"Abraham asks God to spare Sodom until Lot and his family can leave. God sends two angels to help Lot and his family escape. Once they have safely fled the city, God rains fire and brimstone upon Sodom and Gomorrah, completely destroying them."

From the look on Phil's face, the pastor knew his time was limited. Speaking more rapidly so as not to be interrupted, he continued, "You announced in Paris that transport ships were coming to evacuate three thousand people. Many of us are wondering if you are as the angels sent by God in this Old Testament account. Are you here to remove the most righteous three thousand people of Earth so that it can be destroyed by fire and brimstone?"

Darius shook his head. He was taking the question very seriously. "No, Pastor Taylor, we are not angels. We predict the fall of societies and planets through social evaluation, science, and statistics. God has not commanded us to visit Earth."

Pastor Taylor looked both self-conscious about his question and disappointed at the answer. Darius put a hand on the minister's shoulder and continued, "However, Pastor, I want you to know that most all Parmithians do believe in God. In our exploration of space, we are constantly reminded that the physical laws of nature—from the shape of molecules to the gravitational pull of suns—are precisely tuned to allow the development of intelligent life. The odds that such a benevolent universe was created by chance is infinitesimally small. The only explanation is that a Higher Power established those laws. Our findings in science and space travel rather demand it.

"We also believe in the good works done by churches like yours in encouraging people toward religion. Religion encourages people to repent and live better lives. In much the same way, we ask world governments to repent of their failures to become stable societies where people can thrive. As you may know, we have asked governments to halt the proliferation of single-parent families and prejudices due to race and gender."

Pastor Taylor responded as if on cue, "We believe those requests are righteous. We thank you for your efforts. Yet I must ask, if we meet your requirements of us, must the three thousand people still leave?"

Darius nodded. "Yes, the colonizers must still be allowed to leave. Having three thousand people colonize a second planet is a safety precaution. If Earth is ever made uninhabitable, the people of Earth will be protected from extinction."

Pastor Taylor nodded, contemplating these words and the apocalypse described in the book of Revelation. "We also came here today to tell you that we don't believe our planet is yet as bad as Sodom and Gomorrah. There are still many good people here."

Darius nodded and looked over the pastor's congregation. There was little doubt in Phil's mind that Darius had orchestrated this exchange. He was talking to the world, not just to Pastor Taylor.

"Yes, there are still many good people on Earth. But in our experience, when even a small part of a planet descends into anarchy, the rest of the world follows quickly. Pastor Taylor, your planet has some difficult times ahead of it. Many people seem to blame God for those difficulties. God is not responsible for those calamities, but He will not stop their consequences from happening either. Earth's populations have a decision to make and only a few more days in which to make it."

San Francisco, United States

The interviews in San Francisco ended early on their second day there, wrapping up at around 4:00 p.m. Liftoff of the *We Come in Peace* would not occur until midnight. Allie, however, announced that she had a special field trip planned for the group and hustled everyone into the caravan vehicles that drove directly to the airfield. Everyone was so tired from the schedule of the past several days that no one questioned the plan even as they boarded the spacecraft. As soon as the last Parmithian team member clambered aboard, Amelia lifted off and accelerated the ship away from its dock at Vandenberg Air Force Base. The flight was short. Less than an hour after takeoff, Amelia announced their imminent landing. They set down in a large but empty parking lot.

Allie had remained quiet about the destination of this side trip. She opened the hatch door and encouraged everyone to join her outside. The group found themselves unexpectedly...in a forest. The air was crisp and alive compared to the city air they had just left. Giant trees surrounded them. After everyone had gathered outside, Allie welcomed the group.

"I decided that we all needed a mental and emotional break. I talked to Amelia, and she told me that the most ancient forests on Parmithia are often used as places for meditation and reflection. She told me that such locations have a certain spirituality about them, making them a place to revitalize one's spirit."

Allie gestured toward largest trees directly behind her. "Welcome to the Giant Sequoia National Monument. The oldest tree here is over 3,200 years old. This forest is an ancient place, and to me it has always felt like a cathedral. I thought it would be a good place for a spiritual rest. Everyone is free to wander wherever they wish. We should all be back in, say, two hours?"

Everyone in the group paused for a moment, listening to the silence of this place, enjoying the smells of the forest and feeling its calmness seep into their very bones. Darius walked up to Allie and, in a rare expression of deep emotion, embraced her for several seconds. Then he started to walk into the forest, instructing his cell phone to set an alarm for two hours. He stopped at the first large sequoia at the edge of the forest and reverently placed a hand on the bark. He bowed his head for a moment and then disappeared deeper into the forest. The rest of the Parmithian team all approached Allie, most to simply touch her arm and whisper their thanks. They all chose separate paths and disappeared into the trees.

Matthew lingered behind to talk to Allie for a moment. "Our visit to this place has deep meaning for us, especially now. The strain has been hard on all of us but especially so on Darius. Thank you for this consideration." Matthew blinked away tears and set off on his own quest.

Phil ambled over to Allie, examining her thoughtfully. "Allie, you never cease to amaze me. This was a wonderful idea. Our guests needed this. How did you know?"

Allie smiled and shook her head slightly. "I talked to Amelia, and she described—"

"No, Allie, how did you know what to ask Amelia?"

Allie hesitated, putting her thoughts into words, "We learned in Rome that the Parmithians are a spiritual people. They attribute the success of their civilization to their spirituality and their continued quests to find God. To them, meditation is not a process to get in touch with their innermost feelings. Meditation and contemplation are means to seek communication from a Higher Source, to seek encouragement to be good and moral. If you take such people away from that communion, they lose the emotional support of that spirituality." Allie nearly whispered her last sentence, "It would be rather like asking my grandmother to stop praying."

Phil contemplated this for a moment. He had not been raised in a religious family and realized he didn't understand this pursuit of spirituality. He finally asked what seemed to be the most obvious question. "Couldn't they just kneel by their bed at night and pray there?"

Allie hesitated and then responded, "They might pray like that. It wouldn't surprise me if they do. But we must think of Parmithians as missionaries as well as explorers. They need more spiritual meditation than a now-I-lay-me-down-to-sleep prayer at night. The Parmithians have come to Earth to save souls. But they must deal with the welfare of the whole planet, not just a few individuals. It must be a strain on them to change a world."

Allie took a deep breath and put her hands in her jacket pockets. "Parmithia is both trying to save Earth and convince us to seek greater spiritual understanding. A stable society supports the individual's search for the celestial, which in turn produces a more stable society. They have to change the people, not just government policies."

She glanced up at Phil and continued, "Anyway, I thought it would be…helpful for them to come here. This forest is special. These giant, living sequoias have marked the passage of time with their very size. There is a spiritual feeling to this grove. Even I can sense it. I believe the Parmithians can too."

Phil was shocked when a small part of him whispered that maybe he, too, might go into the forest. He examined the desire, the first such yearning for spiritual peace that he had felt for many years. What effect were these Parmithians having on him? Not ready to admit his prompting to Allie or even himself, he slowly walked away, announcing, "I think I'll go for a walk."

Allie looked up at him, thinking he had read her exact thoughts. She turned on her heel and set off in an altogether different direction. "Me too," she whispered.

São Paulo, Brazil

The visit to São Paulo had followed the now well-established routine. An assortment of government administrators, farmers, engineers, mechanics, and their families had appeared for their interviews. As usual, a few interviewees missed their appointments. Some walked away from their interviews shaking their heads, apparently deciding they did not have the will to board the transport ship. Phil overheard a couple of interviews. Darius was not pressuring anyone to accept his offer to colonize a new world. It was their decision.

After the interviews, everyone was shuttled back to the *We Come in Peace*. Friedrich had remained on the ship all day to finish up some work and prepare dinner. Since the visit to the Giant Sequoia National Monument, the mood had been significantly more relaxed. The end of the colonizer ship interviews was a relief to everyone. However, they knew that the hardest part of the journey still lay ahead of them.

After the dinner dishes had been cleared, Darius rose. Conversations stilled, and he began his address, "I would like to thank everyone for their hard work of the past ten days. In total, we accomplished over five hundred interviews. We have the names of the three thousand people that we expect to board the transport ships in two days. There is a waiting list of several hundred people for each ship to take the places of anyone who makes a last-minute decision not to emigrate. Leaders and administrators have been chosen. Classes in English are already scheduled. One people, one language.

"The resettlement planet is the third planet of a sun called M789 in the Gemini system of the galaxy. It is just a bit smaller than Earth, but climate and natural resources are very similar. Two civilizations of humans evolved on the planet, but they both destroyed themselves as they developed the technology to do so. The planet is vacant, and the environment has recovered. It is an ideal location for the resettlement.

"Tonight, Amelia will fly us to Washington, DC. Tomorrow, Friedrich and I will attend a meeting with the five permanent members of the United Nations Security Council—the United States, China, France, Great Britain, and Russia. Besides their ambassadors, most of these nations will also have their presidents in attendance. President Gordon Schaeffer and General Theo Bart will attend for the United States. We are still unsure about Russia's and China's plans.

"After her stop in Washington, Amelia will fly Matthew and Teresa to Paris. They will supervise the boarding and join the Parisian transport ship for its voyage to New Earth. Amelia will then fly Newton to New Delhi so he can supervise embarkment and lift off the transport ship from India. Finally, Amelia will fly our ship back to Washington. The *We Come in Peace* will serve as a support vehicle for the three transport ships during their trip. However, my team probably but won't see each other again in person until we meet at New Earth in six months."

Allie gasped. Tonight would be their last night with half of the Parmithian team, with the other half departing on Sunday! Her friends would be leaving her, never to be seen again. Her heart ached, and tears welled in her eyes. Allie did not have many friends. Her job and a naturally introverted nature prevented much socialization. She bowed her head and pinched her tear ducts, trying to force the tears to stop.

Darius continued his briefing, "Unless decisions in our meeting with the UN Security Council changes our plans, the transport ships will arrive around nine o'clock on Sunday morning, July 9. It will take about three hours to board everyone. It's not much time, but the shorter the stay, the less chance there is for problems and violence. According to the media, protests are being planned by hundreds of organizations. Some of these groups are prone to carry weapons and incite violence. The city governments of New Delhi, Paris, and Washington have promised to provide security for the embarkments. However, we must expect and prepare for attacks similar to the one that occurred in Washington on the day of our arrival."

Phil spoke first, "Darius, I would like to send two of my security team with Matthew and Teresa and another two with Newton to provide personal security for them during their embarkments. They can catch commercial flights home after the liftoffs. Major Heroux and I will accompany you and Friedrich to the meeting with the UN Security Council and the boarding of the Washington transport ship."

Darius nodded his head approvingly. "Thank you, Major. That would be appreciated... In fact, speaking of appreciation, now would be a good time to present you and Major Heroux with tokens of our appreciation for your dedicated support over the past month."

Amelia jumped up and stood beside Darius, obviously very happy with her assignment to present their gifts. She anxiously awaited as the two majors rose from their chairs and joined her.

"Phil and Allie, we would like to give each of you a present so you can remember our visit and our team. We will certainly never forget you." She gave each of them a round disk about five inches in diameter and one inch in height. The top appeared to be a finely etched diffraction grating, breaking white light into a dazzling array of colors that changed as the disk was rotated.

Allie stammered, "This is beautiful. Thank you!"

Allie leaned in for a hug, but Amelia held up her hand and started giggling uncontrollably. Shaking her head, Amelia reached over and touched a nearly invisible button on the side of the Allie's disk. A hologram of the Parmithian crew, astonishing in its clarity and vibrant color, immediately filled the six-inch space above the disk. As they watched, the projection changed to an individual photo of Darius, then one of Matthew, and each of the rest of the team. Unstaged photos of their visits to New York, Washington, Rome, and Paris were then displayed. There were even a few photos of the team at the reception dinner in China. Finally, there were photos of beautiful landscapes, modern cities, and picturesque neighborhoods.

Allie looked at her friend quizzically. Amelia was gazing at these last photos longingly, overcome with her own emotions.

"Those last photos are of Parmithia," she said softly. "We thought you'd like to see some images from our home world."

Throughout the trip, the Parmithians had refused to answer any questions by media outlets about their home planet. Part of this resistance seemed to have been an attempt to maintain their planet's security. But Allie recognized that part of their refusal came from a reluctance to discuss a sacred place with a people who would not understand what a planet should mean to its people. The Parmithians obviously loved their planet, and sharing pictures of it was a deeply intimate thing for them to do. It was an expression of love and trust.

Allie's trick of pinching her tear ducts was going to do nothing to stop the tears this time. She extended her hug with Amelia, trying to control herself. How ironic, Allie thought, that one of her best friends in the world wasn't really from this world at all.

The party lasted late into the night. Knowing that tomorrow would be a long day, the Parmithians gradually said their goodbyes to their friends and retired to their rooms. Everyone realized their partings would be permanent. Just before midnight, Amelia said her goodbyes and headed for the ship's bridge to fly the ship to Washington, as planned. Phil quickly bid everyone farewell and hurried after her.

"Amelia, do you mind if I join you? You really should have someone to help keep you awake while you're driving."

Amelia smiled as she glanced over at him. "I would be glad to have some company, thank you."

They walked onto the bridge, and Amelia sat in the pilot's seat. Phil took a seat beside her, probably a copilot's chair, he thought. However, there was no array of switches and lights common to military aircraft cockpits. It was a simple keyboard, with a three-dimensional interactive hologram hovering above it. Phil watched as Amelia spoke to the ship, "Hey, Siri, prepare the ship for launch."

Phil sat back in his chair. "Wow, we call some of our computer systems Siri as well!"

Amelia just smiled and gave him a sideways glance.

After he calculated the odds of this being a coincidence, Phil groaned, "But you already knew that, didn't you?"

Amelia chuckled. "We learned about your computer activation words during our travel here. 'Hey, Google' sounded ridiculous. Who names a computer Google anyway? 'Hey, Siri' has a nice ring to it, so I changed the name of the ship computer to commemorate our visit to Earth."

Phil took a deep breath. He looked down at his hands and then turned in his chair to face this woman who had so intrigued him. He had known her for only one month. He realized he was going to sound like a lovestruck teenager, but it was now or never. He had to know.

Speaking quickly so as to not lose his nerve, Phil asked, "Amelia, is there any way I can convince you to stay on Earth? I don't know if such a thing is even permitted. I just know that you are the most fascinating woman I've ever met, and I don't want you to leave. I would have liked to have spent the past weeks building a relationship with you but have had to deal with congressional hearings, mob attacks, a kidnapping, and a trip around the world instead. We have been cursed with…major distractions. There has been no time, and now you are leaving in two days. I want you to stay."

Amelia hesitated, busying herself with the ship's controls and not speaking for two of the longest minutes of Phil's life. She made her last keyboard entries and finally spoke, "Hey, Siri, calculate our course to Andrews Air Force Base in Washington, DC."

"Done," the computer chimed.

"Initiate liftoff and flight."

The ship bumped slightly as the ship rose into the sky and started its acceleration, which was barely noticeable from inside the ship.

Amelia turned her chair to face Phil. "Phil, when I first met you, you saved my life. Afterward, I felt…an immediate attraction to you. Naturally, I thought your allure was just a crush I had on the superhero who flew through the air to rescue me. Then I thought my attraction was due to the similarities you share with my deceased husband. After I had some time to get to know you…the attraction just deepened. Like Drake, you are committed to protecting the lives of those around you, whatever the odds."

Unexpectedly, Amelia threw her head and hands back in exasperation. She started yelling at the ceiling, "Then I thought, well, this is just stupid! I can't have a relationship with an earthling! We were only to be on this planet for four weeks. What could I expect to accomplish by having feelings for you?" Shifting her eyes from the ceiling to Phil's face, she smiled at fonder memories. "Then we were kidnapped to China, which gave me a few days to think. I decided to mentally break off my feelings for you. But then, after the reception… I remember the kiss, Phil. I didn't know if my life was in danger, but I knew I wanted to kiss you before it ended. I'm sorry."

Phil frowned and shook his head. "Wait, what are you sorry—"

Amelia kept talking, too emotional to notice the attempted interruption. "The past ten days have been wonderful. Exhausting, but wonderful. We talked between interviews, had lunch together, and shared dinners. It was almost as if we were…actually dating." Amelia started talking faster, trying to stay ahead of the tears that were welling in her eyes. "I think I may love you, Phil. I certainly respect you, and I admire you. You're everything a woman could want of a man…in this galaxy anyway. We just need more *time* to figure this all out... But I can't stay on Earth. I've made a commitment to Parmithia and to my team. It's my responsibility to pilot the ship to New Earth and probably on to Parmithia from there. Again, I'm sorry."

Amelia was silently crying, but as Phil expected of her, she refused to allow herself to break down. She focused on the screen and keyboard in front of her, furiously wiping away tears so she could see what she was doing.

Though he was delighted by Amelia's confessions of her feelings toward him, Phil could only process her final answer. Phil understood the requirements of duty to one's country. Amelia was being honorable in her personal sacrifices. What else could he expect of her? But this could not be the final goodbye.

"Amelia, could you come to my quarters after you've landed the ship?"

Amelia glanced over at him, smiled, and shook her head. "No, I can't do that, Phil. For centuries, Parmithian culture has taught that a widow dishonors her late husband by becoming...intimate with another man before remarriage. It's a very old tradition, but it has been deeply instilled in me since childhood. I could never dishonor Drake like that. I'm sorry...yet again." She sighed.

Phil stood to leave, and Amelia arose with him. He moved to give her a simple goodbye hug. Her answer was no, and he had to accept that... Then Amelia turned up her head and kissed him. Phil recovered more quickly than he had from Amelia's first unexpected kiss in China, and he was able to return this kiss. Yet it was not a passionate kiss. It was a goodbye kiss, a what-might-have-been kiss. After just a few seconds, Amelia pulled away and rested her head on Phil's chin.

"Goodbye, Phil." Amelia gently extracted herself from the embrace and sat down in her pilot's chair. She checked the screen for status updates and made an entry.

Phil took a deep breath and composed himself. With nothing more to be said, he walked out of the room.

Chapter 23

BACK TO WASHINGTON

The next morning, two Suburbans pulled up to the spaceship that was safely docked at Andrews Air Force Base. Given the imminent arrival of the Parmithian transport ship in Washington, it had been decided to hold the meeting with the United Nations Security Council in the most secure location available—the White House. It was a surprisingly crisp morning for a day in early July. As they drove past the location where the *We Come in Peace* had landed on the White House lawn, Phil could not suppress a feeling of déjà vu and sadness. Had it really been just five weeks ago that he had been so thrilled to be standing by an alien spaceship? It felt like years had passed. Phil wondered if he could ever enjoy a science-fiction movie again. Reptile aliens? How ridiculous.

Phil, Allie, Tyson, Darius, and Friedrich walked through White House security entrance with no problems. The group was escorted to the conference room selected for the meeting. Before entering the room, they were required to surrender all firearms and cell phones.

As they entered the chamber, Phil immediately recognized Commander Alex Xi a few steps away. He stifled a reflexive impulse to check his sidearm. Phil reminded himself that Xi was here for the meeting, so it was doubtful he would try to kidnap anyone. Beside Xi stood Vice-Chairman Zhang and Technical Secretary Chung Guowei. China was obviously represented by leaders who could make decisions for their country. Phil recognized Jeremy Cline, the prime minister of Great Britain, and Vladimir Shamalov, president of Russia. The prime minister of France, Franc Dubois, stood beside their friend from Paris, Jacques Dimont. Monsieur Dimont bowed toward Darius in greeting. The ship that was to land in Paris would be loaded with the treasures the Louvre had decided to send to New Earth. The masterpieces would be safe from whatever destructions might occur on Earth and would provide inspiration to the colonists for centuries to come. Dimont was probably here to make sure everything proceeded as planned in Paris.

Phil and Allie approached General Bart and President Schaeffer, stopped, and saluted their two leaders. General Bart returned the salute and asked for an update.

"So, Majors, are there going to be any surprises in this meeting?"

Phil vacillated, "I would like to say no, but…"

"Darius has surprised us before, General," Allie finished the thought. "Repeatedly, actually."

Officially, this was a meeting of the United Nations Security Council, so UN Secretary General Guillermo Himes conducted the meeting. At precisely 9:00 a.m., he asked everyone to take their seats.

The secretary general spoke cautiously, fully aware that his last meeting with the Parmithians had gone terribly wrong. He welcomed everyone to the meeting, reciting the names and government positions of each person in attendance. He rehearsed a few of the events that had led to this meeting and then summarized the goals of the meeting, "We have two questions for the Parmithian team today. First, everyone here would like an update on your plan to bring in three transport ships tomorrow to resettle three thousand Earth's citizens to another planet. Second, we wish to discuss the status of your requirements for Earth to partner with you in applying Parmithian technology to solve Earth's food supply and environmental crises. If such an agreement was made today, would it not eliminate the need for the resettlement?"

The secretary general gathered his notes and moved to the side of the podium. "Ambassador Darius, we will be pleased to hear your report."

Darius was wearing one of the suits provided by Allie. He looked tired, but confident, and happy to have met the deadlines imposed by this meeting.

As he walked to the podium, he stopped, and as if it had just occurred to him, he asked, "Has everyone surrendered their cell phones? I will be presenting some confidential material that cannot be leaked to your governments or the public. I'm sure you all understand."

Everyone nodded as Darius surveyed the room.

"Excellent," he said. He placed his stack of papers on the podium and casually lifted off a paper weight that looked like a hockey puck. Just as casually, he pressed the center of the device as he put it aside. Phil, recognizing the multifunctional paperweight, looked around the room expectantly.

Sure enough, two pops went off in the back of the room, sounding like the first kernels of popcorn to burst on a hot skillet. An aide to the Russian ambassador yelped as he leaned forward to avoid the heat of a melting cell phone in his suitcoat pocket. An aide from Great Britain was even louder and more disruptive as he endeavored to remove his melting cell phone from his front pants pocket. At a nod from Phil, Tyson stepped forward and politely motioned the two men toward the exit. He followed them out and closed the door behind them.

As Darius checked his notes, Alex Xi caught Phil's eye. Commander Xi smiled, mouthed the word "Rookies," and shook his head.

Barely missing a beat, Darius began, "In regard to the resettlement effort, as most of you know, we have conducted hundreds of interviews across your world. We have visited New York, Washington, Rome, Paris, Johannesburg, New Delhi, Sydney, San Francisco, and São Paulo. Those approved to board the transport ships will be allowed to bring up to five family members or friends. These family members were also vetted and approved, of course."

"Please let me emphasize that those who have agreed to come with us are not being coerced, drugged, or brainwashed in any way. With this invitation, we are not breaking any international laws or moral codes. We are offering select citizens of Earth a chance to start over on a new planet. These colonists all *want* to come with us."

Without saying a word, President Shepherd raised his hand like an obedient student in elementary school. The room quieted.

"Ambassador Darius, can we know the names of those people who plan to board the transport ships?"

Darius reached down and flipped a switch on a projector. A list of names, broken down by their country of origin, appeared. Many of the names were recognizable. There were government leaders, corporate directors, and several heads of charities and philanthropic agencies. There were a couple of Nobel prize winners and other well-known scientists. Phil noted there were no movie stars, sports heroes, or other famous entertainers.

Darius turned to Russian President Shamalov. "President Shamalov, since Russia has banned its citizens from joining the colonization, we will not be making their names public."

Shamalov did not respond, not ready to explain the response of his government to the boarding of transport ships. Russia, like China, had felt excluded from the whole Parmithian affair. Shamalov nodded, and his face actually softened a bit at the news that some of his citizens were to be included in the colonization of a New Earth. Phil guessed that Russia would do nothing to further hinder its citizens from the exodus.

Darius continued, "We cannot save your whole world, but we can save your species. The people on this list are considered essential for the success of a new colony. They are also some of your most conscientious citizens. Beyond their accomplishments, this group of people are a good representation of the variety of DNA that this planet has produced. In our records, your species of humans will be known as *Homo sapiens terra*."

Darius cleared his throat. "Concerning tomorrow's landing, boarding, and takeoff, the transport ships will drop down directly from space. They should not have to enter any country's airspace except those of the countries where they will be landing. We have a rather important question for those three nations represented here. Will our transport ships be fired upon?"

President Schaeffer was the first to reply. "You will not be fired upon by the United States. I know many of the people on your colonization list. If they go with you, I will miss them. But I am happy to know they will be colonizing a new planet and giving *Homo sapiens terra* a new home. Parmithia is providing us a way to preserve our particular version of the human race of the universe despite what happens here on our home world. I, for one, appreciate your efforts, and the United States will do nothing to impede them."

Representatives from France and India echoed President Schaeffer's statement.

General Bart spoke up without raising his hand. Gruffly, he cautioned, "Ambassador Darius, we have numerous organizations that have announced they will actively oppose any efforts of our citizens to board transport ships. They believe that you are stealing citizens for experimentation…or as a protein source for Parmithia. We are expecting protests, and we fear they will be violent protests. We will provide police and army troops to provide security for the boarding, but it may still not be peaceful."

Darius looked thoughtful but responded immediately. He declared, "The time and place for the boardings cannot be changed. We have made promises to the people we have interviewed. We appreciate your offers of protection and gladly accept them. In any case, we will proceed with the boarding as planned."

Darius checked his notes and looked up at his audience. In a disappointed tone, he announced, "In regard to Earth's response to our requirements for Parmithian assistance, I have heard nothing. It appears that the United Nations has done nothing to assure children have two-parent families. We have not heard of any political efforts by the United States to prohibit special treatment of its citizens due to ethnicity, race, religion, or family name. We have not heard of any progress in establishing religious freedoms from China." He summarized, "It appears that when the transport ships leave tomorrow, my team and I will be leaving with them. We will not return."

General Bart did not take this news calmly. His face turned red, and he kept running his hand through his hair. He declared accusingly, "Ambassador, you are leaving this world without a clean energy source that would bring comfort and survival to millions of people. I realize that Earth has its problems. Problems have always been a part of life. I suppose we will handle them as we have always handled them before."

"Actually, General, you will *not* be able to handle problems as you have before. Sir, do you not think it strange that of all the scientists we could bring on first-contact missions, we choose to bring a social statistician?"

"Ambassador Darius, I don't even know what a social statistician is."

"A social statistician takes events from the recent history of a world and creates predictive models that extrapolate what is going to happen to that planet in the near future. I would like to introduce you to Friedrich, our ship's social statistician. Friedrich has been studying your planet for five years now by intercepting your broadcasts and running them through his computer models. Since arrival, with full access to your Internet, he has continued his study. I have great confidence in his projections…and I don't think Earth fully appreciates what Friedrich can tell you about your future. You need to listen to him."

Darius backed away from the podium, inviting Friedrich to take his place. Friedrich was apprehensive, but he realized he had spent the past five years of his life preparing for this moment. This was no time to hesitate or to soften his conclusions. The statistician stepped up to the podium and cleared his throat.

"General Bart, no offense, but your country and your planet have never before had the kind of problems you are facing today. You have an overpopulated planet, constantly balanced on the tipping point of mass starvation. You have millions of refugees across the world permanently housed in hundreds of refugee camps, continually drawing resources away from the countries to which they have fled.

"At the same time, industrialized countries like the United States are divided and in constant turmoil. The constant bickering of competing ethnic groups, religions, races, and political parties leaves these countries with no time or resources to address serious global issues. China isolates itself. World economies are crumbling, but there is no evidence that your country or anyone else will confront these problems until it is far too late."

As he spoke, Friedrich's voice became more emotional. He clicked off Earth's problems and their consequences, "Global warming has reduced agricultural output as vast areas of farmlands have become deserts. Food supplies and distribution are breaking down in your more impoverished countries, which ignite protests and attacks on food storage facilities. When that food is gone, new refugees will spill into neighboring countries in search for food. Unless your militaries are prepared to kill thousands of homeless people, they will flood into your industrialized nations. Their demands for food and shelter will be impossible to meet."

"According to my projections, your Earth's civilization will tear itself apart within ten to twelve years. Most of your problems today are social problems, which is why Darius has demanded solutions of the United Nations, the United States, and China. But the social problems of today will lead to your survival problems tomorrow."

General Bart had been staring at his hands. "Why are you just telling all of this now?"

Friedrich looked at the general, incredulous that he could ask such a question. "What?" Friedrich sputtered, "First, we *have* been telling you since we arrived! Secondly, you should already know all this. You have social statisticians of your own on Earth. I have read their reports!"

Darius stepped forward and placed a hand on Friedrich's shoulder. Friedrich glared at the general for a moment longer and took a step back, surrendering the podium to Darius. Darius restated Friedrich's conclusions, "As I have stated previously, by far the greatest benefit we bring to you is Friedrich's predictions of your future should you not act now. As I told the congressional committee, if Earth is not willing to eliminate the social structures that are tearing it apart, then Parmithia does not want to invest its resources in your planet."

Resigned to the realities of the situation, Darius closed his remarks. "Of course, our first choice would have been for Earth governments to agree to make the changes we requested. We could have established technical solutions to deal with the demands of feeding your population. After the rejection of our requirements of the United Nations, Congress, and China, I concluded that Earth would reject our offer and its requirements. Our backup plan was to provide transport ships to preserve this human species and give it a second chance on a new planet. When we leave Earth tomorrow, the loss of millions of lives is practically guaranteed."

A lone voice, with a familiar Chinese accent, came unexpectedly from the back of the room. "China agrees to meet your demands."

All heads turned as Vice-Chairman Zhang Chow Kai slowly stood up from his chair. The Chinese delegate bowed slightly to the assembly.

In a heavily accented but authoritative voice, he calmly made an earth-shaking announcement. "Ambassador Darius, you have asked China to stop repressing religion and to allow our citizens the freedom to seek spiritual growth wherever they wish. You want us to partner with the United States in bringing Parmithian solutions to Earth. I am authorized to tell you that China's premier leader and government accepts your terms. Legislation is being put in place to allow complete religious freedom in China. Charitable organizations and volunteer service clubs will also be unrestricted in their operations. Our people may choose how they wish to worship. We also agree to fully cooperate with the United States and all other governments in applying Parmithian technology to Earth's problems. We hope our decision will encourage you to not abandon Earth."

Vice-Chairman Zhang took his seat in a room of world leaders who had gone silent. China was not known as a nation where change was readily accepted, but they had just reversed a policy of religious suppression that had endured for decades. How would this affect tomorrow?

Darius considered his next words carefully. "Vice-Chairman Zhang Chow Kai, I thank you for this announcement. This is indeed unexpected and will be a good change for your most honored nation... But it is not enough to change my decision. China is very powerful, but it is still just one country. This policy change is not enough to alter Earth's course toward self-destruction. I realize my decisions condemns billions of Earth's people to desperate times and even death. The guilt of this choice will stay with me rest of my life. I am sorry. In fact, I cannot bear to ever do this again. After tomorrow, I am retiring from leading first-contact delegations. Earth will be my last mission."

Darius closed his eyes and seemed to be mentally reviewing his decision. Apparently finding there was no other conclusion he could have made, he sat down in his chair.

Secretary General Himes was caught by surprise at the sudden turn of events. He stood up, thanked everyone for their attendance, and brought the meeting to an end. There was nothing else to be said.

*****

The rest of the day was uneventful. Amelia was delivering her comrades to New Delhi and Paris and would not get back to Andrews Air Force base until after midnight. Allie had booked rooms at a nearby hotel for Darius, Friedrich, Phil, and herself. Darius advised everyone that he was locking himself in his room, where he would be taking his dinner. Friedrich announced that he would be reviewing his social constructs and prediction models now that the Chinese had accepted their terms. Phil made assignments of his security team to stand guard outside of Darius and Friedrich's rooms.

A couple of hours later, Phil was sullenly catching up on his own email. Suddenly, there was a frantic knock on his door. He opened it and found Allie there, catching her breath from an apparent sprint through the hotel to his room.

"You need to see something." She gasped as she darted past him into the room.

Allie grabbed the remote control to his television and turned it on. A few seconds of channel surfing took her to a local news network. Under a banner announcing, "Late Breaking News—Parmithians Report Their Decision to World Leaders," Phil saw a video of Darius, giving his final decision at the White House. This was the same meeting that had concluded just a few hours ago!

Allie explained, "The news networks have this video on continuous play. It shows the whole meeting at the White House, including the declaration of China's decision by Vice-Chairman Zhang."

Phil sat down on the bed, thinking wildly. The meeting had been held in the highest-security building in Washington. Darius had proved there were no functioning cell phones or battery-powered recorders in the room. How could this have happened? The audio was high quality, and the image of Darius speaking was stable. Could someone in the room have possibly shot this video? Directional long-range microphones outside the building would not be this clear and could not account for the video. There was only one logical conclusion.

Allie stood with her hands on her hips, waiting impatiently for Phil to arrive at her conclusion. When he finally looked up at her in understanding, Allie beat him to the announcement. "The White House leaked the video! No one else has taken responsibility for the disclosure, but the White House is refusing to admit that the meeting even occurred!"

Phil asked the obvious question, "But why would President Schaeffer do that?"

Allie looked out the window still flooded with summer sunshine and contemplated the question.

"I don't know. Maybe he is trying to control the political fallout from the Parmithian departure? He doesn't seem the type to do that..." Allie squinted and tilted her head. "Let me check something."

A few seconds of channel surfing took her to KUTV and a special edition of *The Tom Blackstone Show*. Tom sat on the edge of his barstool with the large-screen television behind him showing the muted video of Vice-Chairman Zhang making his speech. Tom was the only person on the stage, and he was in the middle of a rampage.

"China, a country we have disparaged for years for their repression of their own people, *has agreed* to the demands of the Parmithians! But *our* own government refuses to address the requirement made by the Parmithians to make our nation a place where all men and women are to be treated as equals!

FIRST JUDGMENT

"The Parmithians leave us *tomorrow*! You have just heard their predictions of what will happen to our planet within the next decade. Not three weeks ago, Ambassador Darius called upon Americans to make the changes required for our world to continue its existence. In the past, the silent majority has had the luxury of remaining silent. But Friedrich has explained to us that old rules *no longer apply*. We, the silent majority, must respond and we must do it now!"

Tom paused to take a breath and calm himself. He announced, "We will now replay the entire video of the final report of the Parmithian team to our world leaders. Thank you for watching."

Allie turned off the television. Phil thought for a few moments and finally offered his conclusion. "Allie, this really changes nothing. I don't know why the White House leaked the video. I don't know if General Bart asked his question to get Friedrich to restate his predictions for the end of the world…though it now seems likely. In any case, the schedule for tomorrow is set. The transport ships will arrive in the morning. Nothing has changed."

"We could call General Bart…or the president may even take our call."

"Allie, do you expect the general or President Schaeffer to apologize for their oversight in not informing us? Apparently, we are not on the need-to-know list, or we would have been advised earlier."

That evening, Allie, Phil, and Tyson had dinner together to review the next day's schedule. They all agreed that nothing could be done about the leaked video. Tomorrow's events would occur as planned, and their assignments as traveling companions of the Parmithian aliens would end.

Chapter 24

DEPARTURE DAY

Also called President's Park South, Washington's Ellipse is a fifty-two-acre park, shaped, not too surprisingly, like an ellipse. The Ellipse was surrounded by the White House, the Washington Monument, the Lincoln Monument, and the Reflecting Pool. During the Civil War, the grounds had served as a campsite for Union troops. The area had been used as a baseball field and a park for over a century. Yet for several years, fewer and fewer people visited the Ellipse to enjoy the park. It had become the gathering place for a continuous stream of demonstrations and riots. Sunday afternoons there could actually be dangerous. Phil could almost feel the negative energy of the place as he recalled some of the worst demonstrations held here and the hatred expressed by conflicting groups. Maybe today's event would bring some positive energy to the place, but somehow he doubted it.

Boarding day for the colonists in Washington dawned bright and clear. Sunday mornings were usually the quietest time in the capitol, and today was no different. Phil and Allie, both outfitted in full dress uniform, stood in the middle of the Ellipse. Phil could not decide if this setting was appropriate to conduct an evacuation of American citizens or not. In some ways, this was a bold step forward for the nation. In other ways, the event was an indecisive step backward that would bring disastrous consequences to the nation.

FIRST JUDGMENT

The planned landing site for the Parmithian transport ship was by the National Christmas Tree directly in front of him. Phil and Allie had just inspected the ground where the spaceship would rest and found nothing amiss. All the streets that entered and surrounded the park were closed off.

As far as security requirements went, this was the worst possible location for the boarding of the alien transport ship. No one knew what violence might ensue today nor the damage that might be done to irreplaceable national monuments. Someplace more rural would have been more logical. However, the decision had been made by the president himself. Phil could only guess President Schaeffer was making a statement to the world that America supported the rights of its citizens to depart the planet and to form a New Earth colony. Apparently, he felt they deserved an appropriate sendoff from the center of the nation's capital.

Barricades had been set up along the sidewalk that formed the circumference of the park. Army Rangers were stationed at each entrance. Today they were under Phil's command. Phil had delegated responsibility for the security of the outer perimeter to Lieutenant Tyson Young.

The press was just starting to arrive. Camera crews were setting up cameras behind the barricades nearest to the landing site. Reporters were reviewing scripts of their reports that would begin well before the descent of the transport ship. Early-bird passengers were milling near the entrance to a gravel access road that would serve as waiting line to board the spaceship.

Until the transport landed, no one would be allowed into the Ellipse. Most colonists were pulling regulation-size roller bags behind them. The volume of belongings each colonist was allowed to bring had been limited. Each person had to consolidate their wardrobe and personal belongings from their lifetime into two cubic feet of space. Many passengers were accompanied by family members or friends, there to bid a last farewell to their loved ones.

Darius, Allie, and Friedrich walked up to join Phil. Darius had news that he wanted to share.

"I have spoken with Newton. The boarding in New Delhi is complete. Almost all invited colonists arrived and boarded without incident. Newton reports that several hundred extra people showed up with baggage, hoping to board the ship without invitation or background checks. They were turned away without the need for violence. I also spoke to Matthew and Teresa. The boarding in Paris started two hours ago. There are multiple protest marches, but they are being successfully contained by the French police and military. Lastly, my sister Diedre's ship will land in one hour, as will Amelia in the *We Come in Peace*."

Allie added her own update, "Police, National Guard, and security forces are all in place. We are hearing reports of a lot of foot traffic headed toward us. Some of them are colonists…but most of them are not."

Indeed, protestors were already arriving at the far end of the Ellipse. Placards were plenteous.

Resist the Brain Wash!
Don't Be Assimilated!
Don't Trust Parmithian Lies!
Judge Not, Aliens!

At 8.30 a.m., a dark spot appeared directly above the park. This was not the glide path of a normal airplane. The dark spot gradually grew larger. Coming straight down, it was hard to distinguish the ship's size, shape, or speed. Finally, the transport dropped low enough to get some perspective.

The huge spaceship was shaped like a bullet. It looked to be about fifty feet in diameter and two hundred feet long. The back quarter of the ship was dedicated to engines and storage. The uppermost floors had small, regularly spaced portholes, so most assuredly contained the cabins that would house the passengers. The tip of the bullet ship was transparent, giving the bridge visibility in all directions.

The ground under the ship started to flatten when the ship was still about fifty feet above the ground. The depression was soon a foot deep and visually deepened as the ship gradually descended. There was no roar of rockets or windstorms of rotors as the base of the ship settled into its preformed sinkhole. Only a high-pitched whine could be heard that gradually faded away as the ship cut its thrusters. The whole descent was weirdly quiet.

A few seconds later, the *We Come in Peace,* dwarfed by its predecessor, settled onto the other quadrant of the Ellipse. Its doors opened almost immediately, and Amelia emerged. Phil could not catch his breath for a moment. The joy at seeing her face was crushed by the realization she would be leaving him today. Amelia came down the stairs and started walking quickly toward the group. She brought herself to a halt in front of them, standing at attention in front of Darius. Parmithians didn't salute each other.

"Darius, I am reporting back to duty. My trips to Paris and New Delhi went fine, and the ship is operating within optimal parameters."

Darius smiled and nodded. "Thank you and welcome back, Amelia."

Amelia turned to Allie, standing next to her and gave her a hug. Then she turned toward Phil and unabashedly gave him a hug as well. This was the first public display of affection Amelia had given Phil.

"I missed you," they both said in unison in each other's ear.

When they finally broke their embrace, they looked around a little self-consciously. No one appeared even vaguely surprised. Allie giggled, leaned close to Phil, and whispered, "What…you thought we didn't know?"

One floor well above the engines appeared to be the main entrance to the ship. The massive doors opened, and a large ramp extended out and unfolded to the ground. An older woman with white hair led a procession of about ten other officers down the ramp. The group walked in a loose military formation but were gaping at Washington sites like tourists in Disneyland.

Darius held his arms out as the group neared. The woman with white hair, obviously his sister, smiled and did not break stride as she walked into the embrace. They held each other, obviously having to control deep emotions at being together again. Several of the transport bridge officers approached Amelia and Friedrich to give them hugs and handshakes. It had been at least five years since they had seen one another. Most of Amelia's greetings were hugs, but Phil did not feel any jealousy. This gathering resembled a long-delayed family reunion. It was obvious these people cared for one another and were truly delighted to be together again.

None of this bridge crew spoke English or any other Earth language. Amelia, Darius, and Friedrich were all speaking to their comrades in their native Parmithian language. To Phil's trained ear, the cadence and tones sounded like a combination of French and Arabic. Phil and Allie were introduced to everyone. Phil noticed that most of the names were lengthy, but at least they sounded somewhat similar to Earth names. Parmithian appeared to be a speakable language. Officers began to return to their ship to begin their duties.

At 9:00 a.m., colonists started to form a line. Allie had recruited a couple dozen of her coworkers from Army administration and the State Department. They had set up canopies, tables, and chairs and were prepared to begin the registration and boarding process. Translators lounged around, waiting to be called upon for their assistance.

Parmithian crew and staff stood outside of their ship waiting to welcome and escort their guests to their cabins. When Allie concluded that everything was prepared and organized to her expectations, she motioned for the first colonists to come forward to begin their processing. Most all the colonists had decided to arrive early, perhaps nervous that the ship might fill up and they would lose their reservations. The queue had lengthened to several hundred people.

After a few moments, Darius and his sister, Diedre, left to board and inspect the transport ship. Friedrich had gone with them to translate and supervise the dispersal of passengers to their rooms upon boarding.

Amelia stood by Phil, arm in arm, both realizing they had just a few hours left to be together. Phil was in awe of the technology apparent in the starship in front of him. Only the movie *Star Wars* had ships that approached the size of this leviathan.

"What's the name of this ship?" Phil queried. "I've never seen anything like it."

Amelia nodded and tilted her head appreciatively. "This is the *Inspiration to Greatness*. We Parmithians tend to name our ships with motivational messages."

"You are proud of your people, aren't you, Amelia?"

"Yes, I am. Please understand, we're far from perfect. Our history is filled with mistakes and bad decisions. But our people have good hearts. It has taken generations to mold us to become a united population that cares for one other and our world. It is still a struggle, and I worry about what our society has become since we left it. But yes, I am proud to be Parmithian. We are trying to be…a people of Zion, as you call it here."

Phil nodded, unsure about the reference, but determined to look it up at his first opportunity. A guttural shout behind him turned his attention to the opposite end of the Ellipse. The shout was the kind you might hear at a football game, a roar designed to elicit physical courage and destructive zeal. Phil turned. Protestors were gathering around the Haupt Fountains. There were about a hundred of them so far, but Phil could see more people with placards…and clubs…gathering from all corners of the park.

Phil squeezed Amelia's hand. "Maybe you should go and see if Allie needs some help in registration. I think I need to go to work now."

Amelia squeezed Phil's hand in response. She glanced nervously at the gathering mob and placed a hand on his jacket lapel. "Be careful," she whispered, and she turned and walked toward the canopies and tables.

Phil took a short moment to admire the retreating shape of this extraordinary woman. He took a deep breath, turned about in a military pivot, and started his march toward the gathering protestors. He doubted a verbal warning would do any good, but these protestors needed to know that the rules had changed. People could die here today. In his peripheral vision, Phil saw someone approaching him from the side, jogging at a speed and angle to meet up with him. It was Tyson Young, who had been supervising the security personnel around the periphery of the Ellipse.

Phil kept walking, and Tyson fell into step beside him. Phil observed dryly, "Lieutenant Young, I don't remember ordering you to accompany me."

Tyson smiled and explained, "No, sir, you did not. But if you are going to approach an enemy force *by yourself*, you obviously need someone to cover your back."

"I should order you to return to your duties."

"Yes, Major, you could. But with all the noise the mob is making, I doubt if I would be able to hear the order."

The apparent leader of the protestors who had been standing on the wall of the fountain jumped down. Accompanied by two wingmen, he walked over to confront Phil and Tyson. The man wore an ancient Rolling Stones T-shirt and a leather Harley-Davidson jacket. His hair was long and greasy, and he smelled of cigarettes and alcohol. He stopped about ten feet from Phil, lazily twirling a wooden baseball bat. He greeted the two military men.

"Hello, officers… You aren't here to deny fellow Americans our right to peaceably assemble, are you?"

"Heavens no," responded Phil amicably. "As long as you remember and obey the peaceably part of that First Amendment, we should have no problems. But you should know that the activity at the other end of the park is especially important to our country. Any attempt to disrupt that activity will be met with force."

Mr. Rolling Stones squinted his eyes and started flipping the bat again. "So," he drawled, "you have no objection to that alien ship kidnapping our citizens and then returning with soldiers to invade our planet? You don't think we should take out those two ships now before they can be used in a war against us?"

Phil folded his arms in front of him, trying to remain calm in the face of such active paranoia. He responded patiently. "No one is being kidnapped. The Parmithians are providing transportation for colonists who have agreed—"

The bat slipped out of Mr. Rolling Stones' hand during its upswing. The Louisville Slugger flipped on a direct path toward Phil's head. Phil started to duck his head to the side, realizing he would never be able to avoid the blow. Then the bat stopped in mid-air, parallel to the ground, and seemed to float there motionlessly.

Tyson had shot out his hand, catching the bat at its heavy end, just a few inches from Phil's face. The bat had not been released by accident. It was too well aimed. Tyson had seen the plan in Mr. Rolling Stones' eyes the second before the bat had slipped his grasp.

Tyson growled and pitched the bat back at its owner. Mr. Rolling Stones lifted his arms to protect his head, raised a leg to protect the rest of his body, and squealed in alarm. The bat bounced off his shoulder harmlessly and clattered to the ground. Several protestors laughed, and comments of "Squeals like a girl" could be heard from the crowd.

Phil resisted a strong urge to grab and throttle the protester. Instead, he pointed at the man and commanded, "Tell your friends to stay on this side of the park. Cross the midline and there will be consequences. Are we clear?"

Mr. Rolling Stones mumbled several profanities and stalked away. He had been humiliated in front of friends and now withdrew to plot his revenge. Phil and Tyson turned and started walking back to the boarding area.

Tyson glanced over his shoulder, watching for any other thrown bats or attacks. But the protesters were happy to see them go.

"Boss, they're not going to stay on their side of the park. Their numbers are growing. They're already passing around bottles in brown paper bags, and we've just embarrassed one of their own."

"Not to nitpick, Lieutenant, but I think it was *you* who humiliated one of their own… I'm not complaining, of course. I appreciate the fact that I'm not nursing a broken nose right now."

Tyson grinned, basking in the praise from his friend and commander. But his joy was short-lived. More boisterous roars echoed behind him. Alcohol and paranoia were working the crowd into a frenzy that would soon overflow its boundaries. Protestors were openly waving clubs, bats, flags, and even shields, but Tyson knew there were guns hiding in shoulder holsters, waistbands, and green duffel bags as well. Nothing could be done to stop it; there would be violence soon.

*****

An hour later, the registration process was in full swing. About three hundred people had registered and boarded the *Inspiration to Greatness* transport. Nevertheless, the line had continued to grow and now continued outside of the park. Phil stood alone, using binoculars to observe the movements of the gathering mob. Tyson had returned to his responsibilities on the periphery of the park. Amelia and Allie were fully engaged in overseeing the registration process. Phil felt detached as he watched the scene unfold before him. It seemed as if this drama was part of a movie again.

Unexpectedly, General Bart had arrived, also attired in full dress uniform. He was accompanied by a squad of army regulars, who were carrying pieces of a portable aluminum platform. The general indicated the spot he wanted it placed, directly between the transport ship and the gathering dissidents. Within minutes, the platform had been built, leveled, and provided with fold-out chairs. This was not a speaker's platform; the general had installed an observation post from which he could follow the movements of the aliens and of their enemies.

Once his observation post was complete, General Bart climbed the stairs and, catching Phil's eye, motioned him over. As Phil arrived, he saw Darlus and Diedre approaching from the transport ship. The general seemed to be gathering his command team in preparation for a battle.

The ranks of the protestors had grown to over five hundred. There were more bottles in brown paper bags being passed around as the protestors worked up their courage to become a mob. Someone had broken out a couple of megaphones, and the shouting and chants were nearly continuous now.

"What do we really know about these aliens? Will we allow them to take away our citizens so they can make them their slaves?"

"*No!*"

"Should we allow these ships to leave so they can be used in the invasion of our planet?"

"*No!*"

"Are we here to protect America!"

"*Yes!*"

The speaker, who Phil recognized as Mr. Rolling Stones, had apparently regained his swagger. As he worked up the crowd, the self-appointed spokesman worked his way closer and closer to the middle of the Ellipse. His fellow protestors, emboldened by their numbers, alcohol, and patriotic duty, had pulled themselves to their feet and were moving with him.

They had crossed about a third of the Ellipse, quickly approaching the borderline that Phil had warned them not to cross.

Phil licked his lips. "General, do I have permission to have our Rangers take up position in front of this mob?" He was already moving his hand to his headset to give the order, so he was surprised by the general's response.

"No, Major, not yet. We need to see how this will play out."

Phil had to consciously stop his motion to thumb his headset. *We need to see how this will play out! Wasn't that pretty obvious at this point?* General Bart watched the approaching mob, which was gathering more confidence with each step. The protestors were not slowing as they approached the barriers set up halfway across the Ellipse. They obviously expected only token resistance here in the middle of Washington. Phil glanced over at his commanding officer, waiting for the order to deploy their troops. The general was watching the advancing enemy line and kept surveying the park as if he expected someone else to arrive.

All of a sudden there was a roar, not from the mob but from outside of the park. Phil looked up and down the street, expecting to see a couple of Blackhawk helicopters fly over the park. The roar came again, and Phil realized it was not caused by machinery but originated from hundreds of human throats. The protestor line stopped, many taking defensive positions against whatever was creating such a horrendous noise. A third roar filled the park.

Phil's detachment from reality deepened as he saw lines of marchers pouring into the Ellipse from both sides of E street. Incredibly, the marchers were not in uniform, but they were all dressed similarly. Everyone was wearing a white shirt! These were not soldiers from any US military force nor police. These were civilians. The glare of the light reflecting off the white shirts, blouses, T-shirts, and jackets was nearly blinding. Phil shook his head to clear it. No, he told himself, despite all appearances, these were not angels.

Many of the men looked like they had come straight from their office jobs. Others looked like production workers who had never worn a white shirt before in their lives. There were lots of soccer moms wearing shorts, sandals, and white blouses. There were professional women, some wearing high-heeled shoes. There were elderly men and women, several of whom needed walkers or canes to negotiate the curbs and rough spots in the streets. There were church groups singing "Onward Christian Soldiers" as they marched into the park. Some wore hats that identified them as veterans or members of Kiwanis clubs. Ranchers wore white cowboy hats; several construction workers wore white hardhats. There were no baby strollers. In fact, there were no children at all. This was not simply a large, peaceful protest march that had lost its way. Most of the marchers carried bats, clubs, and batons. The cowboy contingent wore their handguns in holsters on their hips, while others carried their handguns in shoulder holsters. These people knew why they were here, and they knew this was no place for children.

General Bart put his walkie-talkie to his mouth. "Lieutenant Young, this is General Bart. Please remove the barricades to the park. Also, have your men stand down. They are not to move in or interfere with this group unless I give you a direct order."

"Yes, sir, General," Tyson's awed but confused voice responded.

Army soldiers immediately started removing barricades, allowing the white-shirted army to flow like a river into the Ellipse. They flowed around the *Inspiration to Greatness* starship and the general's observation post. They filled the gap between the protestors and the two Parmithians ships. Soon less than twenty feet separated the two front lines. The marchers continued to fill in the space behind their comrades. Since the first three roars, the white-shirt army had been remarkably quiet. It gave the whole scene a very eerie quality. Phil rubbed his eyes, having no idea what was going on. If this was a dream, he needed to wake up. The registration process had been put on hold. Allie, Amelia, and Friedrich quietly joined Phil, General Bart, Darius and Diedre on the observation platform.

FIRST JUDGMENT

There were now over five hundred protestors preparing to attack the Parmithian ships and about two thousand white-shirted defenders who stood in their way. Everyone waited. It was the protestor's move.

Intimidation had worked for men and women like these protestors for their whole lives. Simply implying violence with profanity and in-your-face aggression always prompted the meek to walk away. Implicit threats had always worked, and they fully trusted them to work today. A large, heavily bearded protestor with a sleeveless Ghost Rider jacket stalked forward. Tattoos covered his forearms and hands. The man was glassy-eyed and apparently more than a little intoxicated. He walked up to a small balding man sporting round glasses and a red bow tie with his white shirt. Though he now stood his ground on the front line of a battlefield, one could predict this man had probably been bullied his whole life. The Ghost Rider fan had recognized such an optimal target immediately. This man would certainly run away, as would they all. No problem.

"*LITTLE MAN, YOU NEED TO GET OUT OF MY WAY...,*" the hulking man said slowly.

The balding white-shirted accountant stood his ground, though he could not bring himself to look his tormentor in the eye. He started shaking visibly.

The bearded protestor bent at the waist so he could get into the littler man's face. Nose to nose, he came within a few inches of his target, using the physical intimidation of his size to terrorize this insignificant obstacle that challenged him. He roared, "*LITTLE MAN, GET OUT OF MY WAY, OR I WILL WALK THROUGH YOU!*"

Spittle flecked out of the big man's mouth, flying onto the smaller man's glasses and lips. The bow-tied man flinched, but he did not move. The large, bearded man stood up straight and then, not understanding how the rules of life had changed, grabbed the little man's shirt with both hands and lifted him off the ground. The attack had now become physical. Four pairs of hands reached out from the crowd and grabbed the protestor's arms before he could pull back. Other hands grabbed the man's jacket. The protestor was pulled bodily into the crowd and flung to the ground. He disappeared under a flurry of white shirts. Clenched fists, batons, and bats appeared above the fray, descended, and reappeared. In a few moments, the hairy assailant was bodily ejected from the white-shirt army. Ghost Rider landed on the grass, bruised and battered, but still alive. Terrified, he forced himself to his feet and staggered back to the ranks of his mob. The white-shirted crusaders apparently did not want to kill anyone, even in self-defense. The small, bespectacled man with the red bow tie slowly and politely returned to his place on the front line.

Phil's walkie-talkie beeped, and he answered it, "Major Casaverde here. Go ahead, Lieutenant Young."

Tyson was agitated. In a controlled voice, he reported, "Major, we have Washington, DC, police here, SWAT teams and multiple officers in flak jackets. They believe the protests are turning violent and want to clear the park of everyone, including us. They are demanding that we leave! What are your orders?"

General Bart grabbed his own walkie-talkie. "Lieutenant Young, under no circumstances are the Washington police to be allowed to enter the park. Tell them the Army has jurisdiction over this operation. Do whatever you must, but keep them back. Do you understand me, Lieutenant?"

"Yes, sir… I'll tell them we have jurisdiction. I really don't think they're going to like it…"

"General Bart out." Distracted by the conflict in front of him, the general tried to clip his walkie-talkie to his belt, requiring several tries before succeeding.

The outcome of the attack by the bearded man in the Ghost Rider jacket had stilled the raucous shouts of the protest mob for a moment. But the dissenters rallied themselves, and the noise grew louder, though a bit more desperate. With shouts, screams, and raised clubs, a group of about fifty protestors, led by Mr. Rolling Stones himself, ran to attack the front ranks of the white-clad defense. They had every reason to expect the soccer moms and office geeks to scatter in the face of the violence of such an attack. For a moment it seemed their assumption was correct. The front of the defense gave way under the impact of colliding bodies, clubs, and swinging arms.

But no one broke ranks. No one ran away. On the observation platform, Phil felt tears welling in his eyes. This was courage in a place no one would expect to find it. He had to restrain himself from joining the battle.

In a few moments, the white-shirt front line recovered from the effects of the initial blows. By sheer numbers, a sea of white shirts overwhelmed the protestors from all sides. Soccer moms in sundresses were striking at their attackers with softball bats. Office workers were pounding away with table legs and golf clubs. The white-shirted defenders were getting in one another's way in the chaos, but it didn't matter. The silent majority was dispensing with the vocal minority.

A few of the attackers managed to pull themselves free of the chaos and stumble away from the battle. Many crawled their way back to safety. Like bouncers throwing drunk patrons out of a bar, white-shirt defenders tossed their assailants back into the neutral zone. Those attackers who could manage it limped back to their friends. On the other side of the battlefield, the white-shirted guardians reassembled themselves into their ranks.

The protestors now finally understood they were outnumbered by a determined opponent. Physical intimidation was not working to remove this barrier to the alien ship. But the mob had one more card to play, literally one more weapon in their arsenal. Guns had solved their problems before because the ultimate threat was the threat of gun violence. Guns were loud, violent, and deadly. Few people stood up to the threat of being shot. Thinking that fear for their lives would certainly remove the defenders, rioters along their front line pulled their weapons. There were no police around, and they all knew that a shooter could remain anonymous in such a large crowd.

Over one hundred protestors opened fire, each committing a felony to support the propaganda they had been fed by fellow anarchists. Phil jumped at the sound of the gunshots, reaching for his own sidearm. He was ready to run into the fray, but the general grabbed his arm and shook his head. Phil watched helplessly as defenders dropped, red bloodstains blooming on their white shirts. This confrontation had now become a shooting war. Battles that determined the fate of a nation almost always demanded spilt blood.

But the Parmithian defenders had come prepared to respond to such violence. Hundreds of handguns were pulled from holsters, pockets, and purses. The guardians focused their return fire on those who were actively shooting. When an attacker fired his weapon, ten to twenty guns fired back in response. For about thirty seconds, a gun battle raged near the steps of the White House. Finally, the firing slowed and then stopped altogether. The attackers were all lying flat on the ground. Some were dead, some were wounded, but many were hugging the ground because it was the safest place for them to be.

Phil watched in awe as the small man with the red bow tie pushed himself up to his knees. Then he slowly stood, curiously examining the bullet hole in the middle of his white shirt. In fact, many of the white-shirt army who had been shot were now struggling to their feet. Phil looked closer, and under the white shirts, he could see the black outlines of bulletproof vests on the first five rows of defenders. Hundreds of people, who apparently owned body armor, had put themselves in the front lines of this battle, fully expecting a firefight. The forethought of wearing body armor had saved many white-shirt lives.

His pent-up emotions finally overflowing, the small man in the red bow tie stepped forward. He shouted at the mob still lying prone on the ground, "WE ARE PEACEFUL CITIZENS OF THE UNITED STATES OF AMERICA! WE ARE CIVIL PEOPLE WHO SIMPLY WANT A SECURE FUTURE FOR OUR CHILDREN! DO YOU THINK THAT MAKES US WEAK?"

Phil's mind jumped back to when Darius had shouted almost exactly the same words at Commander Xi in China. The message was the same. Because a people try to act civilized and be moral, one should not think them weak.

The small man in the red bow tie spoke for all those who surrounded him and, Phil realized, most of the country. He finished with a command to those whose paranoia would have ruined the world's chance at redemption. *"NOW LEAVE!"* the small man with a red bowtie and a bullet hole in his white shirt bellowed.

The protestors who could move arose quickly. Running in a low crouch to avoid more gunfire, the banished rioters retreated to the safety of the streets. Glancing over their shoulders to assure they weren't being followed, they forced their way through onlookers who were regathering now that the shooting was over. The battle that historians would later recognize as a major turning point in the future of the United States…and the world…was over.

*****

Emergency vehicles were immediately allowed to pass through the barricades and drive up to the park. Paramedics attended the most grievously wounded and covered the dead with sheets. Some of the white-shirt army volunteers helped their wounded comrades to walk to the ambulances. It appeared that the whole event was over.

But then…it wasn't. Instead of scattering or leaving the park, most of the white-shirted recruits simply turned to face General Bart's observation platform. Standing at near parade rest, they all appeared to be waiting for something. In his confusion, Phil looked at General Bart, who didn't look surprised at all.

From the middle of the crowd, one man, nondescript except for the white Stetson fedora he wore, walked toward the platform. The white-shirted army parted in respect to allow his passage. The man climbed the stairs and removed his hat. Only Diedre didn't recognize the man. The spokesman and apparent leader of the white-shirt army was Tom Blackstone.

Chapter 25

THE APPEAL

Tom Blackstone fiddled nervously with the hat in his hand. Tom was used to large audiences, but he had changed. His hair was not slicked back as it had been on his television show. It was shorter and simply combed. Blackstone was less the used car salesman and more the concerned environmentalist. Tom was here to request something, and most of his army was waiting to learn what the answer would be.

Darius stepped forward and shook Blackstone's hand. "Tom, it is good to see you again, but your appearance here is...unexpected."

Tom smiled. "Darius, I apologize for the grand entrance. Your appearance on my show sparked an idea that has taken on a life of its own. It's why I am here. I have a story to tell you, and then I have a request. Do you have a minute?"

Darius smiled, finding amusement in the request. He nodded his head toward Tom's two-thousand-strong white-shirted army. "Considering what has just happened here, yes, I think we can spare you a few moments. I think there is more to this story than the street battle we just witnessed."

General Bart pulled up a folding chair, sat down, and leaned back. Diedre sat in a chair beside him. Amelia took Phil's hand and leaned against him. Tom rocked back and forth. This was not his usual format for reporting the news. He took a deep breath and launched into his report.

"Darius, after your interview on my show and the attack on the studio, everything was in shambles. But that day, we started getting calls and emails from viewers asking how they could join the silent majority uprising that you had described. We didn't know how to answer them at first, but we set up our website to register anyone who wanted to join the cause.

"Word got around quickly. Between the attacks on you and your team, your visit to the Pope, and then your announcement in Paris, you were in the news almost continuously. Your warnings about the state of the Earth and the need for stability resonated with people. We ran several shows with environmentalists and farmers to confirm that the Earth is truly on the brink of its own destruction. The American people came to believe you when you said you would leave the planet in its crisis mode."

"Entertainers, heads of major corporations, religious leaders, and thousands of others from across the country publicly united with our cause. Our website crashed from the number of people logging on to sign up in support. Within a couple of days, we had to triple our broadband capacity and then triple it again."

Tom looked out upon his army of followers and seemed to draw strength from their presence. Getting a little choked up, he continued, "We didn't know what we were doing. What were we going to do with all this support? Were people taking this seriously, or did they think they were just signing up to receive a political newsletter? I knew our efforts could do nothing within the current political system...so I started a new political party. We called it the Silent Majority Party. Our platform is that our country's government needs to recognize the truth of our dire situation, admit that we need Parmithian help, and decide to do something *now* to receive that help."

"I sent an email to all those who had registered on our website, asking if they were ready to register themselves as members of the Silent Majority Party. The response has been...well, overwhelming. Voter registration websites and phone lines were swamped with callers. Our studio suddenly became the headquarters of what was becoming a major political party. Then we started getting calls from companies like Google and Microsoft offering their help in handling registration. As of this morning, it appears we are the chosen political party for almost 20 percent of the nation's electorate. In three months, we expect to double that. In six months, we are on track to become the majority party in the United States. Donations are pouring in, and we've not even asked for financial support yet. There really hasn't been enough time."

Blackstone took a deep breath. There was a lot of story to tell, and it had all been packed into two exhausting weeks.

"Darius, we knew that today would be our last chance to convince you that the US was sincere in its commitment to make the changes you have requested. So in the name of the Silent Majority Party, we sent out several thousand emails asking for volunteers to show up for the transport ship departure today. We explained that rioters were expected…and that they should know there was a strong possibility of violent conflict. Everyone was asked to wear white shirts, as a sign of both purity and unity. We wanted to demonstrate to you, Darius, that we were willing to fight for our county's future. We didn't expect this level of confrontation, but everyone performed admirably, I think."

Blackstone was fighting back deep emotions now. The response and sacrifice of his followers had been unbelievable. He took another deep breath and plunged ahead. All this effort would be wasted if he failed to communicate now.

"So, Darius, I am here today to ask you for *time*. I know you are leaving with the three colonist lifeboats today. We don't want to interrupt that effort. It really could be mankind's last chance for survival as a species. But we want you to come back in a year before you issue your final judgment of our planet. Within one year, the Silent Majority Party will introduce a new equality protection amendment called the Self-Evident Amendment to the Constitution. If passed, it will forbid any organization from attempting to provide advantages for one minority group over another. No preference or penalty will be given due to a person's ethnicity, gender, race, religion, or other belief system.

FIRST JUDGMENT

"On top of that, we will pressure the United Nations to meet your request that all children be provided two-parent families. We will drive legislation from here in Washington and support initiative efforts within the governments of our allies. I have talked with several Chinese leaders, and they, too, will support the effort. The United Nations will be...strongly encouraged to enact and enforce these laws throughout the world. In a year, we plan to meet the requirements you have given Earth to share your technology. But we *need* you to give us a year. Get the colonists settled onto their new planet and then come back to Earth. You have mobilized our silent majority. It will not be silent anymore. We have the power to do this. Please give the Earth a second chance."

Tom fell silent, exhausted from the emotions behind his plea. Most of the people on the observation platform knew the anguish that Darius had gone through in making a judgment against Earth. All of them expected that he would be overjoyed at this new development.

Darius looked across the white-shirt army, closed his eyes, and took a deep breath. He wanted to believe, but still Darius wavered, considering his response. Finally, he explained the difficulties behind his decision, "Parmithia has never sent transport ships to a planet to resettle a colony of human refugees and then decided to share technology and help stabilize that same planet. I don't know that I can even get approval to return. I don't want to make promises that I can't keep. Besides, Tom, there will be *other* requirements besides those I have made public. You will have to meet those as well to qualify for full assistance and technology transfer."

Blackstone lowered his eyes, not knowing how to respond. There had been so much sacrifice in the past three weeks to arrive at this moment. It seemed it could be all for naught.

From the back of the podium came a new voice, "Then let me stay on Earth to guide them." As one, everyone on the platform turned.

Friedrich stepped around General Bart's chair and stood in front of Darius.

"Darius, for the next year, you will be on a colonizing run that does not require the skills of a social statistician. I can stay on Earth and advise Mr. Blackstone on what needs to be done to prepare Earth for Parmithian collaboration. I can help ensure that Earth will be ready when you return. Having me here gives Parmithian leadership yet another reason to allow you return to Earth. If I do say so myself, good social statisticians are extremely hard to come by."

Then Friedrich looked directly at Allie and held her eyes for a moment. "Besides," he said pensively, "I think I would like to spend some time planetside."

The whole group standing on the observation deck now turned to look at Allie. She blushed furiously at both the attention and the thought that Friedrich might stay on Earth. Amelia put her arm around Allie's shoulders. Allie took a deep breath to handle the embarrassment, but she did not respond. Everyone turned back to look at Darius.

Darius finally spoke again, "Friedrich, your offer is appreciated, but we have a year's voyage ahead of us. With Newton, Matthew, and Theresa on the colonist ships, my ship's crew is down to four of us. We need you to help Amelia in Navigation, monitor Engineering, *and* to cook our meals."

"I can cook!" Phil blurted without thinking. *Anyone can cook*, he thought. Heating up a can of soup counted as cooking, right? "I can do engineering too…if you explain to me what to do. We'll have ship-to-ship communication with Newton so he can talk me through procedures."

Darius looked at Phil and cocked his head sideways. "You'd have to learn the Parmithian language to read our engineering manuals… and recipes," he finished dubiously.

"I am actually quite good at learning new languages. Really. Ask General Bart…"

Phil froze in midsentence. He'd forgotten about the general! Phil was not great at remembering military protocol, but he could guess one needed permission before making a commitment to a foreign power. Phil turned and stood at attention in front of his commander.

"Sir, requesting permission to be assigned as a military advisor to the Parmithian delegation for the next year…if they'll have me."

General Bart looked back and forth between Darius and Phil. He started nodding even as he spoke. "Major Casaverde, speaking for the United States Army, your request is granted. I think you can best serve your country…and your planet…as an advisor, engineer, and cook for our foreign friends. I agree with Mr. Blackstone. We need the Parmithians to be willing to return and give us a second chance. If Ambassador Darius approves, your assignment will be to facilitate that return." From his chair, the general looked up at Darius and asked, "Are you willing to return Major Casaverde in a year?"

Darius did not look up. From his pocket, he had pulled out his pair of red dice and was rolling them in his hand again. Darius was obviously fighting his emotions, but no one could tell if the emotions were of sorrow or relief.

Diedre put her hand on her brother's arm. In halting English, she said, "I will support whatever decision you make before the High Command. I have some small influence with them."

Darius started a side conference with his sister about the particulars of such an arrangement. Phil took the opportunity to lean toward Amelia. He whispered, "I won't do this if it will disrupt your life too much."

Amelia was now blushing in pleasure and smiling from ear to ear. "I would love for you to join us," she whispered back. "But can you really cook?"

"Sure, I can. I…may need a little help with Parmithian ingredients…" Phil lowered his voice even more. "And how to turn on a stove. But I will learn to cook anything if I can be with you." Amelia lowered her head and then looked up again. She smiled…and winked at him.

Darius finished talking to his sister, who was nodding and smiling. General Bart cleared his throat, obviously trying get the negotiation back on track.

Amelia caught Darius's eye and, nodding her head toward Phil as if he had just passed a job interview, she prompted his decision. "Darius, I support Major Casaverde's proposal." Her voice softened, "However, this is not my decision to make. You will have to answer for any repercussions of your choice. Sir, what do you want to do?"

Blinking away tears, Darius smile and shrugged his shoulders as if this was a simple decision. "Okay. We'll return in a year."

Tom Blackstone raised and pumped a fist, and two thousand people cheered the dawning of a new age.

Chapter 26

LIFTOFF

Two hours later, the interrupted boarding of all passengers onto the *Inspiration to Greatness* was complete. Most of the white-shirt army had left, though a few of them still needed to stop by a hospital on the way home. The Washington police had finally worked their way into the park and assisted in the grisly business of cleanup. Two police officers approached Phil and General Bart, escorting a handcuffed Lieutenant Tyson between them.

With a furrowed brow, General Bart looked down his nose at Tyson. "Lieutenant Young, what did you do?"

Tyson looked miserable. He looked at the general and Phil, knowing he needed to choose his words carefully in front of the two police officers.

"General, there was a disagreement and misunderstanding about the military's jurisdiction of the…events that were taking place here. SWAT teams were responding to reports of a conflict in the park. I was trying to delay their entrance from interrupting a delicate and important negotiation…"

One of the police officers interrupted, "The lieutenant here ordered his men to *hold my men and me at gunpoint* as we tried to respond to reports of a confrontation within the park. He is going to jail, and he will be charged. We are here to see if one of his commanders should accompany him. Was Lieutenant Young under orders to hold our SWAT teams at gunpoint for the past hour?"

General Bart sighed audibly and addressed the ranking police officer, "It appears that Lieutenant Young may have misunderstood his orders. Regretfully, I don't have time to deal with this right now. The Washington, DC, attorney general's office will be in touch with you before the end of the day."

The general turned back to Tyson. "Thank you, Lieutenant, for your service today."

Tyson looked from his arresting officers to the general. "But, sir…"

Phil felt bad for Tyson; he *had* been following orders after all. What he had done had required courage, but the general could not resolve the issue without making a few phone calls. Phil could at least wish his friend goodbye.

"Lieutenant Young… I am accompanying Darius and Amelia to New Earth to drop off the colonists. I'll be back in a year."

Tyson's face broke out in a grin, understanding the importance of the announcement to his good friend's personal life. "That's great, Major!" As the two police officers hauled him away, Tyson added, "I'd love to hear the details before you go!"

General Bart pulled Phil aside as he watched the retreating officers escort Tyson away.

"Lieutenant Young is a good man. Don't worry, Major, I'll make sure that he is cleared of all charges."

"I appreciate that, General. Tyson followed your orders precisely. But you couldn't let the SWAT team come in and spoil the showdown, could you? General, I am curious. When did you make the decision to arrange for all of this to happen?"

The general registered a little surprise but then gave up the ruse.

"Major Casaverde, this is still very confidential, but since you're leaving soon, I should probably bring you up to speed. Tom Blackstone called me when he started organizing his new political party. He needed some help from President Schaeffer to handle political and bureaucratic approvals, which the president did provide. We have been assisting Mr. Blackstone ever since then. We decided a new political party was our last chance at getting Parmithian assistance to avert a global tragedy."

The general shrugged and admitted, "However, we needed to publicly demonstrate to Darius that the Silent Majority Party was sincere enough and powerful enough to do what Blackstone said it could do. We knew protests were forming to disrupt the Parmithian departure, and we decided to use the opposition to accomplish a demonstration of our resolve."

General Bart turned to look at the White House.

"As you have probably guessed, we recorded and then leaked the video of Darius's final report at the White House. Neither Darius nor Friedrich knew anything about it. I pushed back on Darius to force him or Friedrich to review the future of Earth without Parmithian assistance. I needed the American people to understand the consequences of inaction. The silent majority needed to be jolted into action, and the leaked video was designed to do that. But nothing was said that wasn't true."

General Bart glanced over his shoulder to confirm no one could overhear their conversation. He continued with his confession.

"And...you're correct about Lieutenant Young's role. If the SWAT teams had interrupted, they would have forced the protestors to leave without allowing a confrontation. The Silent Majority Party could never have shown its mettle. Darius had to see that he could safely agree to return in a year and give Earth a second chance. Seeing our military or police force in action would have convinced him of nothing. Defense of the colonists had to be accomplished by normal citizens."

The general sighed. "So it all worked out. There were a few surprises. I wasn't expecting Friedrich to stay or for you to leave for the year. However, both decisions will help our cause. Friedrich will be invaluable. You will become our ambassador to Parmithia if they will allow such a thing. Major Casaverde, your assignment is to assure that the Parmithians return. As our ambassador, you must establish relationships, learn their language, and learn of their culture. Marry one of them if you wish."

Phil tilted his head in surprise, but then he smiled. "Actually, thank you for that last part."

Allie approached the two military officers. "Major Casaverde, they are starting final boarding. Liftoff is in twenty minutes."

Phil looked at General Bart and gave him a full salute. "Thank you, General for…everything. I won't let you down, sir."

General Bart returned the salute. "Safe travels, Major. We'll see you in a year. I'd better go see if I can get Lieutenant Young out of jail." With that, General Bart turned and walked away.

Major Heroux turned toward Phil. "I saw the general talking to you. He explained everything, didn't he?" she announced conclusively.

"Yes, he did, Major," Phil responded. Allie let the silence extend for several seconds.

"Are you going to tell me what he said?"

Phil grimaced theatrically. "Heavens no. I really don't have the time…and it feels so good to finally know something that you don't."

"Wow, you are so—" Allie's return banter was interrupted by Phil's sudden embrace. Tears sprang to Allie's eyes as she returned the hug.

"Phil, please take care of Amelia. She has become one of my dearest friends, and I think she may be in love with you."

"Ah, Allie, and what's not to love, right?" he asked as he broke off the embrace. "Don't worry, I love Amelia too. If she can put up with me for a whole year in close quarters, we may have a future together."

Allie beamed, happy for her two good friends. She announced, "I think the general is going to let me work with Tom Blackstone and Friedrich in a new government division. I think we should call it the Department of Parmithian Affairs. We have so much to do. A year is a very short time to change a world."

From the direction of the ship, an announcement came over a bullhorn that Friedrich had accommodated. "This is the final boarding call. Doors close in five minutes. This means you, Major Casaverde."

Phil looked at Allie and gave her a full salute. Allie returned the salute, her eyes misting up yet again.

"Goodbye, Allie." Phil started to walk away. He turned around and, walking backward, pointed to Friedrich, who was waiting at the bottom of the stairs to the *We Come in Peace*.

"By the way, Allie, I really like Friedrich. You have my blessing if you decide to date him."

"Thank you, Phil. I really like Amelia too. You have my blessing if you decide to *marry* her because you're *never* going to be able to last a whole year as just friends!"

Phil chuckled. Ouch. "Touché, Major Heroux!" he called back, not breaking his stride.

As he approached Friedrich and the ship, Phil reached into his pocket and pulled out his keys. He tossed them to Friedrich as he walked up to him. "Friedrich, here are the keys to my apartment. You're going to need a place to stay. My address is in my file."

"Thank you, Major Casaverde. In return, all my recipes are in the kitchen computer. Just run the English translation program and follow the instructions. You should be fine, whether you can really cook or not."

"That, Friedrich, is the best news I have heard all day. Thank you."

With that, Phil shook hands with the alien who was no longer an alien. He climbed the stairs to start his science-fiction adventure that was no longer fiction.

Chapter 27

NEW EARTH

Six months later, New Earth

On January 5, 2035, Old Earth time, the three transport ships and the *We Come in Peace* arrived at New Earth, the third planet of a sun identified as M789 in the Gemini system. The trip had been relatively uneventful. There had been a few disagreements. The ships were huge, but with one thousand passengers in each, quarters were still tight. Yet most of the passengers recognized the honor it had been to be chosen for this colonizing effort. The passengers were an appreciative group who were willing to sacrifice some comfort to pursue a better life.

During the voyage, classes had been taught in agriculture and crop selection on the new planet. As planned, English classes were taught during the flight so that language would not be a differentiator between New Earth citizens. Classes in the Parmithian language were optional but well attended.

The sun of New Earth was a little redder than that of Old Earth. The planet was a bit smaller, so everyone felt a bit lighter as they disembarked from the ships. Offloading of the passengers, shelters, supplies, and farm equipment began immediately.

When the ships were in dark-energy propulsion or at warp speed, as Phil called it, the fine targeting required for communications with Earth was impossible. Once they arrived at New Earth, Phil and Amelia could finally reestablish communication with Earth, specifically through Friedrich's specially adapted computer now sitting in the Department of Parmithian Affairs.

Phil and Amelia downloaded and watched every Tom Blackstone show that had been broadcasted since their departure. They were delighted to see Allie as a guest on the show, not once but several times. In her first appearance, Allie described to viewers what had happened at the White House Ellipse on that fateful Sunday of the transport ship's departure. Because of the bravery of members of the Silent Majority Party, she explained, the transport ship had launched as planned. Using her new holograph projector, Allie showed photos of the crew and some of the scenes taken of Parmithia. Viewers started to feel a connection with the alien planet.

Friedrich was also a guest on Blackstone's show. He explained in detail the technologies that Parmithia could provide Earth. He described advances to provide clean power to reduce and eliminate the carbon footprint of burning oil and coal. He reported on methods to provide free and simple birth control to third-world countries. He discussed treatments to improve agricultural lands and their outputs. However, Friedrich warned, these technologies could do nothing to fix the current social problems that existed on Earth. It would be up to Earth to correct those issues. When he returned from his voyage to New Earth, Friedrich warned, Darius would look for proof that this social transformation was a reality.

Blackstone even invited JinJing Soon from China to be on the show. The fact that the Parmithian visit to Beijing was not voluntary would never be revealed to the world. JinJing spoke in glowing terms about the tours and reception during the visit of the Parmithian delegates. Dressed in a beautiful Chinese silk gown, Jin charmed the studio audience and millions of television viewers. She reported that laws to implement religious liberties throughout China were well underway. JinJing only hoped that the United States would meet their requirements as well and partner with China in this great undertaking. For weeks, *The Tom Blackstone Show* was the top-rated television show in the country and in most foreign markets as well.

As Tom predicted, the Silent Majority Party continued to gain members at an astonishing rate. Politicians in Washington, DC, were very good at detecting the winds of change in their states. Proportionally, this change was a hurricane. Senators and congressmen vied for time to call press conferences to announce their decisions to change political parties. President Schaeffer was one of the first to join the Silent Majority Party, stating it was the only party willing to address the threats to the nation. In states that allowed it, the Silent Majority Party initiated recall elections of officials who disapproved of the Parmithian measures.

The United Nations, under pressure by the United States, China, France, and Great Britain, announced a new global program to enact laws to hold negligent parents responsible for the upbringing of their children. No longer could children be cast adrift by inattentive parents. Social service and child protection programs saw their budgets doubled and then tripled in the course of a few months. Naturally, there were complaints about a system that imprisoned parents for dereliction of their family duties. But few organizations or law firms wanted to be linked with supporting the rights of deadbeat parents.

Six months after the Parmithian departure, a new amendment to the Constitution was brought to the floor of Congress for debate. The phrase "We hold these truths to be self-evident, that all men are created equal" would no longer be debatable under the law. Called the Self-Evident Amendment, it specifically prevented any organization from promoting the special treatment of anyone because of their birth circumstance.

Protests were rampant at first. Too many organizations would be disbanded or negatively affected by the new legislation to expect otherwise. Marches and protests were organized. The Silent Majority Party responded just as they had to the protest against the Parmithian launch. When a demonstration drew five hundred protestors, the Silent Majority Party provided a thousand of their own to attend. The party affiliates all dressed in white shirts to distinguish themselves. When the protests were peaceful, there was no conflict. But when the protests became violent, when protestors tried to draw news coverage through destruction or intimidation, they were stopped by an army of white shirts. A few demonstrations ended in exchanged blows. One protest drew rioters who resorted to gunfire to express their outrage. Only a few of them survived the resulting firefight. Such was the power of a silent majority that would no longer be silent.

In the final minutes of the last downloaded broadcast they could get, Phil and Amelia watched as Tom Blackstone admitted that he was very concerned about the future. The Silent Majority Party had grown but did not yet have the votes to pass the Self-Evident Amendment to the Constitution. Opponents of the party had realized they didn't need to stop efforts to remove prejudice from the nation. They only had to *slow* the process down enough so that when Darius returned, Earth would not meet his requirements. If Darius left for good, it was likely that the Silent Majority Party would dissolve, and the country could go back to business as usual. The Self-Evident Amendment languished in House committee meetings.

Chapter 28

BACK TO OLD EARTH

Nine months later, Old Earth

On the evening of Monday, October 8, 2035, fifteen months after its first visit, the extraterrestrial ship *We Come in Peace* once again settled onto the front lawn of the White House. The ship was almost three months late in its arrival. The transport ships had been needed elsewhere, so they had left earlier than expected. Settling the colonists had taken more time than planned. However, as they neared Earth, Amelia had communicated their imminent arrival. There was a small crowd of onlookers outside the fences, many of them wearing white shirts. But most were there just to take photos of the landing of the airship and dispersed immediately after its touchdown.

The weather was cooler than the last time the Parmithians had visited. No trouble was expected, but the ship's perimeter was secured by Army Rangers. A welcoming committee composed of Allie Heroux, Friedrich, President Schaeffer, and General Theodor Bart waited as the hatch door opened. Phil was the first person out of the ship. He stepped out onto the stair platform and scoured the area. He noted the Army Rangers and the welcoming committee and visibly relaxed. He started down the ramp, followed closely by Amelia and Darius.

FIRST JUDGMENT

Though it had been just over a year, Phil noted that President Schaeffer and General Bart both looked older. It had been a difficult year for them, and they both showed signs of wear. However, Allie Heroux looked the same. When Phil stepped off the steps, she saluted quickly and jumped into his embrace. Phil had never had a sister, but this, he was sure, must be what it felt like. He moved on to salute the president and General Bart. Laughter and delighted squeals witnessed to the reuniting of old friends behind him.

The meeting was soon moved into the warmth of the White House. The president invited everyone into the Oval Office, where they found Tom Blackstone waiting for them. Eventually, everyone sat down and looked at the president expectantly.

President Schaeffer, smiling broadly, reported, "We have asked Tom Blackstone, chairman of the Silent Majority National Committee, to report on our legislative accomplishments of the past year. Tom…"

Blackstone arose. "Thank you, Mr. President. Darius, Phil, Amelia, Newton, Matthew, and Teresa…welcome back to planet Earth. We have been anxiously awaiting your return for the past few months. At first, we were going to schedule the vote for the Self-Evident Amendment for after your return. When it was apparent you had been delayed, we decided to go forward without you."

Blackstone took a deep breath and announced, "One month ago, the Twenty-Eighth Amendment to the United States Constitution was approved by the Senate and the House of Representatives. Since then, forty-five state legislatures have ratified the amendment, making it the law of our country. Implementation is in full swing, though hundreds of lawsuits are trying to delay it. None has succeeded. The Constitution is actually very clear about the fact that all men are created equal. The United Nations has pushed its Two-Parent Families Initiative into over a hundred nations, including our own. Our youngest generations are receiving the attention they deserve.

"China has fully integrated religious freedoms into their society. Religious leaders still have to be careful not to criticize their government. However, church buildings and worship services are now allowed and protected by the government. Around the world, people are experimenting with the whole concept of seeking more spiritual lives. Religion is seeing a resurgence in popularity. Parmithians showed Earth that though they may not see God, they can believe in what God stands for and work toward greater consciousness and empathy."

Blackstone smiled and sat down. He'd been rehearsing this report for over a year, and he was glad it was over. Darius smiled and arose. It took him a moment to find his voice. "Congratulations to all of you. This progress makes me…very happy," Darius exclaimed. "Friedrich and I have been in communication the past week. He has informed me of the other programs that have been successfully initiated by the Department of Parmithian Affairs. His models illustrate that nations of planet Earth are accepting new responsibilities to care for the planet and one other. From all I have seen and heard, Earth has met the initial requirements for Parmithian assistance and technical support."

Darius's eyes misted up as he realized that the millions of souls on this planet would not weigh on his conscience for the rest of his life. Fighting back his emotions, he continued his update. "For our part, we have been in contact with Parmithia. Our high command has requested that I stay planetside for the next two years to oversee the technology transfer. The dark-energy generators will take about a year to arrive. Unmanned ships can accelerate, travel, and decelerate much faster than manned ships. However, this time will not be wasted. It will take at least a year to remodel your power plants to accommodate the new generators. Technologies such as our soil remediation and carbon dioxide removal are in storage on the *We Come in Peace* and can be incorporated almost immediately. Friedrich has requested that he also stay here for the next couple years to continue to facilitate technology transfer."

"Why does he want to do that?" Amelia interrupted, giving Allie her what-have-you-two-been-doing smile.

Allie blushed, took a deep, patient breath, and looked at Friedrich. "Yes, Amelia we're…dating."

"We're dating *steadily!*" Friedrich happily corrected. Everyone laughed, and light applause filled the room. Darius waited out the interruption and continued to detail their plans.

FIRST JUDGMENT

"The *We Come in Peace* will lift off in one week to continue its exploration. Matthew has been promoted to be the new ship's captain. Teresa will now be the ship's expert on religion and cultures. Newton will continue as ship engineer, and Amelia will continue as our pilot. Phil Casaverde has asked to remain on as our social statistician, engineer, and cook."

"And why does he want to do that?" Allie interrupted, giving Amelia some of her own medicine.

Phil smiled, took Amelia's left hand, and removed her flight glove. No one could miss the diamond ring and wedding band on Amelia's ring finger. Cheers and applause greeted the announcement.

Phil explained, "Apparently, only on Earth does a ring on the left hand indicate you are married. But Amelia has agreed to honor the tradition. I made these rings on the ship with a laser sintering unit and some recycled gold dust. It's like 3D printing in gold. Fortunately, Parmithia and Earth do share the tradition that a ship captain may perform marriages. Darius conducted our wedding ceremony while we were orbiting New Earth. By Parmithian law, we are married."

Darius added, "As the first alien crew member of a Parmithian ship, Phil may also be the first earthling to ever see the planet Parmithia." He continued, "Thank you all for your roles in making this moment possible. For a long time, this outcome appeared impossible. The road ahead for Earth will not be easy, but with your efforts, the road ahead exists."

After a moment of silence, the Oval Office was filled with tears, laughter, and congratulations. Everyone related their most exciting moments of the past year. A few minutes later, Lieutenant Tyson Young burst through the door, and all the stories had to be retold. The meeting that would secure the safety of the planet Earth was over. Its first judgment had been passed. Unspoken, but understood by everyone, was the knowledge that more judgments were to come.

The End

ABOUT THE AUTHOR

Scott R. Frazer is a career analytical chemist with a lifelong interest in science fiction and seeking to understand the universe. Born in Iowa and raised in Colorado, Scott earned his PhD in chemistry in Arizona. His career in corporate research and development then took him to other corners of the country. During that time, he married his wife, Cheri, and together they had four children.

Scott has always been fascinated by the overlap of science and religion and has written three nonfiction books on the subject. *First Judgment* is Scott's first fictional novel. While science fiction must first be exciting and engaging, it is also a great forum to compare mankind's technical advances with his accumulated wisdom and empathy. Breaking the science fiction mold of reptilian aliens bent on conquest, Scott endeavors to tell a story of not so fictitious science fiction set in the not so distant future.

Printed in the USA
CPSIA information can be obtained
at www.ICGtesting.com
CBHW031927090824
12961CB00009B/287